the possession of celia

m. s. valentine

The Possession of Celia
Copyright © 1998 by M. S. Valentine
All Rights Reserved

No part of this book may be reproduced, stored in a retrieval system, or transmitted in any form, by any means, including mechanical, electronic, photocopying, recording or otherwise, without prior written permission of the publishers.

First Masquerade Edition 1998
First Printing October 1998
ISBN 1-56333-666-9

First Top Shelf Edition October 1998
ISBN 1-57333-930-7

Manufactured in the United States of America
Published by Masquerade Books, Inc.
801 Second Avenue
New York, N.Y. 10017

during such sensory-stimulating encounters, the astute Jason preferred to save the rhapsodic moment of pencetration for the very end when Celia would cry out in shameful ecstasy —when his carefully calculated attack had finally become far too much for the well-cleaved knurl to bear and it was at last forced to abandon its struggle. Hence in the splendor of her indignity, Celia would truly be ready for him....

Also by M. S. VALENTINE:
The Captivity of Celia
The Governess

the journey...

The gentle rolling green hills and valleys festively patterned with large squares of the brilliant springtime yellow of rapeseed fields soon began to replace the familiar bleak grays and sinister bogs belonging to the Yorkshire moors. As their train raced and rattled through the Kent countryside on its way toward Folkestone and the famous white cliffs of Dover, Celia and Colin briefly found themselves unable to bring to mind the handsome contours of Moorland House, nor the handsome contours of its manipulative owner. The similarly handsome young man seated across from Celia wanted nothing but to wipe from memory forever the libidinous image of his cousin's face and form, whereas she would be unable to do so even if she had wished.

Indeed, every manly detail of Sir Jason Hardwicke was forever etched upon her brain and body. The lush landscape beyond the rain-spattered window of their car was a landscape that went mostly unappreciated by its female observer, for Celia's thoughts had returned to an earlier train journey—a journey which had delivered her to a life the likes of which she could never have dreamed, and to a man the likes of whom her wildest imaginings could never have conjured. She allowed her china blue eyes to close against the hazy morning light—eyes that had once looked so innocent and now, whenever Celia observed them reflected back to her in a mirror, looked so corrupt, so sated, indeed, so filled to overflowing with shameless sensuality. Suddenly she could see the striking figure of Sir Jason silhouetted against the protective shades of her lids—the raw masculine need with which he always beheld her. She could still taste the briny sweetness of this need, and without even being conscious of doing so, she dragged the tip of her tongue across the strawberry plump of her lower lip, taking up the flavorful memory that had so often a time been left upon them.

An abrupt clearing of a throat abruptly startled the distracted young woman from her reflections, and the heavy lids of her eyes popped open, only to reveal her travel companion staring oddly at her. She smiled at him shyly, hoping he would assume that the burn on her cheeks stemmed from the closed-in warmth of their car rather than from any erotic mental meanderings. Colin returned her smile and reached forward to pat her hand which, for some reason, trembled in her lap. A distinctive throbbing had commenced within what had at one time been Celia's most secret of places until her beloved's iniquitous cousin had forced her to reveal all that she might once have held private. Indeed, she no longer harbored any secrets from Sir Jason Hardwicke; they had been pried from her like the furled petals of a newly born rose that refused to blossom without coercion. For Sir Jason simply could not abide secrets of any kind.

All at once Celia realized that Colin was speaking to her. She did not even need to listen to know what was being said, for he had been speaking the same words ever since his older cousin had seen them off at the station in York. She could still see Jason standing on the puddled platform with the cold English rain pattering down upon him, turning his beige trench coat a muddy brown and making inky curls from the already dark waves of his hair. His ivory-handled umbrella remained at his side, unopened. Had his eyes glittered with unshed tears or was it merely an illusion created by the water droplets on the dirt-streaked window of their car? For suddenly he had seemed so alone to her. Then his broad shoulders had stiffened with a practiced aloofness and he had turned away from the two nervous passengers awaiting the first rude lurch of the train which signaled its departure, his impressive figure striding purposefully back in the direction whence they had come. What made Celia wonder if she would ever see him again?

Rather than responding to her beloved's hopeful chatter with verbal confirmation, she nodded absently, not really agreeing with him, yet not really disagreeing either. Despite all that had gone before, Colin was still somewhat naive when it came to his elder cousin. As for Celia, any naïveté she might once have possessed with regard to her young man's enigmatic relative had been thoroughly vanquished from her a long time ago—indeed, vanquished the instant she had stepped over the threshold of Moorland House. She entertained no such childlike beliefs that Sir Jason had grown tired of his games and, out of the kindness of his heart, decided to send the young couple off on the road to freedom—away not only from his wicked ways, but from the authorities as well, for they were still pursuing Colin Hardwicke for a murder he did not commit. Granted, the investigation had lost much of its steam; many months had passed and other murders had taken place which now needed to be solved. Why, a mad ripper was right at that very moment on the loose in the south, leaving as his calling card a bloodied trail of victims from Gloucester to Brighton. Nevertheless, poor Colin would never be free so long as he remained on English soil—not unless the real killer came forth, which appeared highly unlikely at this juncture. Although Celia still wished to remain optimistic that the case would one day be put to rest, she just could not rid herself of the nagging sensation that Sir Jason had somehow lent a hand toward its creation. Yet as their train transported them farther and farther from his realm of control, she began to wonder if maybe Colin might be right after all—that maybe his cousin *had* finally grown weary of his twisted games.

Indeed, all Sir Jason Hardwicke appeared to be growing weary of was the endless cold, damp, dreary days and nights of the Yorkshire moors. Had he not said so many times? His dashing plan to spirit his fugitive cousin out of the country had not been born out of the goodness of his heart, but rather from a selfish desire to move on to lands more hospitable to his needs. How could Colin possibly think that the man had taken his fill of Celia's ripe young body and now simply wished to relinquish her back into the eagerly waiting hands of his younger cousin? Surely Jason would not have undertaken the risk of doctoring his own passport with the tiny black-and-white photographs of a temporarily mustached and goateed Colin and a stern-lipped but still sensual Celia if he no longer had any use for them. Why, he could go to prison for such tampering!

As it happened, Sir Jason had matters timed so perfectly that the moment their Channel steamer was scheduled to dock in Boulogne, he would be reporting on the unexpected loss of his passport and simultaneously applying for its duplicate. If, as Colin was so keen to believe, his older relative did not have any plans to join them later, then why should he go to the bother of securing for himself a replacement document? Indeed, Celia knew the reason why, even if her poor befuddled Colin did not.

Yes, perhaps it was extremely generous of Jason to offer his passport to the couple so that they would be able to travel as Sir and Lady Jason Hardwicke. How shocked Celia had been when she learned that her wicked captor had once been married, however briefly.

Jason Hardwicke did not often reflect upon his failed marriage, let alone discuss it—if indeed, it could even have been called *a marriage*. Vivian had gotten the deed annulled quicker than he had managed to pull his trousers back up. The newlyweds had not even enjoyed a full night together as man and wife before the silly thing had gone running off on the eve of their wedding and back into the overprotective arms of her family. Never would Sir Jason have imagined that such a flirtatious vixen would balk at her new bridegroom's salacious desires. Since Vivian came from a titled family in North Yorkshire, her occasional romps with his peers were no secret to him, and he presumed that the lady of his selection would be well up to his masculine demands. For those lips that had repeated the well-worn nuptials before the local vicar were not the lips of an innocent, and the lush womanly curves of her body were not hidden so chastely beneath the frivolous layers of shiny white satin. She had looked like a lamb being led to slaughter, save for the knowing glint in her eye. Why, even that whisky-flushed buffoon of a vicar could see that she had indulged in acts of a far less reputable nature than the one he proposed!

In what was to have been the couple's marriage bed, Jason unwrapped as much as he could manage of the extravagantly swathed parcel of his new bride, ceasing his efforts when he encountered the complex series of laces crisscrossing the front of her corset. For indeed, what he intended would only require the use of her lower half. Bending Vivian's half-clad form forward, he endeavored to slip it into her from behind, only to find the stately gift of his penis rudely rebuffed by a most unwelcoming backside. Instead the silly woman kept fidgeting about as if subtly to reroute her handsome young husband into her more traditional thoroughfare. Surely she did not imagine that *he,* Sir Jason Hardwicke, was so unskilled in the ways of Eros not to have realized which opening he was in the midst of pursuing?

Hence the determined gentleman decided to make matters clearer. To induce his bride into being more cooperative, Jason reached round to massage her clitoris—an act he noticed was not in the least bit repulsed by her. Although pleasingly silken in texture, it felt rather small to him and, despite his unceasing efforts, it steadfastly refused to puff up against his fingertip. Nevertheless, Vivian appeared to relax, her clenched buttocks losing much of their tenseness. With her attentions thusly occupied, Jason was now ready to claim the territory that had previously shunned him. Like the most expert of archers taking aim at the bright red bull's-eye of a target, Jason launched the angrily swollen head of his penis into the mouth of Vivian's unsuspecting backside, her protests for him to desist from such actions falling upon unhearing ears. Indeed, he had no intention of producing an heir just yet, a fact which he assumed had been well understood and agreed upon by his bride. But apparently it was not, for the new Lady Hardwicke ran off into the misty night, never to return to Moorland House again.

Vivian's rejection had wounded Jason deeply. When had any female dared to refuse such a fine male specimen in her bottom? He could only attribute it to the young woman's parochial upbringing in the Dales. *These Yorkshire lasses!* he mused sourly. Never again would Sir Jason Hardwicke bother with the likes of them.

As if to cuckold the abandoned bridegroom, their joint passport arrived the following week in time for what would have been their honeymoon in Corfu. Needless to say, Jason would not allow himself a moment of defeat. Hence he set sail alone for that seaport island, ready and willing to bury his sorrows within the bronzed, sun-heated bodies of the prettiest local girls.

And indeed, his glossy dark hair and flashing dark eyes set so dramatically against his fine white English skin dazzled the knickers off the female residents of the isle; thus he had no shortage of fleshly entertainment—entertainment which included the delicious deed that had been denied to him by his ridiculously provincial bride. Yet not for a single instant did he deceive himself that such attentions were born out of love. No doubt many a woman who sought his sophisticated company harbored the hope that the handsome young Englishman might be willing to take her back home to his land of pale flesh and continuous rain and four o'clock cuppas. For although the island might have appeared a paradise to a tourist, it could frequently be a hell for girls of little means whose only future was to grow fat and squat like their mothers as they spent their lives cleaning up after their sweaty fishermen husbands and their dirty-mitted children.

Thus it was no wonder that these pretty young females who blessed the saints daily allowed the visiting Englishman to commit acts which would have surely gotten them banished from the church and, indeed, banished from the pious bosoms of their families. Despite his single-minded pursuit of personal pleasure, Sir Jason was not totally immune to their sad plight. Even though he had no intention of bringing one of these island Gypsies back home to Yorkshire with him, he always made certain to sprinkle enough drachmas into their always-upturned palms so that they might eventually make their way off the island and perhaps on to a better life. His generous reputation quickly became known, providing his randy penis with an endless supply of supple posteriors ready and willing and, indeed, eager to be deflowered. Yet no matter how much she may have pleaded, never once would he service a woman in the sanctioned manner, for Sir Jason Hardwicke did not relish the idea of being dragged by the collar up the church steps for a hasty Orthodox wedding.

A sheen of moisture dulled the pristine blue of Celia's eyes as she gazed out upon the churning gray seas of the Strait of Dover and back toward the fine green landscape she and Colin had just left behind. Though she tried to convince herself that what she now experienced was a feeling of nostalgia for the land of her birth, somewhere deep within the fundamental core of her being she realized that it was something else. And that something was Sir Jason Hardwicke.

Whilst on the train, she had very nearly told Colin that she wished to go back—that he should complete the journey on his own. Only how could she tell the man she loved—indeed, the man to whom she had been betrothed and very likely still was—that she wanted to return to the depraved arms of his cousin—a man who had made it his daily vocation to dominate and humiliate her? So instead Celia kept her shameful desires silent, watching sadly as the chalky white cliffs of Dover grew less majestic—watching until they merely resembled a child's opaque scribble. Sir Jason had assured her he would be joining them as soon as he deemed it prudent to do so. Obviously he would need to wait for the issuance of a duplicate passport. And this would be conditional upon nothing going awry at their end—on the French authorities in Boulogne would not noticing that the two tiny photographs pasted so recently onto the page did not fit exactly into the ghosts of their celluloid predecessors. However, since Jason was so typically English in his prejudices toward the French, he did not really anticipate any sudden show of astuteness on their part. For everyone's sake, Celia hoped to heaven he was right.

Suddenly Colin appeared at her side. Believing his delicate ladylove's woebegone face resulted from the cold, he led her away from the bow and inside where the warmth could comfort their chilled bones. It seemed impossible that their intended destination could be so warm when the land they had only moments before departed from could be so damnably cold. Indeed, Colin was grateful to be leaving; he, like his older cousin, had had enough of the foul weather of the Yorkshire moors. Yet somehow the cold and the damp no longer affected Celia as much as it had once done. For how could her body feel the bitterness of the elements when she spent her days and nights feeding Sir Jason Hardwicke's unremitting sexual appetites? Even now with the icy wind of the Channel blowing so cruelly upon her, a sultry heat had begun to creep up her body—a heat which had originated between her tightly clenched thighs. She could still feel the inflexible column of Sir Jason's penis rubbing against her as she stood facing away from him, the sharp winter wind sneaking in through a tiny gap below the shut window and stiffening her strawberry-shaded nipples. Her resulting shivers would not be brought about by the cold, however.

That evening Celia had glanced down in grievous embarrassment at the obscenely bulging flap of her clitoris, only to see its lustrous pink being eclipsed by a bulging purple knob equal, if not greater, in its obscenity. The stocky shaft that followed split rudely through a pair of modestly pursed lips which had only moments before been treated to the sharp, exacting blade of a razor. Sir Jason's fingers clutched her buttocks, keeping them apart and utilizing them as a means of support as he slid back and forth within the flooded sluiceway of her perineum. With each of these modified thrusts, the dark springy curls upon his pubis would tickle the exposed notch of Celia's freshly shaven anus in the most provocative of fashions, stirring desires she still felt too shy to express. Fortunately, with Sir Jason words were a commodity not often required, for his instincts on matters of sexuality had never yet been proven wrong. Indeed, one only needed to witness how far the once-chaste Celia had advanced in her erotic tastes to know that his initial judgment of her had been correct.

Celia pressed her quaking thighs together tightly, luxuriating in the concentrated stimulation of her clitoris that was provided with such skill by Jason's slippery organ and his lascivious tongue, for he adored offending her delicate sensibilities with a few well-pointed remarks upon the extremely disheveled condition of her lusty organ. How he delighted in halting his actions in order to more thoroughly examine and comment upon the chaos he had wrought, occasionally drawing the sumptuous bulk into his mouth to incite further disarray. Indeed, nothing could compare to the sudden flush of pink upon Celia's cheeks when he pulled her open to expose the full feminine perfection of her similarly flushed extremity. He would often spend several leisurely and, for the recipient, *torturous* minutes just breathing in its exotic perfume and observing the resulting excited flutters before resuming his seductive penile stroking of her external parts.

During such sensory-stimulating encounters, this astute gentleman preferred to save the rhapsodic moment of penetration for the very end when Celia would cry out in shameful ecstasy—when his carefully calculated attack had finally become far too much for the well-cleaved knurl to bear and it was at last forced to abandon its struggle. Hence in the splendor of her indignity, Celia would truly be ready for him.

Jason urged the still-bucking and -squirming young woman's torso forward and plunged juicily into the palpitating passage of her vagina, the smell of her making him light-headed and greedy for more. For no matter how many times he possessed her or in how many ways, each occasion proved as delicious as the first. The moist sweet kisses Celia's hot folds had lavished upon the gliding vessel of his prick had been nearly enough to bring him to orgasm, as had the piquant taste of her clitoris; therefore it would not require very many pumps for Jason to finalize the deed. He filled her womanly thoroughfare to overflowing, surprised when his reservoir seemed in no imminent danger of being depleted. Several of his fingers found their eager way into the moist furrow whose elasticized perimeter had previously been exercised by parting her buttocks, prompting yet another powerful reaction from the frantic young woman. Aptly rewarded, he continued with these dorsal ministrations, the better to facilitate their next encounter....

Just the sensation of that scorching interior against his immersed fingers was sufficient to stir Jason's spent penis into action. The juices Celia had deposited earlier upon his masculine flesh continued to drip from it unchecked, and he quickly took advantage of this well-drenched condition by plunging into her finger-primed anus in one go. It was an approach this discerning gentleman very much preferred over the more painstaking series of increments that might often be required when a lady's hind port of entry was not yet ready to receive a visitor…although even with sufficient preparation and lubrication, many were still unable to house so stately a specimen as a Hardwicke cock. Nevertheless, he prided himself upon his stature—a stature shared by few men save for his younger cousin who, thanks to Jason's expert tutelage, had learned how best to utilize his manly asset.

Yes, his fugitive relative had certainly journeyed a long way from the diffident lad who had first appeared at the gates of Moorland House seeking refuge. Sir Jason had been a very fine mentor, indeed, however, he still had a great deal left to teach. With this first and foremost in his mind, he bent Celia forward from the waist as far as the limits of her lovely body would permit, thus placing her quivering buttocks and the anxiously convulsing slot between them at his complete disposal. Her honey-colored tresses swept the floor, gathering up any errant particles of dust beneath the faded Chinese rug that the old charwoman had failed to brush with her broom.

To Celia's horror, the man who had manipulated her into so ungainly a pose suddenly called out for Colin. Alerted by the dire sense of urgency in his elder cousin's tone, he appeared within seconds, only to discover his blushing beloved gracelessly contorted with her head dangling between her outspread shins and her hands clamped tightly upon her crooked knees in order to keep herself from toppling over. The commanding figure of Sir

Jason Hardwicke rose up behind her, the proud stalk of his penis stabbing juicily and victoriously into the inflamed opening of her dramatically out-thrust bottom.

Jealousy had long since become an emotion Colin Hardwicke could not afford to cultivate. Nevertheless, he still occasionally deluded himself with the thought that the wicked Jason had forced himself upon the demure Celia—that such a villainous transaction as the one taking place before him would have instantly been met with repulsion had it not been for the circumstances in which they now found themselves—circumstances which would have prompted Colin's immediate arrest had Celia not agreed to allow her body—and indeed, her mind—to be used and dominated and defiled by his unscrupulous relative. Or at least this was what he endeavored to believe as he looked upon the two interlocked figures—one male, one female—his ears burning hotly with the wet smacking sounds of their unnatural convergence. In her degradation, his darling Celia was protecting him, using her poor little bottomhole as a device to placate the perverse lust of a man capable of seeing his own flesh and blood hang by the neck for a murder he had not committed. Surely she could not enjoy this vile deed—a deed Colin himself indulged in with her as often as possible. But of course *that* was different. After all, they were engaged to be married! With Jason it had become an act of force and humiliation—an act its shamefaced beneficiary would have happily refused if such an option had been made available to her.

Yet try as he might, Colin could not ignore the severely inflated tongue of Celia's clitoris that, with every brutal plunge of his cousin's penis, seemed to extend farther and farther away from the dew-covered pods encasing it. Nor could he ignore the desperation with which Celia's fingers had begun to spin it. Indeed, the lids of her eyes had fallen closed in euphoric delight, the delicate softness of her face hardening in concentration as a plaintive series of moans escaped from her saliva-moistened lips.

Unbeknownst to either Hardwicke, Celia had come to love this form of penetration, and indeed, to prefer it over all others. She thrust the perfect mounds of her buttocks back in brazen abandon against her oversized intruder, her fingers moving the slippery flap faster and faster between her parted thighs. Sir Jason obliged in kind, ramming into her with a violence he had heretofore kept under check. Had the aroused young woman's particular penchant for this method of invasion been a fact well hidden, it would be hidden no more. For all at once she pleaded with her cruel lover not to spare her, the words spilling from her lips as raw and rude as those heard from the coarsest Wapping dockworker.

"Tell me again!" cried Jason, his voice strangled with emotion.

Thus Celia's shameful secret was out.

life in provence...

Never would the two weary travelers have expected to discover so charming a house awaiting them. From its blue-shuttered quaintness to its ancient wood-burning stove—not even the eccentric privy could tarnish their joy. Neither Celia nor Colin could have invented a more perfect haven for themselves. Nestled snugly within the fertile wine country between Avignon and Châteaurenard, this typically Provençal dwelling showed itself to be as warm and romantic as Moorland House was cold and indifferent. Indeed, Celia found it difficult to believe that only a few days earlier she had been crying out for Sir Jason to empty every last boiling drop of his seed into her thirsty bottom. Oh, the words she had used!

Even now, in this unsullied atmosphere not populated by sinister shadows or corrupt whispers, she still cringed with shame.

Yet with the passing of days, the taint of shame upon her mind and body began to fade, only to be replaced by a lazy sensuality. For at last Celia and Colin would have only each other to please. There were no crass demands to be met, nor impossible performances to attempt. Here in the late Provence afternoon as a sun like the inside of a blood orange lowered itself over an azure horizon, they would lie languid and naked upon the overstuffed feather mattress of their bed, their bodies flushed and moist from their lovemaking. The shutters on the windows would be thrown open to let in the distinctive singing of the cicadas and the fragrance of lavender from the nearby fields, which combined with the postorgasmic fragrance of their bodies. At moments such as these, Celia could almost imagine living this way forever.

For suddenly they had become like any other young couple in love—walking hand in hand to the tiny village a few kilometers down the dusty road, performing ordinary tasks about the house, frolicking naked in the garden beneath the warm Provençal sun... Sir Jason and his aberrant appetites seemed continents away instead of across the Strait of Dover. Celia began to wonder if Colin might be right after all—if maybe his cousin would *not* come—if this idyllic French landscape was theirs and theirs alone.

Regardless of such simple joys, something nagged at Celia—indeed, nagged at her during those infrequent times when she found herself alone—and that *something* was the person of Sir Jason Hardwicke. Although she loved Colin as much as she had ever done, she secretly longed for the taste of his cousin upon her tongue and the hard hot flesh of him in her backside. The mere thought of such forbidden delights prompted the young woman's trembling fingertips to locate the burgeoning pink bud between her thighs, which she would rub and rub with a heartrending desperation, praying for the day when she could once again be allowed to do so before the all-knowing eyes of the man who had taught her how to revel in her disgrace. Celia made certain to concentrate her efforts most industriously so that the yearning projectile of her clitoris attained a size and flush most becoming to it, and hence most fragrant and alluring for the ruthless individual who so often desired to call attention to this uniquely feminine appendage. Oh, how pleased Sir Jason would be! For, in his cruelty there could be kindness as well. And that kindness did not preclude a long luxurious suckle upon the flickering flame his words and deeds had ignited.

Nevertheless, Celia kept this particular aspect of her life hidden away from Colin, for he would most probably misunderstand her need, interpreting her extra self-stimulation in this region as a sign that he had not done enough to please her. Although this was not necessarily the case, she realized that she missed his older cousin's more aggressive manner and his obsessive hunger to possess her so completely and thoroughly, even at the expense of her pride. She required such treatment in order to experience the violent explosion of sensation that so often came upon her when she least expected—an explosion which always seemed to take place during moments of the most supreme humiliation. Yes, Celia knew what her body and mind craved, for indeed, the two acted in lustful concert. But how could she admit these shameful truths to her beloved?

Ever since fleeing England and the libidinous influences of Sir Jason Hardwicke, Colin's sexual tempestuousness had returned to its earlier gentlemanly dormancy, leaving him in much the same state as his lady-love originally found him. In the gentle springtime warmth of Provence, his touch had grown shyer and more tentative—more temperate in nature than what Celia had become accustomed to and grown to crave in the moors. She often felt as if none of it had ever happened—as if those lascivious days and nights in Moorland House had simply been the subject of some twisted erotic dream, especially if one were to judge by Colin's more cautious treatment of her. Perhaps he felt ashamed of his all-too-willing conspiracy with his wicked relative and now wished to make up for it. Or perhaps his more disreputable desires had suddenly been rendered mute without the corrupting influence of Sir Jason at his side, rallying him on—challenging him, even. Indeed, Celia began to feel that Colin treated her like a wife. Granted, at one time this might have made her very happy. Only now she wasn't so sure.

Despite the regularity of the couple's physical encounters, she discovered them lacking that very special brand of magic she had come to take for granted. Perhaps these encounters had become *too* regular. Although their coming together was as natural as the rural landscape surrounding them, it was the *unnatural* this bereft female desired. To her increasing dismay, Colin appeared to have forgotten all the lusty activities they had once so gleefully indulged in. Irrespective of what had gone on with the two cousins in Yorkshire, Celia was still naturally prone toward shyness when it came to expressing her true desires. And with the absence of Sir Jason, it had become all the more difficult. How could a properly brought-up young lady such as herself possibly ask her young gentleman to put it in her backside or use his tongue on her? Such delights had been the stuff of daily fare back on the moors; at times Colin's depravity had equaled, if not exceeded, that of his cousin. Why, she could even remember how eagerly he had licked out the fingerfulls of sticky orange marmalade he had introduced into the timid opening of her bottom while she had crouched before him, trembling with dishonorable excitement. Yes, her darling Colin could be wicked when the mood swayed him! But he had changed since coming to Provence; he had become more like his old self—the self she knew back in London. Although that man might once have been all she had ever wanted or needed, he was no longer enough. For Celia, too, had changed. And it was all because of Sir Jason Hardwicke.

Hence, when her desires finally became too much for her to bear, she was forced to swallow her pride and whisper shamefully to Colin in the dark of night all the things her body yearned for. He eventually obliged, however, a sharp intake of breath made it clear that he considered such wanton requests well beneath the demure young woman to whom he still considered himself betrothed. How Celia flushed with her disgrace as her handsome beloved fitted the purple knob of his penis into the needful port she had just beseeched him to invade, his journey made all the more difficult by its recent lapse of activity. Perhaps Colin believed she no longer wished for such admittedly base acts and had merely gone along with them in order to placate his blackmailing cousin and, indeed, to placate himself. For had he not also made identical demands upon her delicate young body—and made them with nearly the same frequency?

Indeed, Colin's grudging compliance made Celia feel like a woman of iniquity…although she could not help but notice that such a grudging compliance did not extend to the throbbing column of masculine desire

THE POSSESSION OF CELIA

stretching and straining the presently unpracticed walls of her rectum. Nor did it extend to the bountiful torrent of seething liquid that jetted up through her so deeply she believed she would burst. Nevertheless, he refused to speak to Celia afterward—not even if the tongue that would have formed his words had just finished licking away the creamy deluge from between her thighs. Yet perhaps this silence was a blessing, for afterward, when she promptly absorbed the phallic flesh still hot and fragrant from its rigorous scavenging of her rear conduit into her mouth, Colin replied coldly and with great condemnation: "I am *not* my cousin."

The continual sense of wrongdoing Celia had come to experience with her young gentleman would always make an appearance during such untoward moments. Indeed, the only occasion when it faded into the background of her consciousness was when her beloved took her in the customary manner. How his attitude toward her would change! Suddenly it was as if Colin had been saving it up for a lifetime—as if his recreational defilement of her body in Moorland House had never occurred. Celia considered this recent behavior odd. One might have thought that in Yorkshire he had been denied indulgence in the traditional form of coitus, yet had it not been Colin himself who had instigated any practices to the contrary? For regardless of where they were, whether in the kitchen or vestibule or garden, Celia's knickers would be down round her ankles before she had even realized it, and the younger Hardwicke's ever-voracious penis expanding the moistened interior of her vagina until she felt she would split in two. She feared such boyish foolhardiness might very well get her with child. Unlike his older, and indeed, wiser, cousin, Colin did not seem the least bit mindful of the details of her monthly cycle.

Thanks to a new awareness of her body gotten from Sir Jason, Celia could accurately gauge when it would be the least prudent of her to entertain a gentleman in the sanctioned fashion, therefore she tried valiantly to stave off her beloved's amorous attentions when she deemed the risk to be too great. Surely they could indulge their fleshly desires in other ways—ways she found she now preferred over the orthodox form of male-female joining. For along with the rapture arrived a potent sense of shame—a sense of shame Sir Jason liked to court and inflame; indeed, he knew how best to draw out Celia's humiliation until it became the most supreme form of ecstasy. Perhaps it was the absolute sense of freedom such alternative couplings brought —this ability to take pleasure without having to pay a heavy price for it, other than the price of her dignity. In Yorkshire, this complete liberation of her body and mind had been hers. But Provence had changed everything.

To save herself from the careless application of her beloved's semen, Celia began to develop the occasional well-timed headache, which always seemed to occur at precise three-and-a-half-week intervals and last for approximately two to three days or until the familiar pain in her abdomen had faded. She soon came to resent the sullen pout upon Colin's handsome face—a pout which told her that he did not entirely believe her furrowed brow and slitted eyes. Strange that a man normally so tender should fail to demonstrate the same consideration toward her as his relentless relative during these occasions of fecundity. Had Colin at long last grown tired of sharing his woman with another and now merely wished to lay claim to her once and for all? Sir Jason did not need to prove his total possession of Celia by planting within her womb his fertile Hardwicke seed. For he had possessed her from the first moment he had known of her existence.

Indeed, the senior Hardwicke would not allow a matter of female biology to deter him from his passions. When the time of danger happened upon them, he would amuse himself with the equally pleasurable orifices of Celia's mouth or bottomhole. Ofttimes he would stave off from her womanly thoroughfare completely, reserving himself for the fluid delights which were soon due to arrive. For five days and nights Sir Jason would satisfy his blood lust, relishing the subtle differences the passing of each would bring. As a true connoisseur of Celia's alluring form, he could not allow such a unique opportunity to be lost, for the exquisiteness of the molten heat of her monthly discharges and the elysian passage through which they flowed were rivaled only by the exquisiteness of her shame. After he had finished indulging himself within the riches of her menses, he would wield the bloodied crown of his still-tumescent penis like a paintbrush, the rubies dripping from it creating a dramatic chiaroscuro upon Celia's pale swells and curves—in effect branding her with the visual evidence of her unbreakable bond with him.

Occasionally the physical and emotional exertions they had undergone together would cause them both to fall into a deep slumber—a slumber whose termination would result in yet another sanguinary encounter. The rusty smears of red upon their two perspiring bodies only made Celia realize just how relentlessly thorough was Sir Jason Hardwicke's possession of her. Could she harbor no secrets from this wicked man? For indeed, when he licked the resulting spatters from his fingertips, his knowledge of her would thenceforth be complete.

Indeed, was *this* what Celia now pined for? For all of a sudden she seemed willing to give up the more gentle ministrations of Colin for the more savage ministrations of his cousin. Had she, in her supposed protection of her dearest loved one's neck, finally fallen the rest of the way into Sir Jason's bottomless well of debauchery?

Colin was growing extremely fond of the quiet domestic life with his darling Celia—so fond that he began to fancy the two of them together forever. And it was a forever that would *not* be including his degenerate rogue of a cousin! How his heart warmed at the sight of an aproned Celia standing at the kitchen sink washing the food-encrusted plates from their meal or stretching out her arm to run a dampened cloth over the knotty pine of the table they had just finished dining upon. During moments such as these, Colin could almost imagine a normal life with her—the life they undoubtedly would have had if only his contemptible relative had not taken it upon himself to intervene in their love. They could have been married and living in a house very much like this one, the happy sounds of children filling the air and filling their hearts. But perhaps it was not too late….

Beneath the clear azure sky and the pristine lemony light of a sun unsullied by either cloud or rain, it began to seem as if the degrading acts the three of them had indulged in so readily and frequently and, indeed, *wantonly* at Moorland House were events of years rather than weeks past. How could he have allowed such evils to take place? For in his selfishness to save his own neck, Colin had gone and sacrificed the body and soul of his beloved Celia. It had been criminal enough to play silent spectator while his nefarious cousin forced his salacious attentions upon her innocent young flesh, but to have willingly participated in such transgressions! Not even a mere two days before their feet had left English soil had he and Jason placed themselves before her mouth, their greedy Hardwicke penises side by side in cousinly communion. Indeed, so well versed had Celia become with regard to the erratic nature of their masculine desires that she did not even need to be instructed upon what to do.

In her flushed nakedness, she had fallen to her knees, the strawberry plumpness of her lower lip quivering in what both men had assumed to be anticipation. And their assumption had quickly proven itself correct, for Celia's hands had reached up and grasped these wildly bobbing pillars of brawny flesh, their slender wrists still bound together from an earlier encounter which had involved the application of a nozzle and a great many photographs. Hence, as Jason and Colin propelled their pelvises forward, the seductive pout of Celia's mouth had opened wide to absorb the identical purple knobs whose tiny pinholes leaked with the viscous evidence of their lust. Never before had the two handsome cousins simultaneously shared an orifice and, not surprisingly, they found the one they occupied somewhat cramped. Still, this lack of accommodation did not diminish their enjoyment in the least—not even when Celia's teeth had scraped against the thickly ridged corona of each penis, providing them both with an exquisite torment. *Perhaps this was similar to what she experienced during a rigorous session of buggery,* Sir Jason had mused with a secret smile. For he knew well the merits of blending pleasure with pain.

Thus the shackled young woman had feasted upon the two cousins together, doling out equally loving portions of rapture to both until their manly offerings spewed hotly onto the velvety surface of her tongue and down her graceful throat. How diligently she had consumed this creamy Hardwicke confection, only to pay tribute to them by asking for more. Yet here in the wholesome warmth of a Provençal spring, such previously stolen repasts suddenly seemed vile to Colin. They were the stuff of the moors and of the man whose gloom-shrouded windows overlooked them. They were the stuff of Sir Jason Hardwicke.

Yes! Colin would redeem himself by making Celia his wife.

The image of divine matrimonial bliss her young man proposed did not prove particularly objectionable to Celia either. These recent days had made her realize how their life together could have been had the corrupt Sir Jason Hardwicke not decided to enter it. Only somehow she could not imagine living her life any other way. Even though she adored being with Colin, she could not ignore her pangs of desire for his elder cousin—nor her subsequent need to be dominated by him. Thanks to Sir Jason, Celia had discovered more about herself than if she had lived ten lifetimes...perhaps more than she might ever have wished to discover. Indeed, it was too late. Pandora had opened the box and encountered riches beyond her wildest imaginings—the riches of the flesh. And these riches were irrevocably linked to the man whose hot aristocratic blood also coursed through the veins of her betrothed.

Ergo, Celia would try ever so subtly and gently to deflect Colin's ever-increasing and ever-desperate hints for the two of them to continue with their life of domestic bliss together, especially a domestic bliss which included children. Perhaps one day she might like to have a child...only whose child would she have? Colin's? Jason's? The prospect seemed so remote— impossible, even. No. Being alone with her beloved was one thing, but watching her belly grow fat with his child quite another. Oh, why did he go on about it so? Why could he not allow matters to continue as they were? Surely this kind of talk could lead to no good.

Yet with the passing of time and the fading of memory, Colin's words soon began to make sense to her. Moorland House and its manipulative master had not been real. What *was* real, however, were the vivid hues of the lavender fields and the salty breezes blowing in from the Mediterranean, bringing with them the smell of the sea and the smell of freedom—a freedom which had been denied this young couple for far too long—a freedom they had tasted, albeit briefly. Celia could still see herself skipping along the ancient fourteenth-century streets of Avignon during that first week of their arrival when they had gone to visit the Palace of the Popes, which she had read so much about in school. But it was those moments they spent in the local village that held the most significance for her. How they relished the carefree joy of shopping in the little market square, plucking shiny green apples from their coarsely woven baskets or testing the weight of an earth-speckled potato beneath the affectionately watchful eye of the old gap-toothed greengrocer Madame Roualt. With their purchases placed safely in a burlap sack brought from home, Celia and Colin would move on to the neighboring meat market where they leisurely examined a glistening cut of beef as the whiskey-throated butcher, Monsieur Gastón, looked on with a pride borne of generations of men who have made their livings thusly.

Once they had trudged back to the blue-shuttered house with a sunny morning's worth of shopping straining their arms and a layer of road dust darkening their skin, they would strip off their sweat-moistened garments and run giggling into the flowering garden. And there beneath the leathery-leafed shade of an aged olive tree, Colin would slip quickly inside the woman he loved, the desire-swollen head of his penis easily reaching the end of its course as her vagina melted in the growing heat of the day. The liquescent sounds of their convergence joined with the joyous chirping of birds and the incessant drone of the cicadas, creating a highly provocative choir. Thusly inspired, Celia would roll on top of him, drawing her thighs up and wrapping them about his naked torso so that her buttocks projected sharply out behind her. She enjoyed this sensation of being so exposed—so unprotected from any dangers that might have been lurking nearby. Of course such dangers would usually be in the form of Colin's wicked relation.

All of a sudden Celia would imagine him there behind her, watching...observing...indeed, *studying* the dainty cluster of crinkles that wreathed her bottomhole. Sir Jason would be so close that she could feel the excited heat of his breath blowing upon it. Surely he would not fail to notice how, with every plunge of his cousin's penis, the unoccupied hatchway would burst deliciously open. A man of his salacious sensibilities would undoubtedly have accepted this as a personal invitation—as perhaps it might very well *have* been if only he had been there in person to receive it. Hence, when Celia would turn her head in search of this phantom Hardwicke, she would discover herself bitterly disappointed by his absence.

Burying his face beneath the fragrant curtain of her hair, Colin would lick the salt from her neck, occasionally reaching down and tickling the moist notch of her out-thrust bottom...although this was usually the extent of any such contact unless Celia wished to press the point. Indeed, she soon came to look upon these all-too-infrequent fingerings as a special treat. However, rather than begging her beloved for their elaboration, Celia would shimmy her backside about until it had absorbed the teasing digit in its entirety. If Colin ever detected the furtiveness of her actions, he never once let on. Instead, his finger remained snugly housed within this yearning passage, often thrusting in conjunction with the thrusts of his penis until he and Celia reached the pinnacle of their pleasure. Hot and sweaty, they would cool themselves by taking the garden hose to one another, squealing like a pair of children as the arc of cold water washed over their sex-flushed bodies. Colin would manipulate the moderate stream into a powerful jet and aim it playfully at the bulging knurl of Celia's clitoris, chuckling merrily as she bucked to and fro in shivery orgasm, her aqueous pleasure rousing them both to yet another molten coupling beneath the olive tree.

Nevertheless, such innocent and simple freedoms were scheduled to be ruined by the impending arrival of Sir Jason Hardwicke and his aberrant appetites—appetites which would soon include a far more mischievous use of the garden hose.

Although Celia did not particularly wish to choose one handsome cousin over the other, it seemed that she would have little choice. For in spite of its inherent danger, she eventually agreed to Colin's wild scheme. Indeed, they would flee the blue-shuttered house in Provence a mere two days before Sir Jason reached Boulogne.

celia and colin's flight...

The couple took with them what few francs they had in their possession along with a handful of shillings and precious pounds left over from their journey across the English Channel—all of which had been carefully doled out by Sir Jason Hardwicke—and made their way south toward the Mediterranean. They moved by foot and by the good graces of whoever or whatever happened to be passing, which was usually one of the farmers from the nearby orchards hauling his wares to market. Perhaps in Marseilles they would manage to locate the captain of a fishing boat willing enough to take them across the glittering blue-green sea to Italy. Or at least this was Colin and Celia's hope as they dozed fitfully in the backs of broken-down carts heaped with olives or oranges or the brambly remains of grapevines that had outlived their productivity. On one occasion they were even forced to share space in the rear of a hobbling old wagon, their only company for the journey a truffle-snuffling pig. But they had no choice; Sir Jason had left them with little in the way of funds save for what they would need to live on until his arrival. Most likely such intentional parsimoniousness indicated that he had already anticipated the possibility that the young couple might attempt to make a run for it.

While traveling the dusty road toward their hazy vision of freedom, Celia tried not to think about what Colin's forceful cousin would do once he finally found them. For she had no doubt that he would, indeed, find them. A man like Sir Jason Hardwicke would not be content to let matters rest—to accept what had happened and then do nothing. She could not imagine him relinquishing his claim upon her mind and body as if such commodities were easily replaceable. Of course she dared not give voice to her fears, for despite their temporary physical discomforts, Colin seemed so happy. Perhaps he had gotten lost in the dream of what he hoped would be their future. Celia, however, was of a more practical nature; she knew that they would require food and shelter and a reasonable amount of money to live on. And she also knew that such things were not easy to come by. In the moors, their immediate needs had all been taken care of for them—food on the table, wood in the fire, the sherry decanter always full.... Even those needs not deemed immediate would be met. Away from English soil, she and her beloved were foreigners—indeed, foreigners on the run. What could either one of them possibly offer the round swarthy faces they passed? Could Celia solicit her professional skills as a secretary to these country peasants? Could Colin demonstrate his business acumen from the assistant manager post he never received? Why, they couldn't even speak the language! They would have to go back to England; she could envision no other option before them. Sir Jason would never suspect that the young couple would be so cheeky as to return to the country they had just fled. Only they appeared to be going in the wrong direction. Should they not be heading north instead of south? After all, they were English. What could they possibly do in Italy?

Indeed, Sir Jason Hardwicke was nobody's fool. Had it been at all thinkable for him to do so, he would have happily accompanied the pair on the journey. Needless to say, the likelihood of two different Englishmen departing from Folkestone and arriving in Boulogne on the very same Channel steamer and owning the very same name...well, it would most certainly call attention to them, not to mention increase the odds of Colin's being picked up by the authorities! Yet perhaps that might have been for the best, for Jason often entertained the fantasy of being rid of his miserable cousin once and for all and having the delectable Celia all to himself. Oh, but she could be a woman of mercurial desires...one moment begging for his lascivious attentions, the next turning away in virginal protest. No. He simply could not take the risk. So long as Colin was near, Celia would remain within his realm.

Granted, the dear boy did have his occasional uses. For when Moorland House's lovely captive had shown herself to be particularly amenable to Jason's demands and, as a result, was deserving of a special reward, the younger Hardwicke would thusly be drafted into eager service. Initially Sir Jason had been shocked by the overwrought young woman's apparent passion for entertaining two Hardwicke pricks in her at the same time, especially when one considered the obvious discomfort and embarrassment it seemed to cause her. Indeed, a bewildered Celia would hide herself away in her bedchamber for hours at a time after the last offerings of Hardwicke seed had been deposited inside her, wallowing in a solitary disgrace neither cousin could coax her out of. With regular practice, such delicious dual penetrations grew far easier for their obliging recipient, even if her resulting shame from their acceptance did not. Although such lusty triads required great physical exertion and coordination from all concerned, the participants considered it well worth the extra effort, and it soon became impossible to determine who of the three enjoyed it more. Hence this was the fashion in which Celia would receive her reward, her petite young body sandwiched snugly between the two Hardwickes' wildly thrusting pelvises, her frantic cries of encouragement imploring both men not to spare her...indeed, to fill her as deeply and savagely as they could.

And they would comply without mercy, launching their voracious members into the nearest available passage, their commingled juices easing even the most difficult of journeys. Ofttimes Jason and Colin would switch positions in midstream, replacing vagina with rectum or rectum with vagina, for in so doing, no one would feel the least bit cheated or deprived. Normally the senior Hardwicke would take charge by choreographing how best to accomplish their mission, alternating between placing Celia in a wide-kneed squat with the two cousins to the fore and aft, or lying her faceup or facedown upon either Colin or himself. The latter method posed a minor problem, however, for the gentleman who ended up on the bottom would suffer from a restricted movement of the hips. As a result, the squat method was the one most utilized and mutually agreed upon by all.

It would be in this somewhat undignified stance that Celia would so often find herself shuddering with orgasm after orgasm, her lower half imprisoned luxuriously between the hardworking penises of the cousins

Hardwicke. In the utter thoroughness of her submission, she could truly give herself over to pure sensation. Indeed, the feel of having her neighboring interiors simultaneously plunged in and out of proved so ethereally unreal that she believed herself to be dreaming, for surely these thick columns of masculine flesh could not possibly fit inside her! Nevertheless, the turmoil arising from the repeated chafing of the burgeoning pink bud between her thighs told her that yes, it was all really happening...that yes, those were Sir Jason's and Colin's penises stretching her and splitting her in half.

Always with a mind toward ways in which further to enhance an erotic encounter with the demurely lusty Celia, Jason would situate a mirror beneath her widely splayed feet. By doing so, any participant who cared to look could reap the visual benefits of her dainty slit and anus being enlarged and pummeled by two hardy pricks...although one would need to act quickly, for the reflective tool of their voyeurism would soon become speckled with the impassioned juices raining down from above. He would always accept it as a personal victory whenever Celia bowed her head to investigate what was being done to her, her bashful curiosity eliciting from him the bawdiest of dialogues describing every subtle nuance of the succulent terrain his marauding member was in the midst of investigating. Each newly discovered bump or ridge would receive a highly detailed account designed to put the rouge to Celia's cheeks. Indeed, she still blushed every bit as sweetly as the first time he had subjected her to his flamboyant parlance, hence he would sweep the honey-colored tresses off her face the better to savor the enchanting color of her shame.

After their manly fluids had been thoroughly spent, the cousins would enter into battle to claim their own special prize, for these empyreal triads had a particularly vexing habit of wreaking havoc upon Celia's already-prominent clitoris. To her obvious embarrassment, it would puff up even larger, changing shape so often that it scarcely resembled its original form. By the time the two Hardwickes had finished partaking of their duel penetrations, it would have reached its final stage, the ragged chrysalis cleaving into a beautiful salmon pink butterfly poised in flight. The fortunate winner would capture this sumptuous flesh in his mouth, feeling it fluttering against his lips and tongue like the lustrous wings it resembled. It would taste even sweeter and juicier than the tiny ripe strawberries crowning Celia's breasts. Indeed, what better trophy could a man possibly wish for?

Remembering how it had been to be the victor, Sir Jason decided to depart for Provence a full three days earlier than originally planned…for a fragrant, dew-speckled silken butterfly awaited his kiss.

†††

Celia, too, well remembered these cousinly contests. How she would shiver in rapturous disgrace at the hungry sucklings taking place upon her womanly ornament! For each time she experienced the moist intimate warmth of Sir Jason's mouth, her disgrace would become all the more potent. Indeed, it was a disgrace she lived for with every breath of her being.

Yet even as her plundered passages burned with the ghostly impressions of the two stately specimens which had commandeered them, Celia would already be anxiously anticipating their speedy return—although she would never express to either of the Hardwickes so base and shameful a desire. Instead she would tenderly cradle their handsome dark heads against the ivory pillows of her breasts, her fingers making playful corkscrews of their wavy hair while their lips molded the nipple nearest them into a tiny spike. *How alike they are,* she would muse dreamily, realizing for perhaps the very first time how incredibly happy she was.

Such innocent revelries would quickly be eclipsed by the adroit presence of manly fingers probing about the widely flared lips of Celia's denuded vulva, dipping and sliding and spinning her into a tormented ecstasy. Nevertheless, this would only serve as a teasing precursor for even greater pleasures. For on those comradely occasions when Sir Jason and Colin decided to combine their oral efforts rather than competing against one another in a very uncousinlike fashion, it would be

Celia who emerged as the true victor. *Oh, if only it could always be like this!* she would sigh inwardly, shuddering gleefully and wetly beneath their two wriggling tongues. One would be stationed at the fore and the other to the aft, thereby replacing the more established and sizable masculine presences of their penises. How thoroughly and lovingly the two handsome cousins would lick the shy seam of her labia and the satiny crevasse between her quivering buttocks, slowly and painstakingly dragging their hot, yearning tongues from slit to clit and from bottomhole to tailbone—and all with nary a single hair to bar them! The movements of these feasting appendages would become as perfectly synchronized as those of their previously thrusting members, rendering their squirming beneficiary dizzy with delirium and eager for more.

As the Hardwicke men licked faster and faster, Celia's breath came quicker and quicker, her heart pounding harder and harder until she thought it would finally burst through her chest. A powerful explosion was building up—an explosion which would leave its recipient shaking and weeping and begging for a chance to reciprocate in kind. The two cousins could feel the savory hollows of their lovely quarry reacting to this intense dual stimulus; indeed, they could read Celia's enchanting young body with an expertise the majority of their sex could only dream of. Hence, at the precise moment of climax, Jason and Colin would plunge their desirous tongues deep inside the humid conduits of her vagina and rectum, relishing the orgasmic spasms their actions had incited as both slit and anus gripped these highly dexterous organs with a force great enough to render them forever speechless.

Tears of ecstasy would drip down Celia's flushing cheeks, a somewhat less salty version of which dripped down into the appreciative Hardwicke mouth below. For the first time in her life her innate sense of feminine embarrassment mattered naught. She would willingly endure any shame or humiliation regardless of its intensity just so that she could once again be granted an opportunity to experience such glorious pleasure at their hands—and yes, at their tongues.

Indeed, whatever shall we do in Italy? wondered Celia with a secret smile.

This was a question very much on Colin's troubled mind as well. For he, too, could not forget the impassioned trysts that had transpired in the moors—trysts which had caused him to question himself both as a man and as a protector of his beloved Celia. How could he ever have allowed matters to progress so far with his elder cousin? Yes, it would appear that he was as wicked and debauched as Sir Jason—if perhaps not even more so. For what man of a sane mind would have permitted the woman who had promised herself to him in holy wedlock become the victim of such unwholesome degradations?

But, oh, how deliciously divine were their many pleasures! Indeed, not even the length of the churning gray sea separating him from his fine green English homeland could diminish the pungent memory of his delicate Celia offering up her sweet naked form in submissive sacrifice to the two Hardwicke cousins and the voracious specimens of their manhood. She had torn every thread of cloth from her pale body, her tiny hands clutching at her breasts and spreading her female lips and buttock cheeks as if to advertise the benefits that could be gotten from these parts. How she had begged and pleaded for them to take her—to use her and overpower her until she scarcely knew where her own body ended and either of theirs began. One would have thought that these were to have been their last moments together as a sexual triad, so desperate did she seem. Indeed, never had Colin heard her speak such words!

Jason had bound her most thoroughly on that bleak Yorkshire winter's day—a binding which had rendered her with little movement or will of her own. Yet it had all been exactly as she desired, for Celia had often spoken—albeit with a blushing pink shyness and a distinctive biting of the lower lip—of having her arms and legs, and indeed, even the china blue of her eyes, placed into impotency—of relinquishing her final freedoms—the freedoms of movement and sight—to those who would best understand their value. Although Jason possessed a greater awareness and sophistication of the consequences of such an act, Colin quickly came to share his insight. For indeed, it often seemed as if the two cousins were of one mind!

It was left up to Sir Jason to perform the necessary trussing as a trusting Celia abandoned to him her trembling limbs, a barely perceptible quiver of the luscious strawberry plump of her lower lip confirming her innermost fears. Perhaps she did not entirely place her faith in the senior Hardwicke's ability to distinguish when matters had gone as far as they dared go. Indeed, Jason had often broken the boundaries of human endurance—and still pressed relentlessly forward. Nevertheless, she had endured, had she not? Thus Colin observed in mute admiration as his handsome relative looped a length of silken cord round Celia's slender wrists, shackling them together high above her head and securing the cord to a low beam in the ceiling so she could not move about—or flee.

It proved a rare occasion, indeed, when young Colin was invited inside the private erotic sanctum of his cousin's bedchamber, for he usually found himself on the wrong end of the locked door with his ear pressed desperately to the dark wood in hopes of hearing the orgasmic cries of his beloved. Yet this day he had been granted a special invitation to this hallowed place and the hallowed goings-on therein... which gave him great pause, for had these particular goings-on transpired in the past? Celia appeared to bear her obvious discomfort without complaint. One would have imagined it had become rather routine for her to be dangling from her arms and—when Jason encircled each delicate ankle with a length of cord and attached the cord to the thick pegs of the bed and bureau—routine for her legs to be extended outward like the wishbone of a fowl. Strange that his cousin appeared so damnably comfortable and familiar with these bizarre orchestrations—as if they were not entirely foreign to him, but instead a daily ritual as those of cleaning one's teeth or grooming one's hair.

However, it was the final restraint of all that tore at Colin's pounding heart. Indeed, not even the shocking pageantry of the now-exposed secret inner pink of his beloved's denuded female lips and its desperately distending pink tongue affected him as much as when Jason's silken handkerchief came down over the innocent blue of his ladylove's eyes. He could hear her plaintive whimpers as the last of the light died—whimpers which prompted him to reevaluate the wisdom of this encounter. Perhaps he should have dissuaded her from agreeing to this sacrilege—indeed, of *insisting* upon its unsavory climax. Yet it was surely too late, for the wild light in his cousin's eyes could not be tamed with words, but only with the realization of the actions that had incited it. Yes, he had seen that light all too many times!

Thus Celia abandoned every last shred of her will to

the man who had acted so often to alter it. Although she sensed her beloved Colin was near—for she could hear the raggedness of his breath—she knew he could do naught to protect her; she was now thoroughly in Sir Jason's manipulative hands. With that understanding, the tenseness in her limbs visibly relaxed—as did the pain caused from their shackles. Suddenly the wide spread of her legs felt natural to her—as did the fact that she could not move them closer and more modestly together. Between the moist splayed lips of her labia, her clitoris burned like a red-hot coal straight from a blazing hearth; she did not even need to see it to know that it stuck out as blatantly as a signpost. And, indeed, perhaps this was all it truly was—a signpost indicating the unseemly direction of her desires.

A warm soppy wetness began to make itself known against the hairless notch of her bottom. Although she could not be entirely certain, Celia suspected that its source came from the purple crown of Sir Jason's manhood. For some inexplicable reason she found this playful rubbing of her anus highly soothing—although it rapidly turned into something entirely different as the unseen head of this unseen organ grew ever more aggressive. It was becoming quite apparent that Celia's anxiously twitching bottomhole was being prepared for entry. Only by whom? Indeed, the anonymity of this member proved most provocative to the bound young woman, and her vagina wept in eager accompaniment.

All at once she felt a hot wind blowing against the well-parted insides of her thighs. It was quickly followed by the even hotter sensation of a tongue, for apparently one of the Hardwicke cousins—Celia knew not which—proved unable to resist the sweet nectar burbling forth from the tiny spout of her fully exposed womanhood. She shuddered with pleasure as this invisible appendage lapped at her shaven folds, her juices replenishing themselves as rapidly as they were being consumed by the Hardwicke mouth below. It was then that she felt the narrow passage of her rectum widening. Indeed, so enraptured had she become with the events to the fore that she had lost track of those transpiring to the aft!

Celia's fettered hands balled themselves up into anxious fists above her head as the stinging reality of the overextending ring of her anus made itself known to her. It felt as if someone were attempting to wedge a marble pillar inside her. For no matter how many times she had accepted Sir Jason or Colin in this fashion, each occasion might as well have been the first. How often she cursed the unyielding mouth of her backside for its virginal stubbornness—a virginal stubbornness which had caused it to become the source of so much illicit Hardwicke activity. Hence the adamantine object in her contracting passage pressed relentlessly onward, not satisfied until it had filled her completely—until an all-too-familiar sensation of roiling protest commenced within her aggrieved belly. And only then did this unyielding instrument of manly flesh withdraw, only to begin the process all over again.

As his cousin's penis sluiced in and out of his shackled beloved's pert bottom, Colin licked away the honeyed results of her pleasure. For it had become obvious to him that she very much enjoyed the cruel piercings of Jason's thick organ—enjoyed this cruel stretching and straining of her dainty anal mouth and her hot rectal walls. Indeed, he, too, took great delight in scorching himself within this mysterious terrain, especially when he tamped the conflagration afterward with the soothing application of his tongue. How delicious Celia's lusty little bottomhole would taste after it had been so agreeably opened!

As he sucked from his bound beloved the piquant juices of her excitement, Colin lifted his dark eyes upward, the ecstasy on her blindfolded face validating his love. Celia writhed within her restraints, her hands powerless to lash out, her legs powerless to run; her fluttering eyes could see only the red silk of the cloth that cloaked them. Her powerlessness was so absolute that she could do naught to stop the climax wracking her imprisoned body and filling the appreciative mouth of the Hardwicke kneeling before her—filling it as thoroughly as the filling now transpiring within her plundered backside. For the penis of yet another Hardwicke spewed and spewed its liquid rapture into the innermost core of her being—spewing so much hot, briny froth it seemed to be flowing back out through her vagina. Oh, if only she could know which of the two handsome cousins drank of her! Nevertheless, it had been Celia's personal choice to deaden her sense of sight. And indeed, it had brought with it a pleasure far greater than she had ever imagined possible.

No sooner did Sir Jason's discharged organ commence to dwindle in length and girth than he made a minor adjustment to the cord dangling from the overhead beam, thereby allowing his trussed captive to be bent forward from the waist. Hence he introduced himself to her conveniently repositioned mouth so that he might once again reach his full and dignified tumescence, for he had not as yet had an opportunity to sample the fragrant conduit of her womanhood. Although Celia's initial instinct was to grasp the moist manly object in her hands, it proved impossible to do so. Indeed, she found it extremely awkward not to be able to hold onto the Hardwicke penis which had just plundered with such consummate skill the burning interior of her backside. Only she need not have concerned herself, for Jason held himself out to her lips and, as he recovered his earlier stature, commenced to driving his pelvis to and fro, hence fucking his lovely captive in the mouth.

By this time the blindfolded young woman had come to accept and even welcome such provocative post-anal offerings—which might have explained how she knew that the manly flesh in her mouth belonged to none other than Sir Jason Hardwicke himself. Indeed, he had never made a secret of the fact that he enjoyed Celia's oral attentions after giving her a good hind plundering—a plundering which would continue with the introduction of his cousin's eager member. For just as the wide O of her mouth grew used to the rhythmic thrusts being perpetrated upon it, than a very familiar fullness once again made itself known in the still-burning chasm of Celia's backside—a backside which her modified positioning had caused to thrust out behind her. Her shapely legs continued to remain in their undignified splay, providing her with a sensation of total helplessness and total openness. In such a stance Celia was truly and invitingly open to whomever had a passing interest in using her. Indeed, the idea of strangers happening upon her thusly did not exactly provide an entirely displeasing scenario. Had she only realized how aptly prophetic would be such shameful ruminations!

Had the pleasure of receiving yet another Hardwicke penis in her bottom not been so intense, the anguished recipient might very well have cried out with pain. However, this particular caller appeared to sense her discomfort and, rather than charging forward in battle as his predecessor had done, applied his great length slowly and with considerable care, showing himself to be an artist, not a warrior. The unseen Colin slid inside his beloved's already-widened rear passage in modest increments, his deliberateness allowing him to savor its humid heat. His cousin's contributions had left this provocative terrain very wet and slippery, and the throbbing bulb of his penis had no difficulty in reaching the innermost hinterland of his beloved's rectum. Thusly situated, he began to dole out his masculine flesh in greater and greater portions, finding himself moving in agreeable conjunction with the strokes of his cousin. Of course Jason's seed had already been spent and he would therefore be able to continue pleasuring himself within Celia's inviting mouth for as long as he desired without threat of losing himself. For indeed, he wished to save the second dose of his aristocratic Hardwicke semen for the mouth of Celia's tender young womanhood.

The incapacitated subject of the cousins' dual attentions could feel the beginnings of yet another powerful climax building within her, and she gave herself over to it shamefully and tearfully. The final quivers of her female flesh would be met with the brutal thrust of Sir Jason's penis inside her dripping vagina, his rigid column chafing the greedy projectile of her clitoris. She wanted to clutch his shoulders and enwrap his bucking hips with her thighs—to cling to his muscled body in rapture, but her arms and legs had been completely immobilized, as were her eyes. Despite her previous convictions, Celia still could not be absolutely certain whose rampaging member occupied which of her entryways. Yet perhaps this uncertainty was what had made her shudders so violent.

Hence, as the doubly impaled young captive of the moors hurled her immobilized pelvis to the fore and aft, Colin exploded with a vengeance inside her, filling the welcoming cavity of her bottom as thoroughly as had his cousin before him. He buried his flushing face within the fragrant silken tresses of her hair, smelling scents of a far more intimate nature. So aroused had he become by the alluring perfume wafting upward toward his lusting nostrils that he, too, placed himself within his beloved's sweet lips, only to ejaculate a second time as she suctioned him to a renewed hardness, tasting the forbidden flavors of her backside a second time as well.

Happily depleted, Colin returned to yet another mouth—the smarting mouth of Celia's twice-filled bottom. For he knew well the devastating toll two Hardwicke penises could have upon its elastic flesh. Now he proceeded to lavish the dainty little crinkles with a series of reverent kisses, his thirsting tongue roaming their semen-moistened contours without restraint. Indeed, it mattered not whether the wetness stemmed from his organ or that of his cousin—at the moment Colin's only desire was to cool the fire their explorations had incited. And cool it he did, his tongue curling into itself so that it could reach far into the well-plumbed darkness beyond—a darkness which had proven such a deliciously hospitable home both to his penis and to Jason's. Yes...they had shared her well.

Nevertheless, such activities were now safely and

securely in the past—a past a regretful Colin Hardwicke had no wish to renew. For a new life was beginning for him and Celia—a life which would contain only *two* players.

The couple realized that they had gone as far as they could possibly go by the pungent smell of fish in the air and the brilliant blue of the sky, which seemed to pour directly into the brilliant blue of the sea. They stretched their cramped limbs and sighed, their joy at having made it this far overtaken by their fatigue. Yes, they had reached the end of the line—and in so doing, the end of France. There could be no turning back for either of them now....

Colin eventually managed to locate a fisherman who spoke a few words of nasal English and possessed an affection for English currency—most specifically the precious gold sovereigns that glittered in the hopeful young Englishman's proffered palm. Thus, with the few coins they had remaining to them in the entire world, Colin and Celia were left with the promise of an early morning departure. In the meantime, they would need to seek shelter for the night. As luck would have it, the very same fisherman who had agreed to transport the couple to Viareggio directed them to a weather-beaten inn along the busy quay whose squat-figured proprietor proved more than happy to relieve them of their last few francs in return for a meal and a bed.

As they seated themselves in the tiny café fronting La

Canebière that served both the inn's paltry assortment of guests and the few foreigners who did not know any better, Celia waged a silent battle to ignore the scruffiness of their surroundings and the inevitable scruffiness of the room upstairs which would soon be their safe haven for the night. Suddenly she began to wonder where their next night's slumber would be spent. Indeed, by tomorrow eve, this inn might very well seem like a palace. But rather than expressing her mounting concerns to Colin, she chose to remain mute, not wishing to spoil his obvious good humor with the harsh realities she felt certain were awaiting them. She could only pray that the fishy-smelling, sly-eyed Frenchman who had grabbed their money was not at that very moment halfway out to the Ligurian Sea counting his pounds and shillings...if the rusty old bucket that passed for a boat would even have made it that far.

Perhaps it might have been worry that made her so hungry. Or perhaps it was the potent odor of garlic coming from the inn's little kitchen. Nevertheless, on this sea-scented Marseilles afternoon, neither Celia's nor Colin's stomachs would be hosting much more than a sip of coffee. For just as they raised their oversized cups of café au lait to their lips, the tolling of bells reached their ears—a tolling which was accompanied by a familiar figure joining them at their table.

sir jason's arrival...

With the doors of Moorland House safely locked and bolted and old Ned Biggins placed in charge of overseeing the property, Sir Jason Hardwicke and his new passport sailed the choppy seas through the Strait of Dover on the very same Channel steamer that his fugitive cousin and the delectable Celia had taken only weeks previous. Yes, he was quite looking forward to their reunion, for he had gone without her lusty young charms for far too long.

Indeed, this gentleman of the moors had very nearly forgotten the sweet tang of her little cherry cordial slit upon his tongue—a treat he, in his masculine folly, had denied himself from partaking of until he had finally recognized the error of his ways. Never again would Jason spurn such ambrosial pleasures! Instead he would lavish himself upon the creamy victuals that flowed so profusely from the burbling source of its perfumed mystery, unconcerned with how many droplets might spatter onto his flushing face. No longer did he consider such desires unmanly. For being a man meant experiencing the full realm of pleasure with a woman.

Even now with the chill salt of the sea lashing it, his face still managed to flush hotly with the extent of his desire. Only Jason did not wish to remain inside with the other passengers; he preferred instead to enjoy his moment of silent reverie in private, with nothing but the roar of the wind in his ears along with the distant remembered cry of his lovely Celia. He thought about their last delicious moments alone together when she had lain warm and naked upon his bed, the willing spread of her thighs revealing the moist, hairless folds of her sex. The pouting lips of her labia majora were as smooth and flawless as the finest porcelain, and very nearly as fair, for never had they met the sun. Jason had placed himself in respectful homage before this holy altar, parting the puffy portals with his fingers, thereby bringing to light their glistening inner pink and freeing the salmon pink bud betwixt them. It seemed to grow before his enchanted eyes, surging toward his mouth with a series of anxious twitches. An intoxicating scent teased his flaring nostrils, stirring something so deeply personal within him that his eyes momentarily misted over. Indeed, such unprecedented displays of emotion were as rare to Sir Jason Hardwicke as a tidal wave to the moors. Yes, Celia had made of him a changed man.

Suddenly this ardent admirer took the ripe, burgeoning flesh of his trembling captive's clitoris between his lips, working the tip of his tongue into every flavorful groove. Celia's bare buttocks began to writhe upon the duvet as he used a finger to retract the tawny hood, tickling the rubescent glans this slight adjustment had revealed with his tongue. Jason knew such calculated stimulus nearly drove the poor girl to madness, which was precisely why he chose to do it. However, just at the point where she tearfully declared that she could bear no more, he drew the entirety of the wildly flickering flame into his mouth and suctioned it hard, as if seeking to swallow it whole.

Such oral ruthlessness had incited a rich honeyed flow from the crimson sliver below, and ever so gently he slid the middle finger of his right hand inside the tiny opening while continuing to keep the surrounding sheaths splayed with his left. How delightfully deceptive was this dainty aperture, for who would ever have imagined that so diminutive a slit could house not only one, but several fingers and, indeed, a prick of such magnificent girth as that which belonged to Jason himself? Hence as his lips and tongue continued with their concentrated provocation upon the engorged knurl, he applied his submerged finger as a surrogate sex organ, moving it slowly in and out as if to coax a young virgin opening into receiving the ruthless masculine instrument it longed for. For the wicked Sir Jason could be tender as well....

That evening Celia would come loudly and wetly, her cries of ecstasy echoing across the bleak empty moors. Jason swiftly removed his slickened finger from the quivering chasm of her vagina, replacing it with his mouth and drinking the warm sweet cream that spilled from the spout, his own liquid offerings spurting from him unchecked. He rubbed the desperately throbbing head of his penis against her thigh, driving his tongue deep into the palpitating passage to swab up the final remnants of her climax. For as long as he lived, he would never forget the taste and smell of her on their final night in England together. Indeed, it was a taste and smell this Hardwicke would never get enough of. His only regret was that he had waited so bloody long to experience it!

Standing tall at the bow of the vessel, Sir Jason looked to any observer like the proud man he was. The briny smell of the sea stimulated his nostrils, thusly stimulating the thick stalk of masculine flesh safely sequestered within his tweed trousers—for this smell was bringing him closer to his beautiful Celia. How clever he had been to devise this plot of escape for his fugitive cousin. Why, who would even think of looking for the lad in the

French countryside? Surely not that bumbling detective who had once paid an unexpected call to Moorland House. Of course he had neglected to mention to Colin that the murder investigation had all but ground to a complete halt what with the recent confession of a disturbed young transient new to London and in dire need of lodgings—even if those lodgings constituted the local nick. Needless to say, Jason could not have allowed his reckless relative to go blundering about England on his own, for there was no telling how matters would take a turn. Somehow it seemed wiser to send him away. Indeed, it might have proven rather interesting to see whether Celia would have elected to remain behind without the presence of her so-called beloved. Might she have stayed with her capricious captor in the moors without threat or coercion? It was a question Sir Jason would one day like to have answered.

These occasional doubts as to Celia's true allegiances were often the cause of great mental and physical anguish. Rather than giving in to them, Jason threw back his shoulders, for it would never do to appear weak even before strangers. *If only this infernal vessel would move faster!* he scowled inwardly, annoyed with the unenthusiastic plumes of steam rising up from the ship's funnels. Indeed, he would have preferred to depart a lot sooner, for he did not particularly relish the idea of his handsome young cousin alone with Celia and consequently out of his sphere of influence. Unfortunately the delay could not be helped. The passport office had moved with the usual efficiency of the English—an efficiency which seemed to suit officials rather than members of the tax-paying public, even if that public included those of considerable social standing. Jason could only hope that in his absence Colin had not somehow managed to turn Celia against him. Surely that worshipful fire burning in her eyes as he licked away the last droplets of her pleasure could not be tamped by a few misplaced words from a young man who, try as he might, could never hold a candle to his older cousin.

Sir Jason would traverse nearly all of France from north to south via a series of trains and lurching coaches, much as the anxious couple he had sent on before him had done. A lengthy journey, yes, but well worth the discomfort and inconvenience, not to mention the dust. The sweet scent of the lavender fields laid down in hilly bluish purple grids wafted in through the partially opened window of his car and he shivered, experiencing an overwhelming rush of desire to sample the elusive perfume of the young woman he would very soon be meeting up with again. Celia's fragrant pink blossom was sweeter and more silken than the petals of any flower, as was its distinctive nectar. Did she realize how easily she could drive him to madness just by the mere parting of her thighs?

How the weary traveler's heart hammered in anticipation at once again seeing this hairless bloom unfolding before him. Yet his heart hammered in angst as well at the thought of his undeserving cousin having such lustrous feminine beauty all to himself over these many long weeks. The exhaustive pruning of Celia's vulva and bottom had been entirely Jason's doing, and it angered him greatly that Colin should right this very instant be reaping the benefits. Had the unimaginative fellow been left to his own devices, such enchanting terrain might never even have been uncovered! Nevertheless, the elder Hardwicke's arrival would quickly put a stop to any such unauthorized profiteering.

Sir Jason's anger appeared to mount with the ever-increasing length of the tracks beneath the train's clacking wheels—an anger which would grow all the hotter the moment his shoes landed upon the cool white tiles of a tiny vestibule in Provence, for the silence from within the blue-shuttered house was as loud and cacophonous as the noisiest docklands pub. The empty echoes would pain his ears and, indeed, his heart, prompting a howl of raw anguish that could be heard clear to the Mediterranean Sea. Some said it sounded like a woman's name....

Indeed, such anger would reach a crescendo upon the truant couple's return. For once Jason had finally gotten Celia back within his realm, he would discover that something else had returned as well—namely the caramel curls which had once defied him by sprouting from the porcelain mound whose immaculate beauty cried out to be celebrated. Although admittedly charming in their coiled luminosity, this modest veil would quickly be removed, thus returning to the blushing young woman an innocence both provocative and virginal. For Sir Jason Hardwicke could not abide secrets of any kind. If his fingers wished to touch hair, they could easily be placated by entwining themselves within the honey-colored tresses atop Celia's head—tresses which would placate his penis as well...for he so enjoyed having it wrapped in strands of silk when she used her pretty mouth on him.

Never again would such ethereal purity be marred by the presence of a single hair. How its forsaken devotee had missed that perfect pout! Here in the sensual warmth of a Provençal spring, it seemed to have blossomed even more, as had the lusty pink stamen nestling betwixt the cream-filled lips. Was it only the wickedness of his imagination or had it grown even larger since the last time he had cast an appreciative eye upon it? Perhaps it was the joy of once again receiving his artful attentions that prompted such an extravagant florescence. For Jason knew well how to tease and arouse and consequently drive its charming owner to impassioned tears.

Ofttimes this exacting taskmaster would not even need to lay a single fingertip upon the sumptuous floret, preferring instead for the more modestly inclined Celia

The Possession of Celia

to do so under his highly detailed and usually very lewd instruction. He found it utterly enchanting to watch her stimulate herself, and he always took it for granted that such earnest observations provoked a rapid response. However, one rainy twilight the eruption Sir Jason had been anticipating did not appear likely to reach fruition. The windows had been latched tightly against the chill mugginess of the moors, and the alluring scent of Celia's need grew all the stronger within the closeness of the airless room. Condensation dripped down the leaded panes, corresponding to the continual dripping from her humid slit. To the onlooker, the flustered young woman possessed all the necessary prerequisites for a most satisfying orgasm. Nevertheless, it would appear that her satisfaction required an additional catalyst that evening.

"Please, Sir Jason," Celia whimpered, her wildly oscillating fingers making a ragged clutter of the severely reddened tongue protruding wantonly from between the wide splay of her thighs.

"What is it, my darling Celia?" he responded smugly, quite aware of what it was she so desperately desired from him.

"Take me!"

Jason licked his lips in thoughtful consideration, deciding to draw out the game a little longer. The masturbating woman's nipples had hardened into two tiny strawberries so ripe for the plucking that they caused the saliva to pool in his mouth. He swallowed hard, trying to ignore the insistent pleas from the lengthening beam of greedy flesh straining his trouser front. The sound of tearing fabric accompanied the sound of splashing fingers, nearly destroying his carefully wrought composure and his next words held a slight tremor. "I am not entirely certain I understand what it is you wish from me."

Tears of humiliation tumbled down Celia's frustration-rouged cheeks. "Please, sir, I beg of you!"

"Yes-s-s?" Jason drew out the word in a baiting hiss, relishing his anguished captive's obvious discomfiture. How ravishing she was in her shame!

Turning her flushed face away, Celia shifted her hips so that her callous observer could see the normally bashful pink notch of her anus. On this occasion, its needful mouth was already open, imploring Sir Jason to make use of it. Its desperate owner appeared to be pushing the elastic ring of muscle outward, thus tempting him by exaggerating its circumference. Indeed, this particular Hardwicke could think of nothing better than to delve into the delicious darkness beyond, only he wanted to make the agitated young woman squirm a while longer before bestowing upon her ultimate prize. Such clever if, indeed, *cruel* tactics would surely serve to make the velvety chasm that much hotter and tighter and—if one were to judge by the increasing amount of honeyed discharges from the neighboring orifice—wetter.

Wrinkling his brow in mock confusion, Jason gazed guilelessly into the moist china blue of Celia's eyes for confirmation. In thwarted response, she stabbed the middle finger from her unemployed hand into the twitching portal while those fingers already in use accelerated their frenzied assault upon her clitoris. He raised the dark arcs of his eyebrows, demonstrating a bewilderment that fooled neither himself nor the individual for whom the gesture had been intended. "Tell me precisely what you want, my dear. *Precisely.*"

Despite the sheen of perspiration on Celia's skin, a sudden shivery chill went through her, for she could not fail to miss Sir Jason's pointed emphasis. Indeed, it was not enough that he had made her beg, but that he wished for her to verbalize her shame as well! "I—I—," she faltered.

"*Hmm?…*"

"I want you to—to—to put it in—"

"In *where,* my dear?"

"—in my arsehole!" she wept, tasting the sharp, bitter crudeness of the word upon her tongue. It was a word her handsome tormentor very much liked to use and one which he very much liked to hear her use…among many others of equal crudeness. Yet even after she had finally gained the courage to give voice to her disgrace, a luxurious sweetness lingered upon her tongue—a sweetness born from the act she now found herself pleading with such disreputable despair for.

By this time the stately object Celia longed to have widening the thoroughfare of her bottom was in immediate danger of being unable to fulfill her unseemly request. Jason rose quickly from his chair and went to the sweating window, hoping that the misty sight of the moors could calm him. After several minutes he turned to face the inconsolable young woman, who now lay back upon his bed with her knees drawn fully up to her breasts. The fleshy growth jutting out from the juicy pear formed by her distending labia had ballooned to an alarming girth, its delicate salmon pink become an angry red. Suddenly Jason noticed that two other fingers had joined with Celia's middle one to comfort the yearning fundament below. He followed their undisciplined thrusts with considerable amusement as they tried in vain to imitate the masterful movements ordinarily created by his prick. *The poor darling girl,* he mused, his heart swelling with empathy. *Yes, perhaps he had teased her enough for one night....*

And perhaps he had been teased enough himself. No longer capable of restraint, Sir Jason hurled himself toward the immodestly uplifted cheeks, urging Celia's knees even higher and further apart, thus bettering the availability of the divine entry he sought. His penis would not even require a hand to guide it; it seemed to know precisely where to go, and within seconds its swollen purple knob had reached the innermost core of this frantic female's hungering rectum. As expected, her thwarted desires had made this sacred pilgrimage even more fiery than usual, and suddenly this lone pilgrim feared that the overstretched flesh of his manhood would be irreparably scorched. Indeed, he fully expected to find it charred and blackened upon his withdrawal.

Celia's fingers continued to twiddle and twirl the flap of lustrous pink flesh surging forth from the unjoined lips of her labia. Pleasure cascaded from the unoccupied sliver of her vagina like molten honey, gathering at the repeatedly reamed hole below and inspiring a symphony of aqueous sound. A listener whose eyes did not witness this juicy scenario might easily have imagined him or herself at the beach just before a storm as wave after riotous wave splashed toward shore, only to slam repeatedly against the barrier of a retaining wall.

In a fit of wicked inspiration, Jason drove the three fingers which had earlier served temporarily to pacify Celia's impoverished bottom into her mouth. On this day, she would accept them without hesitation, playing the taunter and exaggerating each lusty movement of her tongue. Sir Jason Hardwicke was not often the victim of torment, regardless of what particular form such torment might take. Nevertheless, the once-demure young woman's intentional lewdness stirred him to a frenzy, and he kissed her hard, his wriggling tongue meeting up with hers and tasting the dorsal delights it had just partaken of. Celia's still-laboring hand became crushed between their two bodies as her handsome captor lowered his weight upon her, their mouths continuing to feed upon each other.

Thusly interlocked, they came together. Jason's boiling liquids erupted from him in an endless geyser of semen, shooting far and deep into her expectant interior. And at last his foiled partner experienced the release she so desperately sought, the celestial pulsations occurring within her radically broadened rear hatchway amplifying the fluttering wings of her clitoris and sending her soaring high into the twilight-lit heavens. The tensile rim of her anus involuntarily clamped its titan visitor, squeezing out any last offerings that might have been more modest in forthcoming, for she wanted to swallow every spumy drop Sir Jason had to give her.

Celia found her starving backside well fed that rainy evening, for within moments she was rolled over onto the graceful curve of her belly with her beloved's wicked cousin plunging into the dilated socket from behind. How delightfully smooth and fluid was his journey, his previous discharge of pleasure having already paved the way for further such ingresses. Celia cried out sharply with each liquescent stroke of his penis, hoisting the flushing mounds of her buttocks agreeably upward to meet them and, in effect, impaling herself on this grand Hardwicke scepter. Indeed, she wished to feel this particular Hardwicke in the most distant recesses of her being.

Pleased at how eagerly this enchanting creature accepted him, Jason placed his palms flat upon her shoulder blades to steady himself, the sensation of shifting bone reminding him of the fragility of life and of the fragility of the young woman bucking and moaning beneath his steadily thrusting pelvis. A light down accentuated the pale ivory of Celia's flesh from the graceful curve of her back all the way to her tailbone, and surely would have continued still farther had it not been for the sharp steel blade of Jason's razor. This filamentous indicator of her humanity drew his eyes steadily downward as well as his hands and they quickly fixed themselves upon the undulating cheeks of her bottom. He dug his fingers into the pliant swells and spread them wide, pressing nearly the full brunt of his weight against them until the hairless fissure had flattened into a polished pink stripe. However, it was the rosy pink pucker between them that captured his fancy—a rosy pink which grew ever more florid and fragrant with the aggressive thrusts it demanded. Indeed, this rapacious mouth had opened so wide for the noble knob of Sir Jason's penis that the dainty little crinkles fringing it had all but been ironed completely away.

Having already so thoroughly and deliciously spent himself, this discerning gentleman now had what felt to him like all the time in the world to indulge even his most lascivious visual cravings—of which he harbored many, for the woman he had lured into his home and, indeed, into his bed had been a very fine muse. Hence, after the entire magnificent length of him had been fully absorbed by Celia's insatiable rectum, he once again withdrew just for the mere amusement of watching the well-breached hollow contracting back into some semblance of its original circumference, its continual failure to do so providing him with the headiest of masculine satisfactions. This formerly diminutive opening seemed to cry out to be filled; if he listened closely enough, he could almost hear its plaintive plea. Indeed, when Sir Jason Hardwicke buggered a woman, she bloody well stayed buggered!

To enhance this dorsal convergence for them both, he directed the weeping eye of his penis back and forth over the slippery port, the resulting serious snaps piquing in him a secret appetite for far more immodest trespasses. Nevertheless, there would be plenty of time for such savory victuals later, for Jason's insatiable member had not as yet taken its fill of this greedy treasure trove. Placing the throbbing purple bulb against the yawning furrow, he urged it right back in where it belonged, pleased at how readily the delicate Celia swallowed his substantial bulk. Her anguished grunts and groans did not deceive him in the least—the tangible proof of her facile acceptance of his manly bestowal was right here before him. Had it been at all physically possible for him to do so, he would have encircled the straining rim with his tongue so that he could, via this more sophisticated sense of perception, feel its elastic tension. Instead Jason contented himself with a finger, using the sentient pad to draw wide circles round the expanding periphery, all the while giving serious consideration to whether his curious tongue might be willing to pursue this particular fancy on an occasion when his cousin's equally impressive specimen was magnifying the perimeter of Celia's anus. For who knew what restraints the lusty heat of Provence could undo?

Sir Jason's fingers trembled as he turned his key in the lock. The clacking of the ancient tumblers appeared to mock him, pointing out to him his folly. Only his ears did not hear their warning, for they still continued to reverberate with the sound of past sighs. Indeed, he had been waiting a long time to possess his lovely Celia again. His penis twitched anxiously within the unseasonably warm English tweed of his trousers, weeping hot viscous tears at the juicy reunion which was very soon to be. The adamantine shaft rose up and away from his muscled abdomen, stretching the warp and weft of the fabric to their limits, and for a brief moment he stood there with closed eyes, imagining his former captive on her knees before him. Weary though he might have been from the long and dusty journey, Jason could think of nothing finer than to linger in the tiny vestibule while the famished young woman pleasured him without any effort on his part. Then later, after he had had sufficient time to rest, he would further reward the greedy girl by feeding the bounteous length and width of his prick to her hungering slit and backside.

Why, he could already see the grateful glow illuminating the china blue innocence of her eyes!

Indeed, the temperature of their new surroundings would undoubtedly add considerable heat to their already impassioned trysts. For there was nothing Sir Jason Hardwicke liked better than to make his lovely young *détenue* sweat—to force her to earn her pleasure and, thus, earn his liquid praise. Because of the bitter winter chill of the moors and the equally bitter drafts that always somehow managed to find their stealthy way inside the thick stone walls of Moorland House, he personally saw to it that the hearth in his quarters always had an abundance of fuel. He would raid the woodpile in anticipation of a private rendezvous with Celia, their surroundings often reaching the level of a sauna before they had even commenced to amuse themselves with each other's perspiring bodies.

Nevertheless, it was the young Englishwoman's heat-reddened form that shimmered the most in the crackling firelight. For as Sir Jason lay comfortably upon his back, she was made to mount him—to lower her dampened pelvis until she had managed to absorb the entire grand Hardwicke length of him inside the slender passage of her vagina. Indeed, no easy task was this for any woman regardless of how practiced she might have been in such an ingress, for his desirous shaft felt even longer and broader than if assimilated from a more customary angle. With her outspread knees situated at both sides of his hips, Celia slid herself up and down along this great beam of masculine flesh, moving either very slowly and seductively or with considerable speed, depending upon the particular whim of its owner. Of course Sir Jason preferred for the breathless young woman to ride him hard—to ride him as one would ride an unbroken horse, with the ivory orbs of her breasts bouncing freely and wildly, their strawberry tips gesticulating toward the east and west and the north and south. Celia's distinctive perfume grew stronger and ever more potent with her every downward slide, offering an unexpected treat to her lover's appreciatively twitching nostrils. Such an intensity of motion prompted the continually chafed sienna tip of her clitoris to become severely bifurcated, and it opened dramatically outward into two prettily scalloped salmon pink leaves—which an astute Sir Jason stimulated with his thumbs. For indeed, he knew how acutely sensitive a well-cleaved clitoris could be!

As their sweat-soaked pelvises locked repeatedly and juicily together, thus did their eyes, with Celia's flickering like a pair of blue flames. The honeyed tresses upon her head swayed as if stirred by a stormy summer breeze, providing a lustrous curtain of silk for the flushing window of her face. A few of the tendrils insisted upon stubbornly adhering to her perspiring brow, and she reached up several times to brush them away with her fingers, the gesture prompting Sir Jason's throat momentarily to close up. If asked, he would have been quite unable to explain this unusual reaction to so commonplace an action. Nor would he have been able to explain how her next words could be so capable of stealing the breath from his lungs. For the ravishing young female he had made such a point to desecrate and dishonor had just whispered to her handsome tormentor that she loved him.

When the battered passage of Celia's womanhood could finally bear no more, she readjusted herself into an unladylike squat over her ruthless keeper's upstanding and richly glossed penis, allowing it to penetrate the quaking mouth of her bottom. Indeed, the strain of her labors was so great that the sheen of moisture Sir Jason had been anticipating at last reached its salty fruition, dripping downward in dainty rivulets through the channel created by the adjacent swells of her breasts. A few of these errant droplets created a warm pond within the rosy indentation of her navel, the surplus splashing onto the fluttering pink pricket below, for there was nary a caramel curl to bar their way. Still more enthusiastic offerings spilled forth from the pale valleys beneath her arms, raining upon both her and her partner's rhythmically clenching thighs. With trembling fingertips, Sir Jason reached out to collect these salty droplets, sampling them with his tongue.

One might very likely have imagined that this vaginally and anally pleasured gentleman should have desired to release his ecstasy effortlessly within either of the two heavenly passages which had so fully and agreeably absorbed him. Nevertheless, it was the taste of this feminine sea of moisture which had incited his passions. Indeed, within moments Sir Jason found himself licking away the dainty beads of perspiration from the dimpled backs of Celia's knees and from the pungent concavities of her armpits. Even the delicate curves of her breasts were thusly caressed, as was the pulsing depression at the base of her throat. Suddenly he placed himself in uncharacteristic submission beneath her parted thighs, crying out with pure masculine rapture as he caught in his thirsting mouth the salty droplets from his lovely cageling's clitoris, which would prove to be all the more sweet and flavorful because of the generous bounties provided by its neighbor. No sooner had the young woman begun to shudder in orgasm than he raised himself onto his knees, his tongue swabbing up the perspiration from her navel and from the musky and drastically prick-widened hollow of her bottom, where this zealous Englishman spent considerably more time than necessary. For it was then that Sir Jason's pleasure juices went spurting from him—indeed, spurting into the fire which had been the catalyst for this salty banquet.

In the more leisurely and sun-warmed atmosphere of Provence, there would be opportunities aplenty for such divine indulgences—indulgences uninterrupted by the occasional cousinly blow or an inept policeman's rude pounding upon the door. Perhaps in their new home the three occupants would finally find the perfection of existence they sought—a perfection unmarred by jealousy or rivalry or the need for threat. In this charming blue-shuttered *maison de campagne* set amongst a cluster of olive trees and a riot of flowers, they might create their own private utopia. And if one day young Colin should desire to move on, so be it. For by then Sir Jason would be certain that his possession of Celia would at last be complete and, indeed, *irrefutable*.

Yes, this demure female had captivated and ensnared the elder Hardwicke most thoroughly. Could it be the comely flush of shame upon her cheeks that, even with the passing of time, never quite seemed to fade? Oh, how Jason worshipped her tiny form! He had made it his life's work to investigate her every peak and crevice —to ferret out her every secret, irrespective of its intimate nature. With Celia he envisioned himself as the intrepid explorer, embarking upon untrodden territory and, in turn, marking it with his flag—a personal sign that he had been there, that he had *been and conquered*. He could spend hour after hour just letting his tongue serve as his divining rod, roaming about in search of new tastes…new textures. They might be within the tight cleavage between her dainty toes or in the dampened hollows beneath her arms—this Hardwicke's desirous tongue would locate them all. How he adored the salty musk of her—a musk which grew ever more fragrant and provocative as he strayed nearer to the source of her womanly mysteries.

Indeed, his lovely captive's enforced hairlessness had made Sir Jason's task all the more rewarding, and he came to discover that his lust-seeking tongue could slide across her pearly flesh with impunity. Yet rather than immediately flinging himself into the juicy feast he knew awaited him—a juicy feast which, when he finally reached it, would be so much the juicier for his having momentarily deprived himself of it—he suppressed his masculine instincts toward impatience. For there was so very much here to pleasure him—and only the most leisurely of promenades would do. He would start matters off by licking along the back of one shapely leg, beginning at the graceful instep and moving slowly and painstakingly upward, tickling the pale crease behind the knee until the quiescent young woman launched her tensing buttocks high into the air in a fit of tormented delight. Accepting this unabashed action as a summons, Jason would seize these bucking swells and pry them apart, hence revealing his prize. Celia's playful squeals would quickly turn into low throaty moans as her handsome bedeviler concentrated his oral explorations within the exposed fissure, dragging the scorching tip of his tongue tantalizingly along the satiny ribbon of recently pared flesh, her fingers raking like claws at the pillows and anything else they could find. Sir Jason might later locate several dried beads of blood upon his person, and their underlying scars would be worn as a badge of honor.

During such deliciously lusty moments, Jason could always sense whenever Celia was on the verge of coming, for she would start to grind her denuded mound against the duvet, these gyrations growing ever more furious with his oral ministrations. Indeed, he could read her exquisite body like a scholar, and at the precise moment of climax, he would plunge his tongue deeply inside her. The rosy pucker of her anus would grip it firmly, compelling him to lose himself as well. Despite his own personal outlay of frothy fluids and the embarrassed yelp from the recipient of such highly improper attentions, this presumptuous explorer had not as yet finished with his amorous travels. As anticipated, Jason would find his efforts loyally rewarded— which he could easily ascertain by flipping the young woman over onto her back. For not only would the impassioned knurl sprouting out from her clean-shaven vulva have attained a magnitude worthy of serious reckoning, but the surrounding sheaths would become completely flooded in the honeyed results of her pleasure. Greatly inspired, he would lick lovingly over these well-glossed puffs of labial flesh, taking up their rich piquant coating before unrolling them with his thumbs and bringing to light their secret inner pink. The frantic twitching of Celia's unveiled clitoris would would tell him precisely what it wanted; at the moment, however, its enamored suitor would have other matters to attend to. Instead, his tongue would paint slow salivary circles round this twittering pricket, confining the brunt of its activities to the fragrant silk of her labia minora. Slipping slightly lower, Jason would lap unashamedly at the burbling cherry cordial slit he found there, the scalloped edges from the needy projectile above nuzzling the already moistened tip of his nose—indeed, reminding him it was there. As if this enchanted gentleman could possibly forget!

Oh, what a fool he had been to have denied himself for so long. He now had so much lost time to make up for—all those moments when he had forced his natural hunger to the background, as if to acknowledge it and, hence, give free rein to it were somehow unmanly. Yet his cousin had known all along. He had known and *not* been afraid. All at once Jason would fasten his yearning lips upon the sentient clitoral flesh of Celia's womanhood, sucking its plump sumptuousness with an uncharacteristic desperation. For it was a desperation born of a man who at long last truly understood what it meant to be a man.

The poignant memory of his recent awakening prompted a melancholy sigh to echo within the tiny vestibule Sir Jason now found himself standing in. The blue-shuttered house in Provence revealed no signs of life. Its modest rooms shouted out their silence—indeed, protested it as if they, too, experienced the loss. It appeared that the traitorous Celia and his thoughtless prat of a cousin had run off together. Nevertheless, they could not have gotten very far.

Yes…Sir Jason Hardwicke would make them pay.

sir jason's wrath...

Indeed, it did not require very much effort to find the itinerant young couple. The people of Provence proved most helpful in directing Sir Jason to their whereabouts, as had the people of Marseilles. What with their fair English flesh and fine English manners, not to mention a painfully inadequate command of the native tongue, Celia and Colin stood out from the locals like two nuns in a bordello.

Hence when their determined pursuer finally located them in a tiny inn fronting La Canebière, it was almost as if their discovery had been expected. Celia herself seemed especially resigned to it, for even though there had been adequate time and opportunity for her to escape from the wicked clutches of her beloved's cousin, she did not attempt to do so. Instead she had remained quietly seated at the scarred little square of table she shared with Colin, stoically drinking what remained of her café au lait, her dainty hands jittering with a telltale tremble as she brought the chipped cup up to her equally trembling lips. Upon seeing her, Jason emitted an audible sigh, the desire to thrust the aching head of his penis between those luscious strawberry-hued lips nearly overcoming his carefully wrought Hardwicke control. If it were not for the taciturn presence of the local villagers, he might very nearly have done so. Indeed, that would surely have awakened the patrons at the sleepy little inn!

Sir Jason could not have devised a grander entrance for himself, for just as he approached the couple's table, the bells from Notre Dame de la Garde chose that precise moment to toll. Upon recognizing the striking figure of the man to whom she had made of herself a veritable sex slave, Celia rose slowly and shakily from her chair, as did an openmouthed Colin. The backs of her thighs had become reddened with the crisscross pattern of the cane seat, reminding the elder Hardwicke of those infrequent occasions when he took his belt to her pert little bottom. Of course the marks he had drawn upon those supple mounds would vanish almost as quickly as they had appeared, rarely eliciting much more than a teardrop or two from their writhing beneficiary. For Jason would never use the leather to harm her, but simply to add additional fuel to the already fiery furnace of her lusty rear conduit... although judging from her most recent behavior, it was patently clear that the naughty girl was in need of substantial disciplining—disciplining which reached far beyond the limited scope of a mere belt. And Sir Jason Hardwicke was just the man to implement it!

On this warm and sunny Marseilles afternoon, Celia had chosen for her attire a modestly printed chemise that this recent arrival failed to recognize. No doubt she must have acquired it at one of the local shops, for the lightly woven cloth with its charming pattern of tiny blue cornflowers and the close-fitting bodice which outlined the gentle swells of her breasts looked far more suited to the local climate than any of the more stiffly tailored garments she had taken with her from England. Beneath the modified and distinctly *un-*English hem of the garment, her legs were devoid of any stocking. They shone with a smoothness that could only have been gotten from a recent shaving, for no silk, no matter how finely knitted, could ever substitute for the provocative gleam of naked hairless flesh.

The sight of this bare-legged apparition proved most pleasing to the gentleman who had gone for too long without, as would the quantity of sleek flesh appearing beneath the gentle drape of cotton lawn. Indeed, only a Hardwicke could know how high the finely honed edge of steel had reached. Usually Jason would perform the divine divestiture himself, drawing the blade along the elegant curve of a calf and over the sudden hump of knee, moving steadily upward toward the bashful V of Celia's converging thighs. With a diligence deserving of far loftier tasks, he worked into her creamy skin his special brand of shaving lather, which he always scented with a few drops of oil of sandalwood beforehand. Sir Jason adopted an artist's stance, wielding the steel with meticulous precision until his apprehensive quarry's legs glimmered in polished perfection. So thorough a polishing was quickly extended to the timorous pout of Celia's labia and the deep inviting pleat formed by the meeting of her buttocks. The elder Hardwicke especially rejoiced in uncovering the snowy flesh of her vulva, for in so doing, he would bring to light an exotic delicacy whose lustrous sleekness did not necessitate a paring. Indeed, this delicacy would twitter most fearfully and—to its calculated unveiler—most bewitchingly as the freshly stropped edge of the razor scraped carefully round it, as if sensing that its safety was at the complete mercy of the man who worked the instrument with such fierce and single-minded determination.

Nevertheless, Sir Jason Hardwicke could not for a single instant allow his anger to be allayed by the depilated contours of a leg nor the intoxicating reminiscences of a pair of plush pinkening lips that the skillful stroke of a blade could render as smooth and flawless as the finest Venetian glass. Instead, he remained standing before the runaway couple's table, the words with which he had been planning to excoriate the astonished pair suddenly superfluous. Celia's breasts heaved with fear and, believed Jason, excitement. Two tiny strawberries pressed impudently outward against the cornflowers, turning their pistillate centers into spikes. Indeed, he could only imagine the highly moistened state of her knickers! Was he mistaken or had the dear girl just squeezed her thighs together?

Colin reached for the young woman's fluttering hand, compressing it with a masculine reassurance he did not feel. For a moment it looked as though he might be about to spirit her away—to launch both her and himself onto yet another dusty country road leading to the unknown. Yet perhaps he finally realized the futility of such a venture, for suddenly his dark Hardwicke eyes shone with defeat, as did Celia's...although hers also appeared tinged with what might have been interpreted as relief. Eventually the visibly shaken couple silently left the inn with the handsome gentleman who only a few short moments earlier had materialized at their table. In all this time, not the slightest utterance was exchanged amongst the three—not even a polite greeting. For indeed, what was there to say?

Taking Celia's arm, Jason indicated with a dismissing flick of his wrist for his flabbergasted relative to remain behind. What he had in mind would not take very long, especially considering the state he was in— a state which had been brought on by seeing the alluring face and figure of his former captive again. The two quickly found themselves in a bustling alleyway behind the inn, where Celia was made to bow down in familiar submission before her beloved's older cousin, her bare knees rubbing against the filthy cobbles. Jason's penis required little direction, for it easily located its former lodgings within the hot chasm of her mouth. Indeed, his sigh from this most harmonious of homecomings was so profound that it could be heard even inside the little café. Hence as Sir Jason lay the great length of himself upon the velvety bed of Celia's tongue, Colin's body stiffened, as did his own great Hardwicke length. It was as if he could sense the connection that had just been made between his innocent ladylove and his nefarious cousin.

As his supplicating pleasurer swallowed him deep into her throat, Jason paid not the slightest heed as to whether man or woman went past. Unlike the laboring young female on her knees, he had nothing to hide. To the contrary, he found it quite refreshing to indulge himself out in the open and before such casual passersby. Some of the bolder ones even paused to watch, barking out their encouragement in harsh guttural tones. Needless to say, this was only the beginning of Celia's humbling—a humbling made all the sweeter by its highly public nature. Why, Jason had half a mind to take her round to the men at the docks and force her to stimulate herself before the grubby fish-scented bulls. Yes, he would make her spread her thighs extra wide for them and, indeed, peel back the plump lips of her sex until every glistening detail of their innermost secrets could be fully seen and appreciated by all. Surely such common laborers had never before cast their sea-weary eyes upon such a lustrous salmon pink clit nor so cherry cordial a slit. How it would weep with shame at having such savage brutes gazing upon it! No doubt their rope-coarsened fingers would wish to execute a friendly tug upon the fleshy tongue that pointed at them with such mocking condescension. Then perhaps if he felt so inclined, Jason might also bend the dishonored young woman forward over a convenient barrel and invite her new admirers to indulge themselves within the scorching slot betwixt her bottomcheeks. How amusing it would be to see them do battle for this distinguished prize!

The mere thought of the delicate Celia being so rudely and deliciously manhandled brought about a climax of such monumental consequence and liquidity that Jason nearly fainted right where he stood and which left his obeisant recipient coughing and sputtering till his fizzy fluids dribbled down her chin. Nevertheless, Sir Jason Hardwicke was nobody's fool. He knew well what such a flagrant display could lead to, and despite his anger toward her, he did not wish for Celia's dainty orifices to become sullied by such crude instruments. But just to offer some proof of what he might very likely be capable of doing had he not been so generously concerned for her welfare, he reached beneath the hem of her chemise and tore off her knickers, only to toss them to the nearest male observer. Indeed, with his bluely inked biceps and a shiny gold ring in one earlobe, the fellow looked quite the ruffian—exactly the sort Jason would have used to frighten Celia with if her sulky mouth had demonstrated a somewhat less accommodating haven for his prick. The man immediately put the knickers to his nose, tipping his ragged cap at their flushing owner in lewd appreciation.

The aptly chastised young woman would be forever haunted by this provocative image. For without her ever having allowed it to be so, some seafaring brute who was a complete and utter stranger to her had been made privy to her most intimate of scents. Late at night Celia would envision him pressing the moistened gusset of her knickers against his flaring nostrils and inhaling her distinctive perfume; why, she could almost hear the dual whoosh of air through the two tiny ducts! Although it horrified her to think that he could do so whenever the desire moved him, it aroused her as well, and her trembling fingers would shamefully locate the already engorged kernel of her clitoris. Indeed, she would rub and rub until the fragile flesh appeared in danger of shredding, only to rub still more until she had at last attained the desperate relief she sought. How Sir Jason liked to tease her upon seeing the chaos she had made, for not only had her attentions left the ragged tongue raw and red and irreparably cleaved, but severely blistered as well. Celia could not have hidden it even if she had tried, for the shaven puffs of her labia offered little in the way of concealment. If anything, her hairless condition served to display the embarrassing growth even more, which had probably been the wicked gentleman's intent all along.

Hence with the humbled Celia's graceful swell of a belly bloated with a meal she had not anticipated consuming on this sunny Marseilles afternoon, she returned on the arm of the Hardwicke, whose briny froth she had siphoned from his penis with such consummate skill to the inn, and to Colin, who had not budged from their little table. Indeed, he looked as if he could have been carved from stone; even his cup of café au lait had not moved from its initial resting place. Celia slipped into her chair, only to reach quickly for a napkin to scrub at the semen that had dried to a glossy crust on her lips and chin, this social nicety not going unnoticed by her beloved. Suddenly he realized what had just transpired. It would seem that once again his vile cousin had rendered him impotent!

The couple's swift return to the blue-shuttered house in Provence proved as silent and uneventful as their capture. Colin was as sullen as ever, reminding the man linked to him by blood of their first weeks together at the manor house in the moors before the poor misguided lad had finally awakened from his sexual stupor and gotten some mettle into him. Only what had happened to that mettle now? Perhaps the peculiar light Jason caught shining in Celia's shyly lidded eyes indicated a desire unquenched—a desire his younger cousin had been sadly incapable of fulfilling.

Be that as it may, the deflated Colin would be receiving no more opportunities to try, for Sir Jason already had his plan of revenge well formulated in his head—and it did *not* include the eager participation of his ungrateful relative. As far as the fugitive Hardwicke was concerned, he could consider himself banished from any and all physical contact with the irresistible Celia. Indeed, Jason found this highly ironic, considering that in the beginning he had done everything he possibly could to cultivate the fainthearted fellow's latent desires. And now he would do everything in his power to thwart them, even if he must personally stand guard outside the woman's door. He had been far too generous with the two lovebirds already—a generosity which had been repaid with the cruelest form of treachery. To think that he, Sir Jason Hardwicke, had actually fancied himself in love!

As the three journeyed northward in a private coach, Jason could not help but smile with smug satisfaction at the evocative sight of Celia's scraped and dirt-smudged knees. He even leaned forward several times to wipe them with his handkerchief, wetting a silken corner with his saliva as one might do for an untidy child. Before they had even reached the outermost fringes of Châteaurenard, he had his trouser front unbuttoned for yet another dose of Celia's oral magic. Was it only his imagination, or did her lips and tongue perform better with an audience? For suddenly he could not recall ever having had his prick treated so eloquently as during those breathless moments in the fetid Marseilles alleyway. Perchance the dear girl enjoyed the company of strangers. Hence, he would see to it that she was *not* disappointed.

In the meantime, there were still several more bumpy kilometers remaining before they reached their final destination. Although the magnificent length of his manhood had been temporarily sated, Jason's eyes continued to hunger for their first nourishing glimpse in all too many weeks of the sumptuous feminine charms he had come to know with such methodical intimacy. Therefore, for the rest of the short journey, Celia was made to take the banquette directly across from the two cousins, such an enforced ostracism consisting of her sitting poised with her slippered feet planted widely to both sides of her. As anticipated, the hem of her chemise rode up to expose what Jason most wished to see. In his absence, the caramel curls he had always kept so meticulously sheared had returned. Only the merest hint of sienna pink was visible—a sienna pink denoting the twitching tip of Celia's clitoris. Her observer's dark eyes flashed angrily, prompting even further anxious twitching from the sequestered node. Indeed, she dared not contemplate what further degradations might later be in store for her...nor would Colin, for whom so improper a vista stirred the length of his own Hardwicke member.

Within the close confines of the coach, the splay-legged young woman's intimate fragrance grew ever more pronounced, prompted both by the heat of the afternoon and by her recent oral lavishings upon the man whose iniquitous demands she felt compelled to obey. Jason threw back his head, breathing of it deeply and with great exaggeration, his aristocratic nostrils flaring with undisguised pleasure. An anguished Celia turned a crimsoning face toward the window, her wetness forming a warm viscous pool upon the leather upholstery beneath her naked bottom. At one time this purveyor of her disgrace might have leapt eagerly and unabashedly forward to bathe his tongue in the honeyed flow, but no longer. For in order to punish the fickle female who had so grievously wronged him, Jason would need to punish himself as well. Yet, in his punishment, he would find many rewards.

In her exposure, Celia's embarrassment was most poignant. Perhaps it was an embarrassment born in part of her earlier transactions with the villainous Sir Jason, for in her enforced subservience to the fleshly symbol of her obeisance, she experienced a joy whose lusty origins she dared not examine too closely for fear she might lose herself altogether—if indeed, she had not already done so. Oh, how she had longed to taste the tears of his manhood! In the squalid alleyway, a frantic fluttering had taken place between Celia's thighs as her famished tongue reacquainted itself with the rigid column of his penis, laving over its satiny surface with scrupulous care. The delicate blue veins pulsing beneath the skin tore at her heart, making her realize that this, too, could be an instrument of great fragility... even if its owner did not choose to use it as such.

As Sir Jason's majestic staff rose up demandingly from the unbuttoned tweed of his trousers, its trembling supplicant drew her lips back and forth over the pronounced ridge of the corona, shamed by the sensations her actions incited in her and indeed, further shamed that such actions were being performed in the most public of places. Celia knew that other men were in the vicinity—and she knew that these men were avidly observing this spirited oral transaction with a vicariousness which might very well have put her in peril. A fearful shiver slithered up the curve of her spine and into her neck, momentarily freezing her tongue. Could this have been the reason her beloved's cruel cousin had selected such a highly inappropriate location—to humiliate her? Or even worse, to pass her into the grubby hands of these common brutes? For even as she pleasured him, his rage glittered darkly in his eyes, telling her that, *yes*, she had a great deal to answer for.

Before Celia could reflect upon this further, her former captor began to hurl his upstanding member into her mouth, driving himself farther and farther down her slender throat. Yet never once did he utter the slightest moan of ecstasy, not even a muted sigh. Indeed, perhaps in the salty Marseilles air his ecstasy had been eclipsed by his vengeance. The broad head of his penis finally came to a rest upon Celia's exhausted tongue, and at the instant of climax, she felt the tiny pinhole at the summit spasming with its expulsion of hot bubbling froth. Yes, Sir Jason had filled her mouth and belly most bountifully on this fine spring day.

Try as he might, Colin could not unstick his burning eyes from the sticky muff of caramel across from him. Nor could he succeed in masking his shock at this unwitting presenter's absence of knickers. Surely she had had them on that morning! The waning afternoon sunlight streamed in through the coach window, turning the copse of once-shorn curls at the crest of Celia's pubic rise a glittering gold. Yet it would be within the secret split below that the hair had darkened nearly to black by her wetness, the saturated tendrils adhering together in a resinous cluster. How could he continue to sit there so civilly beside his older cousin without the

The Possession of Celia

least attempt at protest while his delicate ladylove posed with her milky thighs flung lewdly open, making a flamboyant spectacle of what should only have been viewed by her husband—if indeed, by anyone at all? Within a span of only a few minutes, Colin Hardwicke had once again been reduced to the frightened fugitive who had sought safe harbor in his cousin's home—a frightened fugitive who did not own the courage to put a knife in his cousin's back...not even when that cousin demanded that his disgraced beloved manipulate herself with her fingers.

As the hired coach clattered unsteadily onward and deeper into the lavender-scented heart of Provence, Celia was obliged to entertain her two male traveling companions. Their matching pairs of dark Hardwicke eyes became flames of fire scorching her flared flesh. She waited expectantly for her noble Colin to intervene—to reclaim for her her besmirched honor as the middle finger of her right hand twirled the slippery tongue of her clitoris while a grouping from the left made merry with the moist neighboring mouths of vagina and anus. Even now with her fluid feminine softness courting her fingers, they still continued to tingle from Sir Jason's manly flesh. Indeed, Celia had very nearly forgotten how tightly the translucent skin could stretch over the silken pouch of his testicles, especially as his seminal fluids simmered within them.

No sooner did the first set of cheerful blue shutters

come into view than the flushed young woman's hips were bouncing up and down on the flooded leather seat of the banquette, her desperately digging fingers vanishing altogether inside her two passages. Yet not even Sir Jason's ribald chuckles could compare to what next transpired as Celia stepped down from the coach. For her disgrace was thus complete upon receipt of a Rabelaisian wink from the driver, who had made considerable and, indeed, highly discourteous use of the small window located directly behind his hatted head.

Despite his threats to do so, Jason did not act upon his plan to keep his reclaimed captive under constant watch. Even so, Celia could never be entirely certain when or even if he might suddenly appear in her bedchamber, therefore neither she nor Colin dared risk a meeting. It seemed far wiser to wait—to give the elder Hardwicke's anger some time to cool, for he could be a most formidable foe when provoked. Perhaps she could not really blame him for his wrath; to Sir Jason, the couple's flight had proven the ultimate affront of all. Thus it would come as no real surprise when, on one sleepless night when she desired to take a wander in the garden, she should find the door to her bedchamber locked against her. Indeed, it did not require very much exercise of the intellect to ascertain *who* possessed the key.

Within the still-naive recesses of Celia's mind, this enforced separation from her beloved was undoubtedly the extent of the penalty Sir Jason wished to extract from her—that and the occasional hydrous humiliation amongst the flowers. In his constant quest to cool himself in the foreign heat of Provence, Jason discovered the many bracing merits of the garden hose. Only rather than turning it on himself, he turned it on the shivering female whose garments he had forced her to shuck—indeed, turned it in such a manner as to cool *her* rather than himself. For how best to escape the Provençal heat than from the inside?

Hence this gentleman, who all too often could be anything but, would slip the green nozzle just inside the quivering ring of his naked captive's anus, compelling her to drink. And drink she did, for within seconds Celia was crying out for her handsome tormentor to stop—to cease from his dastardly actions. Yet cease from them he would not. Sir Jason knew well how much the aggrieved young woman could swallow; he had performed similar such operations upon her thirsty bottom at Moorland House with the aid—and even under the direct orchestration—of his eager cousin, operations that had proven most pleasurable to all parties concerned. Yes, Celia would be granted the relief she so desperately sought, as would her precious Colin, whose flustered face was right at that very moment pressed hard against the glass of an upstairs window. It would seem that their garden frolic had awakened the poor lad from an alcohol-induced nap. Nevertheless, this aborted slumber would be opulently rewarded. To Celia's burning shame, her beloved's wicked cousin bade her release the water he had just finished pumping inside her, only to place himself before her spewing spout to cool himself in the resulting spray. Never had this Hardwicke enjoyed so fine a shower! If only its charming conferrer could have guessed that such highly deserved punishments were only the beginning.

Indeed, this delicious douche released far more than merely a torrent of water. It released the last remaining restraints this reclusive member of the gentry had heretofore only entertained in his mind. At long last Jason could give free rein to his most aberrant desires—desires previous circumstance had forced him to control. Newly liberated, he decided to once again elicit the invaluable aid of his Paris contact—the very same Paris contact who had secured the lease on the house in Provence, and the very same contact who had hosted all those delightful soirees he had attended until the rather unfortunate, and indeed, unavoidable incident with the Swedish lad had occurred. Hence a telegram of a decidedly cryptic nature was hastily dispatched to the *maison* of this particular gentleman—a gentleman as mysterious as he was wealthy, and a gentleman whose debauchery rivaled that of his Yorkshire confrere.

Yes, Sir Jason Hardwicke would see the delectable Celia humbled...*completely*.

a perfect humbling...

Within a matter of days Sir Jason's plan was set into motion. In order to secure the cooperation of Celia— for he realized that she would not readily agree to what he had in mind without some *very* pointed convincing, he had taken it upon himself to unearth the name of the head of the local gendarmerie. Indeed, this expert strategist went even so far as to secure one of the fellow's calling cards, which he planned to bandy about whenever a need for it arose. And what with the full schedule of lusty engagements he had organized, the elder Hardwicke expected to do a good deal of bandying.

In this redolent resumption of her captivity, Celia began to feel as if she had suddenly been transported back in time. Only instead of sitting with the two handsome cousins in the chilly Yorkshire drawing room of Moorland House, sipping from her glass of sherry, she found herself seated in the springtime warmth of the little salon in Provence, sipping a glass of Pernod. The occasion still retained the same false element of civility—a civility which would rapidly disappear with the subsequent disappearance of the liquid in their glasses. She very often wondered why Sir Jason even bothered with this stale English custom, let alone continued it in their new home. Such a polite gathering had always seemed so absurdly hypocritical in light of what inevitably follow. Yet never could Celia have dreamed that this daily ritual would soon be necessitating the filling of another glass.

Jason's Paris contact came through in the style and swiftness he expected. For who should he discover ringing the bell of his *maison de campagne* but Inga, the charming Scandinavian girl who had left such an indelible impression upon him all those years ago. For a brief moment he could not quite place her, although there was something alluringly familiar about the face and figure, not to mention an obscure, but no less provocative, mental image of a peach. Time had been good to Inga; it had served to hone and heighten her fair Nordic beauty—a beauty Jason felt absolutely certain would extend to features beyond those most immediately visible. And was not disappointed, for later that evening when this discriminating Englishman was once again treated to the deliciously agreeable presentation of her peachlike sex, he offered up a silent prayer of thanks to his friend Count D'Arcy. Indeed, he could think of no female superior to the lusty Scandinavian to initiate the shame-faced Celia into the savory delights of her own sex.

Sir Jason would never forget the fiery conflagration upon the young woman's cheeks when she had first learned of the true purpose behind the surprise appearance of this very amiable guest. Nor would he forget her frenzied gasps for air as a much-aroused Inga ground her juicy peach down upon Celia's protesting mouth. Celia could do naught but comply with this none-too-subtle prompting—and to comply in the presence of *two* Hardwickes rather than one. Jason watched with undisguised rapture and an element of smug satisfaction as the ungrateful female he desired to humble stretched out her velvety pink tongue to lap tentatively at the sopping folds poised expectantly above her. As if to further her disgrace, they grew ever more liquescent, the resulting droplets raining down onto her crimsoning face and lips like tears of honey. How sweet was the taste of her shame!

Despite her cruel conductor's lascivious fantasies to the contrary, it was immediately clear that the bewildered English girl had no such experience in these cunnilingual matters, although this did not diminish the magic of the scene in the least. To the contrary, Celia's almost childlike probings made it all the more enchanting, for what could be more divinely exquisite than to witness the final loss of innocence? Jason could see that his desperately licking cageling needed some friendly advice on how best to go about her task; therefore he decided to offer up a few kind words of instruction gained from many years of observation. Indeed, his worldly eyes had been made privy to numerous such oral couplings—and by women quite expert in their *spécialité*. "Open her lips with your thumbs, my dear. That way you shan't end up with a mouthful of hair," he instructed good-naturedly, relishing the sharp cry of shame that answered.

Inga balanced expertly on her knees, which were outstretched and planted firmly and decisively to both sides of her unconsenting partner's head. The long honeyed tresses that both cousins so often enjoyed taking a brush to had become hopelessly caught beneath the more experienced woman's weight, holding the disconcerted Celia prisoner. Indeed, she would have been unable to move even if she had tried, lest her hair be ripped from her scalp. Perhaps this imprisonment had been intended all along, for when the beseeching blue of her eyes locked onto the cool gray stones belonging to Inga, she saw that they contained no sympathy for her plight. It would seem she had little choice but to submit to this foreign female's degenerate demands, for neither Hardwicke offered his gentlemanly services to come to her aid. If anything, they appeared to savor her merciless entrapment. Not even her dearest Colin moved forward to rescue her from her fate. Surely that tubular shape at his trouser front was but an illusion created by a fold in the fabric!

Pleased that his demure captive had at last seen fit to take advantage of his many years of wisdom by opening up the peach-fuzzed pout of Inga's labia, Jason inched his chair closer to the festivities, whereas his younger cousin merely seemed intent on ignoring the sapphic proceedings taking place before him—or at least to pretend to do so. Colin remained sullen and mute and staring out the window, the glass of Pernod in his hand trembling with ever-increasing intensity in direct and unmistakable correlation to the lush, liquid sounds of Celia's shyly lapping tongue meeting the Nordic girl's brimming spout. It poured its appreciation into her mouth, the overflow streaming in shimmering rivulets along the graceful length of her neck like juice that had just been squeezed from a very ripe peach. Perhaps it was no wonder that the thoroughly disgraced imbiber of this heavenly nectar would furtively lick her lips afterward. Yes, by the time he had finished with her, Sir Jason would have made of Celia a connoisseur!

Suddenly Colin Hardwicke could no longer bear to look upon the sordid scene of his beloved's humiliation. Indeed, he feared that if he continued to do so, the defiant pillar of flesh throbbing with such needful intensity within his trousers would spurt its masculine delight all over the crisp white linen, permanently marking it with its distinctive stain—and thereby marking *him* with the stain of his ill-begotten fulfillment. For it was a fulfillment he did not wish for his delicate Celia to behold.

Once she had finally understood what her beloved's scoundrel of a cousin required from her, Celia nearly wept. She yearned to spit out the sweet, piquant taste of the pretty Scandinavian to demonstrate her heartfelt contempt for such base and, indeed, highly illicit practices. Nevertheless, she realized that doing so could not erase the ambrosial memory from her tongue—an ambrosial memory which, to her ever-growing mortification, would necessitate frequent and ever more elaborate rekindlings. Instead she stoically held back the threatening swell of tears, not wanting her ruthless tormentor to witness her shame. For Sir Jason had witnessed it far too many times and in far too many ways—and Celia knew it was *this* which roused him most of all.

Indeed, she had presumed that such twisted games were well behind them, left to sink in the bottomless bogs of the moors—that she had at last proven herself a worthy recipient of the elder Hardwicke's love and attention. But apparently she had been mistaken. Since coming to Provence, a high wall of glass had been erected between them, blocking out their mutual sense of feeling—although this did not actually prevent them from being able to observe each other. Celia had become the featured star in a sexual circus with Sir Jason Hardwicke watching from the other side, an excited boy gobbling down his candy floss while his favorite acrobat performed made-to-order stunts for his own personal viewing pleasure. Without doubt, the gentleman's present lasciviousness had well exceeded even his most dastardly deeds of the past.

Yet never once did the severely humbled young woman ever seriously consider leaving, not even after Jason's intentions to continue with his new practice of forcing other females upon her had become known. She was most likely completely free to do so, for Colin had—at least for the time being—been removed from immediate peril. Despite his words to the contrary, she did not truly believe in her heart that Sir Jason would carry out his threat to turn her poor darling over to the local gendarmes. For would he not have done so by now if such were his intent? Had he not already harbored his fugitive cousin from the hangman's noose? Yes, it would appear that the younger Hardwicke's unwitting presence was all part of his manipulative relative's master plan—a plan which involved a systematic and consummate degradation the likes of which could never have been undertaken in Moorland House. Indeed, why not flee from this depravity? No one held her prisoner; her hands and feet were not bound to a chair. Celia could have easily walked out the door and down the dusty road to the little village with its fruit and vegetable stands and its ruddy-cheeked country peasants. Only she did not. For it was not a rope that bound her, but Sir Jason Hardwicke.

As anticipated, Jason's scheme to punish the woman for whom he had nearly abandoned his wicked ways worked extremely well. Far too well, in fact. For it soon became evident to its guiding spirit that the shrinking subject of such well-deserved humbling had gradually come to enjoy this deliciously unique penalty for her transgressions. It appeared that he needed to step up his plan of action lest he allow her to get the better of him!

Indeed, Celia experienced the most supreme form of humiliation for her ill-gotten pleasures with the astonishingly beautiful women Sir Jason procured for her—a pleasure she realized must be kept carefully hidden at all costs, especially from the man who had orchestrated it. For this pleasure filled her with the ultimate shame —a shame far worse than any she might have suffered back in the chilly manor house on the moors. How could it be possible that her tongue should desire the taste of another of her sex? For even in her deepest of slumbers it twisted and slithered in a dreamy creamy paradise of fluid, feminine softness.

This servile participant's ever-increasing skill and ever-growing enthusiasm for the tribadic tasks he had set forth for her with such eagerness prompted Jason to entertain increasing doubts about the wisdom of his plan. Celia's tongue seemed to lick a tad too hungrily over those burbling crimson slits—a hunger which extended to her lips as they wrapped with such impassioned desperation round the proffered pink flippers above, sucking as if the woman to whom they belonged had just been rescued from the desert and given water. Why, only the manly staff of his prick should be suckled like that! Suddenly it felt as if Jason were witnessing the wanton goings-on between Celia and his cousin all over again. Hence it was no wonder that he finally decided to throw himself into the fray. Had he not suffered enough in the past with the girl's woeful disobedience—must he continue to suffer? Needless to say, he steadfastly refused to call the emotion tormenting him by its rightful name —*jealousy*. No. Such childish emotions were well above a man of Sir Jason Hardwicke's station, especially jealousy over the coerced dalliances between two females—even if one of those females happened to be Celia.

Rather than calling an unceremonious halt to the juicy proceedings at hand, this masterful manipulator moved to escalate them, inspired in part by the intoxicating scents emanating from the two enraptured figures before him and by the emotion whose appellation he deigned not to recognize. Whether it was Inga or Celeste or Marie-Claire in a naked greedy sprawl upon the floor, the steady procession of humid vulvae entering the blue-shuttered house in Provence was all the same to Sir Jason. As the delicate creature whose mind and body he had come to know so well performed her recently acquired oral magic upon the complex feminine whorls betwixt the widespread thighs of their invited guest, he moved swiftly and calculatedly into his rightful place behind her. Indeed, he would remind the cunt-absorbed little vixen who was the true virtuoso in matters of the flesh, lest she mistakenly believe it to be her tongue. Hence, after securing himself by firmly clasping her hips, he thrust his angry prick into the eagerly twitching portal of Celia's upraised bottom in one go.

The recipient of this unprecedented implantation yelped in anguished surprise, the sound becoming muffled by the wet pulpy folds in her mouth. Her shapely buttocks wriggled in protest, although she did not labor particularly hard to eject this unexpected intruder. Indeed, it would have mattered not if she had, for Sir Jason had no intention of allowing Celia to rebuff his expert anal advances. To ensure ancillary success in his most favored of endeavors, he spread her quivering rear cheeks wide with his palms, sliding inside the fiery trough of her rectum with even greater ease. He would have been quite content to force his attentions upon her shimmying backside if so infelicitous a refusal had been forthcoming, for Jason considered such imposed plunderings extremely pleasurable, if not preferable. However, so divinely savage a measure was not required on this day, for Celia welcomed the prodigious male length of him inside her with a profusion of pulsating kisses, nearly squeezing from it the boiling juices of his love.

With each deeply wrought stroke of his penis, Jason noted her pink tongue becoming ever more frantic and frenzied as it slithered over the glistening and equally pink terrain of the other woman's unwrapped sex, which its ardent licker kept conveniently splayed with her fingers. Having always considered himself extremely clever in matters of positioning, Jason's post provided him with an unobstructed line of vision from which fully to appreciate the evolving oral talents of his lovely protégée. This came as no surprise, however, for the skills she had learned in Yorkshire had translated easily from the rigid flesh of a male to the more mysterious dips and slopes of a female. All of a sudden Jason realized that he was holding in his breath, so captivated had he become by the ingenious way Celia made a curl of the velvety tip of her tongue in order to scoop up the creamy dribbles her activities had instigated. *Ahh…such sublime artistry!* he sighed inwardly, feeling the immersed knob of his penis give a warning spasm. To Jason, Celia's hunger for her female partner was flagrantly obvious—as it was certain to be to his impassive cousin as well.

Despite the ecstasies that could be gotten from bearing witness to such highly improper acts, what Colin wished most to know was when would it all end?

When would this calculated debasement of his innocent Celia reach its iniquitous conclusion? Indeed, how many more women did his reprobate relative have up his salacious sleeve? For it seemed as if a steady stream of attractive young ladies had paid a call to the blue-shuttered house in Provence, ready and eager to shed their garments and even more ready and eager to allow the shyly flicking tongue of a member of their own sex to poke and prod their most intimate of places—and all this before an audience of two men! Colin would never have believed it possible had he not seen it for himself, for in truth, such unnatural feminine behavior had thus far been unknown to him. Nor would he have believed the uncharacteristic vehemence with which his delicate ladylove approached her task. How could she bear to drink the juices of one like herself—and to drink with such furious thirst? Yes, this time his cousin had positively outdone himself in his depravity!

Sir Jason could detect that Celia was about to come, for not only did the movements of her tongue accelerate in both speed and boldness, but the walls of her rear passage increased in temperature and began to palpitate lovingly against his deeply entrenched organ. He already possessed considerable acquaintanceship with this normally mysterious territory, having explored it and those of other similarly favored females on numerous occasions, therefore his highly knowledgeable prick could detect even the slightest change in its distinctive character. This lusty instrument of pleasure had been a most welcomed guest in many a lady's backside from the day he had become old enough to understand its true purpose. How fortunate indeed was the young woman granted its frequent and exclusive usage!

To guarantee the totality of his captive's shame, Jason reached round to locate her clitoris, encountering instead a billowing flame. No sooner did he position his middle finger upon it than its owner violently hoisted the perspiring cheeks of her buttocks back against his dew-bespattered pelvis, swallowing his manhood clear to its well-thickened root. The wet lips of her freshly denuded labia kissed his overburdened testicles as they collided with her vulva, the lusty smack resounding loudly and provocatively in everyone's ears. With a strangled cry, Jason exploded inside her, prompting a duet of cries to match his as a whimpering Celia pushed her reddening face into the bucking bronze muff of her partner.

There was one more cry within the small Provençal salon on that warm spring evening—a cry as tortured as it was ecstatic. For within seconds Colin's manly liquids spewed unchecked onto the floor, drawing spumy spirals upon the faded wooden slats. How he would have liked to fill his darling Celia with such rich seminal bounties; instead he had been forced to watch his sizzling seed go to waste. His spent penis rose out from the unfastened front of his trousers, its humiliating defeat visible to all, including the nameless female whose sopping folds still held his licking beloved in their fragrant grasp. Yet all of a sudden Colin no longer cared. He would seize his pleasure in whichever way he could, even if he had to do so before Celia and his cousin and whatever stranger happened to be visiting the blue-shuttered house on that day. If stroking his own penis to the accompaniment of his delicate ladylove's degradation was to be the only pleasure granted him, so be it! For he was a fugitive, and therefore he would take his pleasure like a fugitive.

With the piquant taste of this most recent enchantress still teasingly fresh upon her exhausted tongue, Celia began to wonder if it would not be wise to flee before all sense of propriety had become irretrievably lost to her. For indeed, her tongue appeared to be growing far too hungry for this exceedingly exotic and forbidden of fares. Yet what might she have done had she finally decided to leave her life of opprobrium behind? She knew no one—and no one knew her. Who would there be for her to seek out for assistance—to explain the complexities of her plight? How many miles could she traverse on her few nasal words of grammar-school *Français*? The handful of francs Sir Jason kept in the mason jar on the kitchen shelf were barely enough for basic household essentials, let alone sufficient for passage home. Only where exactly *was* home? For Celia discovered that she no longer knew.

The confused young Englishwoman could not understand her unnatural response to these sapphic couplings. Of course she was distressingly aware that they had been orchestrated for the sole benefit and ecstasy of Sir Jason Hardwicke himself. But somewhere along the way she, too, had begun to find ecstasy amidst the disgrace, especially when she felt a pair of soft womanly lips embracing the obscenely protruding flesh of her engorged clitoris. The sensation of those warm, wet lips so enticingly similar to the even warmer and wetter lips pressing so insistently against the yearning facsimile of her mouth stirred something in Celia beyond that of the physical—something just beyond the outer fringes of memory. It was as if she had experienced it all before… in some past life known only to her deepest, darkest, and most shameful subconscious. Yet how could this be possible? Until her feet had stepped over the threshold of this charming Provençal dwelling, her tongue had been ignorant of the flavor of other women, as, indeed, had the swollen knurl of her clitoris and the bubbling crimson sliver below been ignorant of the illicit sensation of another woman's tongue.

Try as she might, Celia could not recall a single instant in her young life when she had been in the company of other females while such aberrant intimacies were instigated or encouraged. The only occasion she ever had cause to be alone with those of her sex other than the members of her own family had been during her course at Miss Waverly's Secretarial Academy for Young Ladies. And surely those naive days of fledgling independence bore no relation to these highly unwholesome unions she now found herself participating in....

Unwholesome unions which Sir Jason saw fit to enhance with the vampish presence of Martine.

a soupçon of martine...

This auburn-haired beauty who spent several days and nights at the blue-shuttered house in Provence at the personal behest of Sir Jason Hardwicke was well known in French society as one of the premier dancers in all of Paris. However, she was even better known in certain smaller enclaves of this very same society for something entirely different from performing the cancan beneath a sweltering legion of multicolored spotlights—a certain *something* the heretofore unversed Celia would soon be made scandalously aware of.

Once Martine received word via Count D'Arcy that her much-celebrated presence had been requested at the temporary country home of none other than the dashing Sir Jason himself, she did not hesitate an instant to put forth her flattered acceptance. Any excuse to leave behind the grit and grime of Paris and the cloying odor of greasepaint and sweaty costumes was all right by her! Having already made the introduction of this very fine English gentleman at the salon of their mutual acquaintance, she felt certain the journey south would be well worth her while, regardless of the unreliability of the trains and the notoriously ill-kept roads of rural France. It just so happened that the talented dancer harbored quite a fancy for this particular Hardwicke, although it would be a fancy her pride would keep silenced. Nevertheless, she hoped that one day he might finally take notice of her and cast his affections her way. For Sir Jason had always shown himself to be the keenest of spectators at the private performances she gave under the count's generous sponsorship.

Martine's unusual and admittedly single-minded preference for having her bottomhole attended to by a worshipful tongue of either male or female origin was no secret to her host. Several of those in Jason's social circle had attained firsthand acquaintance with its reputed delights and spoke of their exploits in the most glowing of terms—and often with a touch of masculine embarrassment, for such an activity was not one that a gentleman usually indulged in, let alone boasted to others of his standing about. Indeed, perhaps the extraordinary attributes of this particular orifice had loosed their conservative tongues. For according to those select members of this exclusive club who had been so fortuitous as to have experienced it for themselves, Martine's anus was the exact shade of a ripe tangerine and equally as tasty. It might also be added that what might have inspired so many of high society to seek out the woman was her rather un-French-like custom of paring the auburn curls from the alabaster flesh of her mons veneris—a paring which would naturally be extended to the coquettish crease between her well-toned buttocks.

The dancer was extremely proud of her limber body and enjoyed displaying its remarkable agility to audiences both public and private alike. However, it would be these private audiences who would benefit the most from her unique talents. For whether on stage or off, Martine loved to dance. And dance she would, the colorful layers of her skirts aflight as she kicked her long shapely legs high into the air, the scent of her perfume wafting toward her devotees along with a subtle musky undertone that could not have been sprayed from any decanter. The shocking absence of petticoat and knickers offered these enraptured spectators an exhilarating peek at the flirtatious vermilion petal crowning the redhead's hairless vulva. Yet there would be still more provocative treats in the offing as she performed a dramatic volte-face with her athletic rear cheeks projecting grandly out behind her and her frilly skirts up to her neck, thereby showing off the famous notch nestling between them—which would be winked with calculated precision at admirers. And indeed, this premier danseuse maintained no shortage of admirers!

Her loose and limber form possessed many more talents besides those most obvious. After Martine had executed the very last of her famous high steps, she would fall to the floor in what might understandably be assumed by the unacquainted as exhaustion. In actual fact, the performance was only just getting started. For within moments, the weight of her body would be balanced expertly upon the broad shelves of her shoulders with her muscled thighs brought to an uncustomary rest beside her pearl-studded earlobes. The extremeness of such a pose should have been considered an utter physical impossibility; nevertheless, the woman appeared to have been blessed with the uncanny ability to bend and fold herself into the most unnatural of shapes. Perhaps she might have enjoyed a highly successful career as a contortionist had she not chosen the more glamorous life of a dancer.

Having thusly mastered the bones and muscles of her nimble body, Martine would urge her head forward toward the moist, hairless cleft between her thighs and—to the astounded enchantment of those gathered—draw the tumescent tongue of her clitoris into her mouth. It required a great deal less effort than one might have expected, for after so many strenuous high kicks and so many appreciative *hurrahs*, the entertainer would have reached a considerable state of arousal, hence making the elongated flap of flesh far easier to grab hold of with her lips. The longer she sucked upon it, the grander and more rubescent it became, making her the envy of all the ladies present and even some of the more modestly endowed gentleman.

Priding herself on her womanly independence, the dancer always found it quite pleasing and, indeed, extremely convenient to utilize this somewhat anomalous option when without the company of a suitable partner. Creamy dribbles would spill inexhaustibly outward from the equally rubescent opening of her vagina, and she would flick the tip of her tongue across this quivering stria, swabbing up what she could manage to reach of her favorite nectar before it trickled down into the deep valley between her buttocks. Had it been at all possible for her to do so, she would happily have licked the twinkling notch of her anus as well. So sadly improbable an attempt would not be necessary, however, for within moments, Martine would be inundated with a host of eager volunteers to do precisely this—indeed, volunteers of *both* sexes.

Having already attended a number of these cultural soirees in the Paris *maison* of his friend the count, Jason considered it a supreme honor, not to mention a privilege, to have the humble salon of his temporary home in the French countryside graced by the presence of so remarkable a lady. Undoubtedly his blushing *détenue* would be likewise affected by the dancer's special talents and would surely wish to take full and complete advantage of them. Yes, he would make certain that the flexibly limbed Martine would be most well received.

Not surprisingly, Celia had no knowledge of the auburn-haired beauty's special claim to fame, only that she was a famous dancer in Paris—a fact which was relayed to her beforehand by Sir Jason himself, whose cunning smirk should have been warning enough to the already uneasy girl. Yet never would she have believed that the man who seemed intent upon her continual degradation should be so despicable as to concoct the unsavory alliances that next transpired.

On the lavender-scented eve of her arrival, Martine performed spiritedly for her new audience, launching her legs even higher than usual and bending so far forward that her aquiline nose grazed the wood-slatted floor beneath her. Celia's face flamed with the embarrassing realization that the woman wore nothing whatsoever beneath her rainbow of skirts. *Surely this cannot be the usual method of costume for the Paris stage!* she declared inwardly, suitably offended by this rude and, indeed, most disturbing display. Nevertheless, the flame upon her cheeks quickly turned into a full-fledged conflagration when she noticed that the dancer's very visible bottomhole appeared to be intentionally winking at them—a winking which, if the horrified china blue of Celia's eyes did not deceive her, was directed specifically and most pointedly at *her*.

Suddenly Sir Jason inserted the tip of the cigarette he had been smoking into this obscenely blinking mouth, stepping back with the exaggerated flourish of a ringmaster in the circus. The puckered rim began to constrict, seeming to draw hard upon the cigarette—indeed, puffing it. Fluffy rings of gray smoke spiraled upward into the too-warm air, only to be replaced by still more fluffy rings of gray smoke. Celia could not help but think about Sir Jason's saliva being on that cigarette and how his saliva was now inside the ripe tangerine of the dancer's bottomhole; only afterward did the prophetic meaning of this actually occur to her. Martine puffed her handsome host's cigarette nearly to the end before she reached behind her to pluck it back out, placing the smoldering stub between her lips and finishing it off. All the while Jason chuckled quietly, the stiffened rod in his trousers obvious to all…as was its duplicate in his cousin's trousers.

How could this vulgar creature possibly be the toast of all Paris? Indeed, Celia could not imagine anyone wishing to procure a ticket for such a foul event, whether gentleman *or* lady. Be that as it may, directly afterward, when she was instructed to remove them, the affronted young woman encountered a moist stickiness upon the once-pristine gusset of her knickers that caused her to cringe with shame. And it was a shame that would continue long into the flesh-heated Provençal night.

Although she had experienced a largess of this unwelcome emotion under Sir Jason Hardwicke's direct patronage, not even Celia's wildest imaginings could have prepared her for so lewd a display, especially from another of her sex. Nevertheless, she was soon made the star of far lewder displays, for no sooner had the smell of burning tobacco begun to fade than Sir Jason made his perverse passions known. Hence, as the elastically jointed dancer bent fully forward and grasped her slender ankles, Celia would at last comprehend what was expected from her on this warm spring eve.

The extremeness of Martine's pose prompted the pearly halves of her muscled bottom to pull away from each other, offering to any and all takers the orange hollow nestling so provocatively between them. Suddenly this gleaming talisman gave its lone female observer a bold wink—a wink which was made ever more impertinent by the complete absence of hair surround- ing this rudely blinking eye. A powerful jolt shook Celia's body, nearly wresting her from her chair. Surely it could not be true that her beloved's cousin should desire such an obscenity from her! Yet as her heretofore unversed tongue encircled the foreign terrain of the other woman's smoke-flavored anus, she realized that *this* was what Sir Jason had planned for her all along. Yes...he had devised a most cunning form of humbling, indeed.

Such would be Colin's ruminations as well. How

could it be that he should sit silently by while his delicate ladylove was forced to perpetrate such grave misdeeds upon a member of her own sex? Worse yet, how could it be that he should grow so damnably rigid from following the progress of the moist pink tip of her tongue as it skated with such childlike uncertainty over the satiny surface of this forbidden burrow? Why, he very nearly leapt forward himself to perform the same act upon Celia, for too many weeks had passed since he had tasted the spicy sweetness of her rosy little porthole. Unfortunately his wicked relative seemed to anticipate such a reaction, and before the younger Hardwicke could extricate himself from the cushioned prison of his chair, Jason's arm shot out, barring the bereft Colin from his flavorful spoils.

After Celia had finally completed her bashful oral explorations of the elegantly fluted rim that had been presented to her with such élan, Jason decided to augment her disgrace by rewarding his guest's saucy tangerine with a visit from his penis. For what could be more delicious than to penetrate the opening his crimson-faced captive had just lubricated with her saliva? Martine could not have been more thrilled to host his fine specimen, although she secretly wished the gentleman would entertain her bottomhole with his hot manly tongue instead of leaving such lusty dalliances entirely to the timid mouth of his wide-eyed female companion. Granted, the English mademoiselle was quite pleasing to the eye and—as the nimble performer would very soon discover—to the tongue as well. Even so, if the handsome Sir Jason preferred to act as spectator to that act rather than performing the task himself—and with this Martine executed an inward shrug—such was the prerogative of the eccentric English!

This was the very first occasion when Jason actually saw fit to indulge himself with one of—as he was so mischievously fond of calling them—"Celia's ladies." Indeed, it seemed silly if not downright criminal *not* to make use of these insatiable temptresses, for why should Celia reap all the benefits from such libidinous unions? Of course it never occurred to him that she might mistake his attentions in this particular direction as a personal affront upon her desirability—a wordless critique that she was perhaps not malleable enough for his needs. Surely the dear girl would appreciate so unselfish an offering of his expertise. All at once he could envision the glorious days that lay ahead of them—the two of them working together, side by side, to achieve their mutual goals. Ahh...what a team they would make!

With this in mind, Jason positioned Celia beneath the dancer's humid vulva, secure in the knowledge that she would find much of merit to occupy herself with there. No doubt she would enjoy the other woman's lush, silken sleekness—a silken sleekness so very much like her own except in the more subtle aspects of shading. As the fairer and more disconcerted of the three participants drew the ripe vermilion flap dangling above her into her mouth, a fully aroused Sir Jason entered the auburn-haired beauty from behind, his plundering penis stationed directly above Celia's perspiring forehead. She slid the startled china blue of her eyes upward, her heart nearly breaking when she saw the throbbing purple knob stretching the tangerine perimeter her tongue had just taken its first shameful tour of. The prodigious cylinder of the shaft quickly followed suit until all that remained was the wildly swinging sac of Jason's testicles. Their movement prompted a heated breeze to wash over the anguished young woman's flushing face, bringing with it the tantalizing fragrance of this union. It was a fragrance Celia would not soon forget. Indeed, it was the fragrance of her humbling.

The Hardwicke whose illicit actions had incited such torment held back from his climax, for he did not wish to lose himself within Martine's agreeable backside. Tonight he had other plans—plans which had been inspired by the recently witnessed ingenuous lappings of the dancer's deservedly renowned hind hatchway. Perhaps the dear girl had not as yet taken her fill of its reputed sweetness! With an uncharacteristic generosity of spirit, Jason withdrew before matters came to their inevitable hydrous conclusion and, reaching for his enraptured cousin's licking ladylove, dragged her out from beneath the hairless mound above and presented her with his penis. To his surprise, Celia made no effort to resist. Undoubtedly he had expected at least *some* feeble show of opposition toward the rather unladylike assignment he now demanded of her; yet instead she took his aromatic organ full into her mouth, her tongue slithering expertly across its well-stoked surface. Indeed, her laving of it proved so painstakingly thorough that it would leave its owner dizzy, and before he even realized it, half his seed had been forfeited down her strenuously gulping throat.

To Sir Jason Hardwicke, his delicate ward appeared to thrive in her humiliation. Although extremely delighted that the important business of her humbling was progressing so well, it also posed a slight problem, for he was constantly challenged to concoct further scenarios with which to humble the ungrateful Celia and consequently put paid to whatever silly romantic dreams she and his equally ungrateful cousin might once have entertained. Rather than relaxing and reaping the erotic bounties of his fertile imagination, his mind was laboring feverishly toward his orchestration of the next lusty encounter. Indeed, it was not always easy being in control!

The unprecedented interjection of Sir Jason's penis into this unwholesome alliance caused Celia much confusion, not to mention a considerable amount of jealousy. She was not entirely certain she appreciated this unforeseen intrusion. For buggering her *own* bottomhole while she occupied herself with the dancer's insatiable counterpart was one thing, but when he went and slipped it into the woman's bottom! Strange that she should suddenly feel so possessive of a man who lived to dishonor her; but she had never before been made to share him—Sir Jason had been hers and hers alone. And Celia had no reason to expect this to change. This recent turn of events disturbed her greatly, for it indicated that the senior Hardwicke was somewhat fickle in his affections. Yes, it would seem that she would need to toil harder than ever to win his love.

Martine's illustrious specimen was Celia's first-ever encounter with the distinctive rear *portière* of another female. How she had burned with shame beneath Sir Jason's inscrutable dark eyes, as had the salivating tip of her tongue, for it desired yet another taste of this savory delicacy. Indeed, she wished to scour the zesty tangerine until it glowed—until she had scraped the finely filigreed rind raw. Such a disgraceful realization nearly prompted Celia to leave the blue-shuttered house that very same night—to take her chances alone on the dusty road to Avignon and on the train she hoped would be waiting at the station the next day. Although she convinced herself that her fear alone prevented her from fleeing, deep down she sensed it was something else—something so monstrously dissolute she dared not even risk allowing it to anchor within the tumultuous waves of her mind.

Unbeknownst to Sir Jason's lovely captive, the flexibly limbed entertainer would be staying on in Provence for several more days. The following morning at breakfast, he chose to pay Celia a compliment on the previous evening's performance. "You did very well, my dear," he smiled mockingly. "Especially for one so inexperienced. I can see that you have developed an unquenchable appetite for our charming guest." And with this, he gestured companionably toward his younger cousin, as if seeking to include him in his opinion.

The cup of café au lait in Celia's hand began to tremble. She barely managed to set it back down on the table before the dark liquid splashed over the rim, staining the pine black. Colin continued to eat his breakfast, seemingly unruffled by the improper subject matter being discussed; one would have thought that his relative had been offering a comment on the weather. The flustered subject of conversation turned toward him for protection, receiving none. Instead he slathered a generous helping of butter across a hunk of brown bread, following it up with an equally generous helping of raspberry marmalade, his appealing Hardwicke features continuing to remain unmoved by the beseeching glances directed his way. Perhaps he had finally become immune to the depravity taking place before him, for now that Celia gave it some consideration, her beloved *had* looked quite euphoric as she was forced to debase herself for his cousin's entertainment. Why, his cry of orgasm had been greater than Sir Jason's! Suddenly her tormentor's liquid velvet voice broke into her reverie. "I trust you will continue to make Mademoiselle Martine most welcome during her stay." And as if to emphasize the true meaning of his words, his right eyebrow quirked upward in a question—and it was a question that did *not* require an answer.

The sentence dangled in front of Celia's disbelieving eyes, each syllable causing an eddy of electrically charged air to disturb the morning stillness. He could only mean one thing—that the redheaded vixen with the tempting tangerine between her bottomcheeks had no intention of departing just yet. Indeed, the woman was right at that very moment upstairs, enjoying a deep, postclimactic sleep. "Our honored guest simply must rest up for this afternoon," Sir Jason added with an overly playful wink, bringing to mind winks of a far less guileless nature. All at once Celia's heart began to flutter wildly, as did the now-agitated flap of her clitoris. It was all she could do to keep from reaching down to relieve its suffering.

The sun was still high on the Provençal horizon when the two women once again met in the light-flooded salon to moisten their lips with Pernod. Needless to say, before the arrival of dusk, they found their lips being moistened with a good deal more. Rather than offering up the desirous opening of her backside on the traditional stage of the floor before her modest audience,

Martine decided to place herself facedown at an oblique angle across her handsome host's lap. She had just spent upwards of an hour preparing herself for whatever amusements the evening might choose to bring, meticulously scraping away even the tiniest of bristles from her intimate folds and crevices. Hence, when she reached back to spread the dance-muscled cheeks of her bottom, her efforts were aptly honored with a profound sigh of appreciation from the gentleman whose thighs she balanced upon. However, the reward she wished for most of all was not forthcoming, for once again the enigmatic Englishman whose oral attentions she sought saw fit to relinquish her yearning bottomhole to his submissive female companion.

Celia could not fail to miss the menacing glint in Sir Jason's eyes—a glint which told her she had better get to it, *and quick*. Indeed, it was one matter to disgrace herself from a distance, but to do so directly beneath his aristocratic Hardwicke nose? Nevertheless, the red-faced young woman did what was expected of her, knowing full well the consequences of refusal. She wedged herself within the generous gap formed by Martine's flared thighs, her palms replacing those of the dancer, who in turn settled her now-unencumbered palms flat on the floor to hold herself steady. Slowly and with great trepidation, Celia began to lap kittenishly at the uncovered dimple, finding it even sweeter than it had been the day before—as was her humiliation at being obliged to partake of it in so painfully conspicuous a fashion.

Jason swept the honey-colored tresses back from the flushed oval of her face so that his view of the proceedings was completely and deliciously unobstructed. His hungering eyes wanted to gorge themselves just as the tremulous girl before him was soon to be gorging herself! "Now, Celia, surely you can do better than that!" he scolded good-naturedly, the underlying brusqueness of his tone inspiring her tongue to move all the faster. Indeed, it virtually flew across the gleaming surface of the other woman's bottomhole, making soft siphoning sounds as it connected with empty space. Always one to take advantage of an opportunity, Jason inserted a pairing of fingers into the unprotected hollow of his hard-working captive's out-thrust backside, twisting and turning them in conjunction with the sinuous movements of her tongue on the cancan dancer's wildly twitching anus. He found himself instantly rewarded by a persistent squeezing of the sphincter muscle, not to mention a highly provocative wriggling as Celia's glistening tongue broke through the brightly hued perimeter she had heretofore only been shyly courting.

That afternoon and well into the moonless black of night Celia labored hard—indeed, harder than she ever had during the entire time of her captivity with Sir Jason Hardwicke. For try as she might, she could not blot out the painful memory of his broadly fleshed organ sluicing in and out of the orifice she was presently lavishing so much oral adoration upon. Perhaps if she did a very good job at pleasing Martine, the woman would not see fit to accept such aberrant overtures again in future—nor would Sir Jason have cause to initiate them. With this childlike hope first and foremost in her mind, Celia stretched out the velvety pink length of her tongue, willing it to grow. The increasing raggedness of Sir Jason's breathing told her that he took great pleasure in seeing it plunge so deeply inside the dancer's anus which, thanks to the clever application of this most recent of worshipper's thumbs, distended eagerly outward like an orange-rouged mouth seeking a kiss.

Nevertheless, such thorough lovemaking did not come without a price, for very soon Celia's jaw began to ache, as did the straining muscles in her neck. Martine's athletic fundament absorbed her with such force that one might have thought its impassioned proprietor intended to yank out the invading appendage by the root. Perhaps it was no wonder that an engagement with this lusty tangerine had proven so unforgettable to so many. Celia raised her perspiring face from between the entertainer's splayed bottomcheeks to gulp in some much-needed oxygen, only to receive a flirtatious series of winks from the abandoned portal. It began to occur to her that the brazenness of this response might not be entirely intentional, but rather a result of the breached rim attempting to return to its normal size. Suddenly she wondered if her own frequently breached rear opening ever exhibited such lewd phenomena upon the departure of a Hardwicke penis, for indeed, the still-innocent English girl had no acquaintance with the manly length and width of any other. The unseemly image of this most personal of bodily ingresses demonstrating so embarrassing a spectacle prompted Celia to whimper with renewed shame. What atrocities the two cousins had perpetrated upon her!

To help distract herself from the hot sting of tears clouding the pristine blue of her eyes—a sting fostered in part by the remembered chuckles from an anally sated Sir Jason Hardwicke—Celia dabbed her fingertip against the ripe tangerine whose ambrosial flavors still danced with scandalous abandon upon her tongue. The wetness of her own saliva excited her, as did the sinewy softness of the elasticized perimeter itself. Like a blind person feeling her way in an unfamiliar environment, she rolled the highly sentient pad in slippery circles over the moistened crinkles, giving herself over to pure sensation. The fathomless void at the center seemed to possess a powerful magnetic field. This twinkling abyss drew Celia's shyly exploring fingertip toward it and, before she even realized it, the entire digit had vanished inside.

An alarming sound reached her ears—a frantic rasping that could only have been caused by someone in great peril. It was Sir Jason, whose breathing had grown dangerously labored...as indeed, had his younger relative's. He grabbed hold of Celia's wrist, squeezing till the flow of blood was very nearly stanched. "Fuck her!" he demanded gruffly, his dark eyes apoplectic with the desperation of his need. Suddenly he took the finger she had used to penetrate the dancer into his mouth, only just as suddenly to thrust it back inside the moist, greedy slot whose violation he desired to witness. So lightning quick were his actions that they might easily have been imagined.

A queer shudder raced up and down Celia's naked body, converging round the bulging lump of flaming flesh that composed her clitoris. She could feel an all-too-familiar wetness spilling onto the insides of her thighs—a wetness which would not go unnoticed or unremarked upon by her two male observers. Colin was nearly drunk in his desire to lap up the creamy dribbles. Before he could attempt to do so, his cousin halted him with a few well-placed words. "See how Celia's little cunt weeps with love for our guest's arsehole!" And as if to confirm his pronouncement, a sparkling pearl of honey filled the opened mouth of her vagina, only to trickle slowly and delectably outward. Such palpable evidence would henceforth keep the younger Hardwicke rooted to his chair—as perhaps had been his heartless relative's intention.

Ever so tentatively Celia began to move her finger within the other woman's rectum, the terrain it inhabited remarkably foreign, although no less enchanting a locale to visit. She had only ever performed so admittedly rude an exploration upon Sir Jason—and his interior had possessed the snugness of one not yet breached by an object of substantial consequence. In fact, the famous dancer had hosted an object of such consequence just the day before in the form of her host's penis. Surprisingly, this fiery chasm grasped Celia's finger with an unexpected affection, giving her reason to doubt the unnatural joining she had earlier been forced to bear witness to.

Martine wriggled impatiently upon the masculine lap accommodating her, her restlessness signaling that a gentle seduction was *not* what she required. Indeed, the refined strokes of a tongue needed to be followed with strokes of a far cruder nature. To the eager recipient, such a logical progression provided a dramatically potent combination, especially when adopted often and repeatedly. In her experience, the continual transposition of tongue to finger or tongue to prick could compare to naught else in the entire realm of erotic stimuli. If perchance it was not in her destiny to enjoy such agreeable attentions from the dashing Englishman upon whose tweed-clad thighs she now lay, then she would happily opt for the fingers and tongue of his charming young protégée. For indeed, the fingers and tongue of a beautiful female could be equally as satisfying in their ruthlessness.

Ever since she had inadvertently fallen under the

wicked aegis of her beloved's older cousin, Celia's instincts in matters sexual had been honed to a sharpness rarely seen in a woman of so tender an age—or indeed, in one who did not earn her living through the temporary let of her body. Without needing to be told, she reached between her thighs, encountering a heated well of moisture with which to lubricate the fingers of her right hand. For it would seem that on this warm spring evening, she would need to employ them all!

As the auburn-haired entertainer continued to maintain her buttocks at their widest possible spread, her blushing attendant urged the prepared digits inside the straining niche that had been made available to her with such consummate willingness. Surely what she endeavored to do must be impossible, if not downright depraved! Within seconds, however, the quadruple assemblage of Celia's fingers were charging in and out of the dilated socket with impunity, her earlier misgivings seemingly forgotten. To uphold the correct angle of attack, she bolstered her wrist with her unoccupied hand, applying herself to this unnatural venture with all the enthusiasm and aggression so often administered to her own intimate openings by Sir Jason himself. Her thrusts might even have been considered cruel, but was she not merely practicing what she had learned at the masterful hands and penis of her handsome captor? So delightfully hospitable was Celia's reception that she very nearly pushed the whole of her fist inside this sweltering cavity and might have easily taken the deed to completion had she not received instructions to the contrary.

"Put your tongue in her arsehole!" Jason cried with uncharacteristic hysteria, the normally untouchable darkness of his eyes bright with emotion. Perhaps he, too, harbored such an unusual desire.

Indeed, just hearing those words sent another mellifluous cascade of creamy honey down the trembling insides of Celia's thighs. She extracted her hand from its tangerine vise, her tongue slipping easily back into the well-stretched aperture just as if it had always belonged there. The vigorous introduction of her fingers had served to loosen this now-yawning ring of muscle significantly, thus sparing her aching jaw and neck from further strain. Since the dancer held herself so invitingly open, Celia's hands had been granted the freedom to pursue other matters. They rapidly found their way between her eagerly spread thighs, only to unroll the twin puffs of labial flesh to give the engorged kernel crowding them as much room as possible in which to move about. No sooner did she position her middle finger upon its ragged tip and commence with a rhythmic jiggling than Sir Jason once again made his wicked presence known.

"Yes, my dear…play with your little clitty," he chuckled lewdly. "Let us see how fat you can make it!" And with this, he encircled one of the swaying ivory globes upon her chest, pinching the tiny strawberry atop it with merciless accuracy. A quartet of fingers furtively moistened by several hurried and extremely pleasurable forays into the hot dripping slit of Martine's vagina returned to plug up the empty mouth of Celia's out-thrust bottom, their attentions equally merciless. Indeed, his knowledge of the humbled young woman's body had by this time become so painstakingly thorough that he could easily locate precisely where in this mysterious and divinely forbidden chasm to tickle and scratch, often inspiring climactic results without even paying the slightest bit of attention to the furiously twitching salmon pink tongue to the fore. Oh, if only his probing fingers could reach deeper!

The dancer's bare belly rubbed against her host's agitated penis, and he reached down to liberate it from his trousers, allowing the needful column to snuggle against her warm, pearly flesh. The taut muscles earned from a lifetime of physical conditioning ground suggestively against him, inspiring thoughts of once again making appropriate use of the woman's brawny and much-lauded bottomhole. For indeed, it had afforded him a most exhilarating fuck, not to mention a highly effective means of punishment for an individual so very deserving of it. Then perhaps after he had finished, he would invite his chastised captive to drink his frothy gratuity directly from the receptacle in which it had been deposited. Oh, what a fine libation it should be!

Before Jason could initiate a move to pursue this delicious objective, the woman on his lap shimmied backward, thereby impaling herself upon Celia's frantically thrusting tongue. This seemingly minor adjust- ment of Martine's limber form prompted the dangerously swollen head of Jason's penis to slip between her breasts, and she reached up to squeeze the supple spheres together, creating a deep gully—a gully he quickly lost himself in. For no sooner did he begin to drive the shaft of his organ forward than he sprayed the entertainer's chest and neck with a sizzling foam. She inclined her head to catch these seminal offerings in her mouth, his liquescent Hardwicke generosity drowning her cry of climax. Had Celia not been so understandably preoccupied with the culinary rewards of the cancan dancer's lusty rear portal, she might very well have observed what had just transpired. Instead, her tongue continued with its shameful plundering and pillaging even long after she, too, had soared high into the darkening Provençal sky in rapturous orgasm.

The once-shy young woman's natural talent for the dorsal tasks set before her greatly pleased Sir Jason. Indeed, it stirred memories of similar such encounters—encounters with him at the helm. Of course he had always been most discreet in these matters, choosing to indulge his oral penchant for Celia's charming little pucker within the strict privacy of his rooms. Although he quite fancied an audience when it came to the happy convergence of prick to anus, the senior

Hardwicke was not about to have the admittedly errant movements of his tongue monitored by either guest or relative. For it was his heartfelt belief that some things should be kept behind locked doors—and putting his tongue to his captive's flavorful bottomhole happened to be one of them!

Yet never would this secretive Hardwicke forget the festive occasion when he had filled a trembling Celia's thirsty rear fundament with champagne. It had been a very fine vintage; in fact, he had been saving the bottle for his birthday. And who better to share it with than his beautiful *détenue?* On this most special of days, they had retired early to his bedchamber, leaving the hapless Colin to his own miserable devices. Unfortunately the two celebrants neglected to bring along any glasses. Nevertheless, the vision of Celia's flawless young body sprawled languidly across his bed with the upstanding pricket of pink poking out from the bashful cleft of her denuded vulva proved more than sufficient to discourage Jason from returning downstairs to the chilly drawing room. Indeed, they could just as easily consume the wine straight from the bottle. Then a sudden stroke of inspiration seized him. Why, he didn't require a glass at all! For who needed crystal with such an elegant receptacle right here at his disposal?

Shivering with the iniquity of his desire, Jason manipulated his flustered companion into a kneeling position, pushing her honey-colored tresses forward until her bare buttocks jutted high into the air and split agreeably and—in his opinion—*invitingly* open. After he had finished arranging the severely crimson-faced Celia in the posture most expedient for his unique mission, he urged the uncorked mouth of the bottle inside the tensing ring of her anus. Deeming it secure, in one swift motion he tipped it upside down, watching with all the boyish eagerness of an excited child as nearly three-quarters of the pale liquid gurgled forth into the vessel of his choosing.

The captive of Moorland House began to emit a series of soft, plaintive whimpers, which her handsome warder took to be an indicator that she had at last swallowed her limit. For good measure, he permitted another inch or so of the effervescing wine to burble forward, exercising great caution as he slipped the lip of the near-empty bottle out from its temporary lodgings and placed it to one side—for this evening its presence would no longer be required. He studied the well-filled trough for any signs of leakage, even going so far as to pluck at the delicately ruffled edges with a fingertip. Despite an increasingly anxious clenching of the sphincter muscle, there appeared to be none. To Jason's delight, the rosy seal showed itself to be both air- and liquid-tight; not even the slightest drop could be coerced to spill from it. After making a few more minor adjustments to the disconcerted young woman's pose so she would be bent fully forward over the edge of the bed, he scurried into place behind her. The flushing cheeks of her backside rose seductively up before him, the brimming furrow between them seeming to aim directly at the birthday celebrant's equally flushing face. "I am very thirsty, my dear," Jason replied simply, taking his overwrought penis into his hand.

Celia's cry of shame could be heard throughout the moors. Although appalled by what her beloved's villainous cousin appeared to be demanding of her, she knew better than to fuss. For no amount of protest on her part, regardless of its vehemence, had ever led to anything other than her complete complicity—albeit *forced* in Sir Jason Hardwicke's depraved games. The fizzy liquid roiled dangerously inside her, imploring her to release it. To Celia such an act might once have been the ultimate in humiliation—and perhaps it still was. Yet it was an act she would perform for her tormentor most willingly. For how could she ignore the frantic flutters of her heart or, indeed, of that damnable snippet of flesh the cold steel blade of his razor seemed so intent upon bringing into full exposure?

The lustful conductor of this birthday fête observed with breathless excitement as the hairless little dimple he had filled began to purse outward, his own heart hammering so powerfully he thought it would cease to beat before he had even stolen his first savory sip of this much-anticipated cocktail. Just as he glimpsed the secret inner pink of Celia's distending anus, an indiscreet gurgle reached his ears—a gurgle this gentleman recognized as his cue to open his mouth for the ensuing eruption. Tears of joy shone in his dark Hardwicke eyes as the bubbly liquid jetted straight from the groaning conferrer's gushing bottomhole. Its inherent effervescence was accentuated by the uniqueness of its serving method, for the instant the first ticklish taste greeted Jason's awaiting tongue, he came. Semen shot from his unwieldy penis in a rapid sequence of violent spurts, painting hot foamy spirals on the protruding pair of buttocks before him. Had his thirst for the vintage been fully slaked, he might very likely have collapsed to the floor in bacchanalian bliss.

As it happened, an uncharacteristically humbled Sir Jason instead found himself collapsing to his knees, for the heavenly flow of liquid had stopped in midcurrent. Certain that the girl could not possibly be empty, he planted his champagne-wet lips upon the still-convulsing spout, only unceremoniously to swill from it what a sudden bout of feminine modesty had deigned to keep from him. The fiery heat of Celia's interior had served to warm the wine, although this did not make it any the less palatable. In this gleeful imbiber's cultured opinion, it had actually improved the vintage. Indeed, Sir Jason would never again be able to drink champagne in the prescribed manner. For no goblet, no matter how fine or costly, could compare to the sacred chalice he had filled and subsequently emptied. How his head had spun in drunken delirium that night—a delirium not entirely brought on by the alcohol. This had surely been the most exquisite birthday toast to ever grace his tongue!

On the final eve of Martine's highly eventful stay—an eve which coincided with the date of his birth—Jason had a special wish to grant himself, one more delicious humiliation to inflict upon the shrinking English violet whom he had been so generous as to take into his care. Indeed, it seemed like such an obvious wish, for what else could a gentleman of his standing possibly desire from two lovely young ladies in possession of such polished pouts but to see them joined together in a kiss? To this lascivious impresario, it mattered not who straddled whom, but only that the straddling be done properly so these impassioned vulvae could come together in all their shaven splendor. Yet not even the most unbridled of male fantasies could have prepared him for the sumptuous reality of two silken tongues fully erect and licking—delicate salmon pink against blazing vermilion, the puffy pairs of labial lips encasing them meeting up with a succulent smack. Jason cursed himself for not having had the hindsight to have packed his trusty camera, for such a sapphic convergence deserved to be caught for all eternity—indeed, to be enlarged and enshrined on every wall of their new home! Nevertheless, it would be forever etched in memory—a memory shared and pondered over in shameful secrecy by the demure young female whose lustrous clitoral flesh had rubbed with such riotous abandon against the lustrous clitoral flesh of another.

The honeyed wetness from the two women's slits mingled into a rich fizzy cocktail that would have put even the costliest of French champagnes to disgrace. After Celia and Martine had experienced their first climax, Jason demanded they partake of the liquescent results, inducing yet another climax of even greater force as the shuddering participants placed their hungering mouths between each other's out-flung thighs. That evening not only Colin, but his cousin as well would spill his spumous Hardwicke seed onto the unworthy surface of the floor. Not even a man of Sir Jason's sexual sophistication could have prevented, let alone slowed, the explosion that threatened—and therefore reached fruition before three sets of ecstasy-blurred eyes, one of which was colored the most innocent shade of blue.

Celia's increasingly educated palate would be forever haunted by the savory memory of the cancan dancer's legendary bottomhole and her sleek hairless folds— folds which reminded her so very much of her own. Perhaps her consumption of these feminine delicacies had been narcissistic, for was she not—much as the flexibly limbed Martine had given so lewd a demonstration of—making love to herself?

Indeed, the thought did not entirely displease her....

colin's secret revenge...

Perhaps he should not have seen fit to indulge himself with that last potent glass of Pernod during—as his wicked cousin so smugly referred to them—"the evening's festivities." Only what could he possibly have been expected to do? For day after day and night after night the much-cuckolded Colin had been forced to witness his delicate beloved's continual and ever-increasing degradation at the hands and, indeed, at the *backside* of her own sex. And if this had not been torture enough, what would prove to be an even greater source of anguish to the younger of the Hardwickes was the gusto with which his once-demure Celia applied her tongue to the upended and highly receptive bottomhole of another...not to mention the corresponding gusto of yet another tongue—the tongue of her fully erect clitoris. Never had he seen it so swollen and livid pink with desire! Indeed, it had fluttered unashamedly within the pouting puffs of flesh encasing it—puffs which the insolent blade of Sir Jason's razor had pared down to a polished perfection. Even with her thighs pressed tightly together, the young Englishwoman, whose carefully calculated humbling was the source of so much liquescent pleasure, could not have hidden her excitement from her observers—which had no doubt been Jason's justification for shearing from her pearly pubis the caramel curls previously providing her sole source of modesty. Surely the demure Celia could not have grown as corrupted as the villain who had orchestrated these unwholesome events?

Yet such was Colin's greatest fear of all—that perhaps his innocent betrothed had become forever lost to him. Oh, if only they had reached Viareggio—their lives could have been so different! For certainly Celia, too, had desired for herself a normal life—a life very much like the one they had enjoyed all too briefly in Provence before his dastardly relative had appeared on the scene. Now instead of only being made to share the dainty orifices of his ladylove with another man—a man linked to him *by blood*—Colin found himself having to share them with another woman as well— indeed, with *several* other women! Never could he have

The Possession of Celia

imagined the complete and utter depravity of his cousin's plan of revenge. Yes, it seemed that he and Celia had been extremely naive when they had taken flight from the little blue-shuttered house, for a man such as Sir Jason Hardwicke would never have taken kindly to what he undoubtedly considered an act of betrayal—especially an act of betrayal perpetrated by his own flesh and blood and by the beautiful woman whose body and, yes, whose *love* they had both shared.

Be that as it may, Colin Hardwicke had some revenge of his own in mind—a revenge he would not make quite so public a spectacle as the revenge being inflicted upon the flushing young woman he had once hoped to marry...and perhaps one day still might. Indeed, he could still taste the piquant flavor of his cherished Celia upon the lusty cancan dancer's lips and tongue as he pressed his dejected mouth against hers in a lingering kiss of sheer masculine despair. Notwithstanding the obvious, Colin quickly made the heartbreaking discovery that this very distinctive piquancy extended to other parts of the much-acclaimed entertainer as well—parts of a far more provocative character.

The multitalented Martine had welcomed her unexpected male caller most solicitously when he had tapped at her bedchamber door late in the evening—an evening which had resulted in many humiliations for those assembled in the little salon downstairs. Indeed, Colin himself had also suffered great humiliations, especially when his pleasure had gone splashing out onto the worn wood of the floorboards for all to see. Never would he forget the glazed look of rapture in Celia's eyes—a glaze which suddenly cleared to a limpid blue as she came to realize that the sizzling spume at her feet belonged not only to the cruel conductor whose lecherous orchestrations had brought its enthusiastic discharge about, but to his seemingly blameless cousin as well. For Colin's equally grand Hardwicke member had dispatched a barrage of frothy fire to rival that of even his nefarious relative's most liquescent endorsement.

From the speed with which she had pulled open her door, one might have assumed that this most recent of female guests to the peaceful French countryside had been expecting her masterful host...or perhaps his little wide-eyed *détenue*. Indeed, Martine would have been quite pleased to have entertained either one of them or even both simultaneously for as long as they desired and in whatsoever manner they desired. For she had found it infinitely pleasurable to receive the monumental prick of Sir Jason Hardwicke and the somewhat daintier fingers and tongue of his charming female companion inside her bottom. Although admittedly smitten with the fine English gentleman in whose humble Provençal salon she had recently been summoned to perform, this première danseuse had never been able to resist a lovely young mademoiselle—especially one with a virgin tongue. Yes, the tangy tangerine of her bottom had deflowered many an oral maidenhead in its day—a deflowering which had never as yet failed to keep them coming back for more! And this most recent of conquests was no exception, for the blushing temptress known to the entertainer only as *Celia* had not proven to be a particularly difficult challenge at all. On the contrary, the English girl's tongue had become a most dedicated aficionado once it had been forced to relinquish its initial shyness. Of course Martine realized that such a maidenly shyness resulted more from the social mores of the day rather than from any authentic aversion to the act. For indeed, the tongue that had worshipped at the religiously tonsured threshold of her bottomhole and deep into its hallowed cloister had displayed not the slightest sign of objection—not even when it was called upon to follow the drastically widened and wetted trail left by the significantly more substantial caller of Sir Jason's manhood. The mere idea of returning home to Paris and never knowing whether she would ever again experience such ethereal ecstasies suddenly caused the dancer's eyes to brim with tears. Oh, if only she could remain behind with them forever in the little blue-shuttered house in Provence! She would make herself worthy of her handsome host, regardless of what physical and emotional indignities it required from her. For Martine greatly admired Sir Jason's peculiar sexual penchants—which might have accounted in part for her secret passion for the man.

As Colin stole inside the tiny bedchamber of the household's latest guest, he found himself wondering precisely whose stealthy knock the rapaciously bottomed and quite unattired Frenchwoman had been waiting for. For surely it had not been his own, if the earlier goings-on in the salon could be considered any indication. Indeed, just the thought of his delicate Celia paying a clandestine visit to the auburn-haired vixen's bed set his blood to the boil. Had she not gorged herself enough on her banquet of humiliation for one night? Yes, he would make his fickle ladylove pay for her recent misdeeds with his cousin's never-ending procession of beautiful young women, even if she were never to know of the price!

Although the anxiously fidgeting figure appearing at her door was not the one whose presence she had been anticipating, the cancan dancer would, nevertheless, not find herself disappointed. Falling to her knees in the submissive posture she knew all men to prefer, the naked Martine grasped her hesitant caller's angry penis in both hands—for she required *both* to contain its unruly bulk—having already loosed the gentleman's linen trousers the moment he had stepped inside her bedchamber. For what else could this extremely erect monsieur be desiring of her but a special sampling of her talents? And of those this erotically charged Frenchwoman possessed a great many. Though she much preferred to apply them to those comelier members of her own sex, this renowned performer was certainly not above a fair amount of self-indulgence with a handsome male—especially if that handsome male happened to be a Hardwicke. Having already taken considerable delight from the grand length and width of Sir Jason's manly member, Martine fully expected his younger relative's to be of equal quality. Indeed, it had appeared a most promising specimen as it had spewed forth its boiling masculine juices earlier that evening. Could it be that she herself had been partially responsible for so magnificent a presentation? For surely the taciturn *célibataire* could not have remained totally immune to the flirtatious series of winks the dancer had directed toward her modest audience of two— winks which continued even long after a certain ingénue's trembling tongue had completed its anal probings and moved on to far juicier fare.

Ever since her arrival, Martine had noted the resemblance between two highly appealing English-men who observed her activities with such naked ardor, for they looked so very much alike in both face and physique. However, it was the majestic sight of Colin's straining organ in her hands which confirmed such idle musings. Of course, as so many had done before her, this visitor to Provence guessed incorrectly, reaching the conclusion that Sir Jason and Colin were, in fact, *brothers*. For surely no two gentlemen could possibly be endowed with the same manly accouterments without so close a blood tie!

No sooner had the dancer's knowing fingers wrapped themselves round the aching shaft of Colin's penis than he fell back against the flower-papered wall—a wall separating the guest bedchamber from Celia's. He watched with unblinking intensity as the spectacular length of his manhood disappeared within the woman's mouth, his enthusiastic moans fighting to reach the sleeping ears of the adjacent room's occupant. It had been so long since a female had pleasured him in this fashion, for his elder cousin had put a swift halt to any such transactions the instant he had discovered the fugitive couple on the quay in Marseilles. Indeed, Colin very nearly withdrew from Martine's welcoming lips, the sense of guilt which plagued him persuading the frustrated flesh of his organ to momentarily soften. Yet why should he not indulge himself with the fiery redhead? After all, his blushing betrothed had done so in ways he would never even be able to bring himself to speak of. Was it not his right to partake of the celebrated performer's unique charms just as Celia had done?

Having successfully absolved himself of his previous censure, Colin could once again feel himself growing to a rigid pillar inside the auburn-headed beauty's hot mouth—a mouth which had fed with an unfeminine gluttony upon the honeyed ambrosia flowing with such abandon from between his ladylove's shamelessly scattered thighs. Indeed, Celia's tender little slit had bequeathed to the dancer a hydrous bounty worthy of even the most liberally discharging male. Yes, Colin would do to the libidinous Frenchwoman everything he had been forced to witness—and *more*.

Martine accepted her male visitor deep into her throat, regretting that she could not entertain both Hardwicke penises thusly at the same time. For the flavor of this particular one proved so deliciously sweet that it only caused her to pine for the flavor of its distinguished twin. It was a rare pleasure, indeed, to enjoy in her mouth a manly member so divinely unencumbered by the distinctive cowl of retractable flesh one usually encountered at the crown. Therefore it was no wonder that the talented danseuse experienced a greedy flicker of desire to fill her hungering mouth with not just one, but two such handsome instruments of seduction. Had the opportunity only presented itself, she would have happily invited this pair of sleek specimens to partake simultaneously of both her front and hind entries—and perhaps to complete this lustful ballet, offered the stiffened vermilion protuberance of her womanly pendant to the English mademoiselle's oft-practiced tongue. Indeed, Martine would have made the flustered little ingénue suck upon it as one would suck upon a gentleman's prick, even going so far as to position the girl inversely to herself so that she might be able to enjoy the moist, savory hollows that could be found between a well-parted pair of female thighs. Oh, the elysian bliss that could have been hers from this luscious *pas de quatre* had she only possessed the courage to impress upon her handsome host her secret desires! Yet would the ever-acquisitive Sir Jason have complied?

The auburn-haired performer licked slowly and meticulously along Colin's impressive Hardwicke length, moving from dribbling pinhole to root, whereupon she absorbed the taut sac located there fully and with surprising impetuosity into her mouth. The oral reception of this uniquely masculine structure was entirely appealing to Martine, and she found herself relishing the excited quivering of his testicles—a quivering quite unlike the rather more ethereal forms of quivering she had grown more accustomed to—a quivering of an aroused female's slit or bottomhole, or the fluttery quivering of a luxuriantly engorged clitoris. Nevertheless, the cancan dancer preferred to open her mind and, indeed, her mouth to new sensations and flavors. Hence, she suckled this tenuous pouch of sparsely filamented flesh with an uncharacteristic gentleness, feeling a subtle shifting as the pairing of glands attempted to readjust to their delightful new home.

Her fingers still scented with the perfume of the desirable young female whose petite body she had earlier commanded, Martine began to kneed the swollen purple knob that pointed up toward the swirled plaster ceiling, the ragged groans emanating from its owner's throat confirming his pleasure. Further emboldened, she squeezed this throbbing orb all the harder, exerting a slightly less aggressive pressure upon the silken sac filling her mouth—a pressure not compromised in the least in its authority. No sooner had she managed to get up a good steady rhythm between hand and mouth than she felt a sudden contraction and a corresponding convulsion against her tongue and along the insides of her cheeks. It was then that a geyser of rich creamy fluid erupted high into the air. Martine immediately released the tensing pouch, only to catch in her mouth the boiling stream before it could become forever lost within the auburn glints of her hair. A grateful Colin sank to the floor in exhausted ecstasy, all traces of his previous guilt spurting down the naked dancer's vigorously gulping throat.

Yet tonight such oral delights would not be the extent of this particular Hardwicke's secret revenge. For try though he might, Colin could not erase from his tortured mind the image of the tantalizing tangerine he had spied between the Frenchwoman's muscular buttocks —buttocks which had been kept so widely and conveniently spread by the dainty hands of his once-chaste beloved. It mattered not whether his wicked cousin had earlier seen fit to indulge himself with such exacting thoroughness beyond its charmingly ruffled perimeter; Colin vowed to eradicate every last sign of his kindred rival's visit—even if this meant expanding the already expanded perimeter to nearly double its size! Although first he would allow his tongue to freely roam these irresistible contours—contours Celia's unbridled tongue had made itself so well acquainted with. Indeed, she had thrust the greedy appendage so deeply inside the performer's athletic rectum that he feared she would never be able to get it back out again. Surely such raw enthusiasm could not have arisen out of simple fear—the fear of reprisal from Sir Jason had she refused to comply with his iniquitous wishes. No. For it had become all too apparent to this despairing young Englishman that his once-demure inamorata had developed a voracious hunger for such exotic feminine fodder—a hunger which could not be quenched with the consumption of a single tangerine.

Well, *two* could lay claim to such appetites! Thus, before dawn chose to break over the Provençal horizon, Colin had already gained intimate and highly detailed knowledge of the cancan dancer's illustrious fruit. The talented Frenchwoman offered her reticent guest a very special display of her much-coveted treasure, for surely this was what the handsome monsieur had come to see—and indeed, to experience firsthand. Returning to her bed after her creamy repast, Martine rolled backward onto the agile curve of her spine, thereby placing the brunt of her weight upon her shoulders much as she had done when performing for the attractive trio assembled in the salon downstairs. How pinkly the licking little mademoiselle had flushed—a pink as exquisitely engaging as the succulent, mouth-watering pink of her fully exposed clit. Indeed, this Paris sophisticate was nobody's fool—she knew a woman primed for the taking when she saw one! For like her discerning host, Martine possessed considerable skill in reading the subtle flutters of this distinctively female pleasure gauge—and even those not so subtle.

No sooner had the celebrated entertainer positioned her body for the younger Hardwicke's ease and convenience than he hurled himself at the widened fissure of her buttocks, his tongue lolling wolfishly out toward the beckoning orifice between them. For some reason Colin had anticipated being more reluctant— perhaps undergoing at least *some* sense of revulsion for what he was seeking to do, for indeed, the anus his tongue desired to invade belonged not to his cherished ladylove, but to another. Yet to his astonishment, his reaction proved to be precisely the opposite. He felt only a powerful and uncontrollable lust as the twinkling orange notch drew his tongue toward it with the promise of the many great glories to be had. No sooner did the eagerly exploring tip break through this already punctured seal than he experienced the perverse desire for fickle young Celia to walk in on them—to discover him with his wet greedy tongue lodged far up the fiery backside of another female, for Colin had only ever performed such dissolute deeds upon Celia's shy little pucker. And indeed, Martine's tangerine-tinted version proved to be anything *but* shy! It grasped her most recent caller's incoming tongue with surprising strength—a strength earned from numerous agreeable encounters of prick, finger and, of course, *tongue*. For the cancan dancer had never made a secret of her preference for the oral appendage—and the one presently breaching the oft-breached rim of her bottomhole did not fail to please.

Flushing furiously both from excitement and a fair amount of genuine masculine embarrassment, Colin gratefully gave himself over to this igneous seduction, all the while silently damning his elder cousin, whose illicit actions were what had finally driven his anguished tongue into the twinkling bottomhole of a strange woman in the first place. Yet within seconds of the first heart-stopping caress of muscle against muscle, he found himself formulating mental comparisons between the insatiable specimen now before him and the one he had already come to know with such loving intimacy—comparisons of flavor and texture, temperature and tone. Indeed, both lovely ladies proved highly appealing to the tongue, although in slightly different ways. For it immediately became apparent that Martine's much-lauded skills as a dancer did not extend merely to how high she could launch her shapely legs into the air.

All at once Colin began to feel that some powerful force was at work, sucking his unsuspecting tongue deep inside the flickering abyss of the Frenchwoman's anus as if seeking to swallow it to the very root. Although he had experienced such consummate joys at the rosy little portal of his delicate ladylove, never had he been absorbed with such sheer potency or, indeed, *violence*. Nevertheless, he met such fierceness with an even greater fierceness, using his tongue as a weapon of war—a weapon of battle. For was all this not but a battle to possess the blue-eyed young female who kept every single one of them—including his seemingly heartless relative—enslaved by both lust and emotion beneath the slanted roof of this blue-shuttered house? Indeed, would any of them survive the bloodshed?

Perhaps what stirred this ever-cuckolded Hardwicke to such extremes of heated ebullience was not just a simple taste for revenge, but also a taste for what had been so freely and generously given to others. For it had become quite apparent from the ease with which she had organized her limbs that the auburn-haired beauty was well practiced in such encounters. Without demonstrating even the least amount of self-consciousness, Martine had wedged her graceful dancer's feet against the rolled underside of the topmost section of the pine headboard, thus forcing her knees to come back to rest alongside her pearl-studded earlobes. As an agreeable result, her naked bottom jutted out at a severe angle, their muscular cheeks splitting dramatically open and offering the orange-shaded chink of her anus to whomsoever desired to investigate its pleasure-giving properties. To further emphasize her dorsal proclivities, she reached round to grasp both buttocks with her hands, wrenching them so far apart that the unbearded mouth between them looked and indeed, *felt* to its owner in serious danger of tearing. Needless to say, this was the lady's most favored position of all, and one which never failed to make her completely irresistible to spectators, irrespective of their sex. For not only did these rather bizarre contortions place her lusty bottom-hole and its desirous environs readily available for every type of ingress, but it served another purpose as well—a purpose as provocative as it was practical. As it happened, Martine so adored the feel and flavor of her own sex that it would be only natural and logical for such emotions to extend to herself. Hence for her crowning achievement, she brought her pretty head forward between her opened thighs, thereby giving her mouth access to the vermilion proboscis of flesh protruding out from the puffy lips of her faithfully barbered womanhood. How fortunate she was to have been born so flexibly jointed, for what woman could claim to be able to entertain the thrusting organ of an impassioned gentleman in her backside whilst simultaneously suckling the excited flap of her own clitoris? Indeed, she had not earned her reputation for naught!

The sprightly cancan dancer had discovered her unusual talents at a very early age—an age when girls went skipping about with their pigtails aflutter, only to huddle together afterward and giggle over the local coxcomb. On the contrary, Martine had no time for such childish pastimes. For she had plans—and those plans did not include staying behind in the backward little village of her birth to work at her family's stall in the market or—when she came of age—marrying some swaggering Lothario with no prospects and even less sense in his head than what he had jangling about inside his trouser pockets...indeed, jangling until he finally came to lose every last coin to a crooked game of chance. No. This girl from such humble surroundings was destined to dance on the Paris stage—and she would do anything to get there.

And indeed, the auburn-headed young beauty would suffer no shortage of sterling gentlemen—and even a few ladies—willing to fill up her tattered pocketbook with francs just for a tantalizing demonstration of her special talent. It was these well-heeled city sophisticates who introduced the untutored country girl to the delights that could be gotten from the penetration of her bottom-hole. Of course such penetrations would not be without a preliminary lubrication from the tongue—an amorous prelude which Martine came to relish above all else, especially when initiated by another female. For no man, regardless of his passion or expertise, could compare to those first tentative exploratory licks committed by a woman—licks which swiftly grew into a frenzied infliction, indeed, a virtual scourging of the tongue. It did not require the wisdom of great years to realize that the prohibited nature of the transaction was what had undoubtedly incited them to such reckless savagery—a savagery far beyond that of even the most ungovernable male. Ergo, such pleasure-inducing oral peregrinations quickly inspired Martine to undertake for herself a thorough removal of the glinting auburn tendrils surrounding this highly sensitive hollow, the procedure promptly being extended to the more traditional areas of erotic interest as well. So provocative a divestiture only added to the appealing young Frenchwoman's popularity—and word traveled quickly within the glittering social circles she found herself being given admittance to.

Yet never could this aspiring entertainer have guessed that her body's unique propensity to bend and contort itself at will would be her real ticket to fame. Although dancing had become her primary method of feeding herself, it was her other appetites Martine chose to concentrate her attentions on. Indeed, there was not a salon in all of Paris which did not welcome her—nor a tongue within it her libidinous bottomhole did not also welcome. Many a generous offer had been put forth to secure the cancan dancer's exclusive company. Nevertheless, she considered herself a free agent and preferred to divide her valuable time amongst those whose lustful attentions she most appreciated. Hence it would be her appearances in the elegant salon of a certain very distinguished gentleman—a gentleman who possessed a nobility of both name and prick—that eventually led Martine to a bedchamber in Provence, and consequently to be pleasured by her own mouth as well as the mouth of the handsome Englishman whose equally handsome relative also frequented this particular Parisian salon.

And such exotic delights were what would, indeed, transpire on this warm spring night. The limber-limbed performer did not even wait for the first spirited stroke of her visitor before she grasped hold of the ripe projectile of her womanhood with her lips, sucking upon it noisily and with unladylike enthusiasm. She enjoyed the sweet piquant taste of herself nearly as much as she did of another—and perhaps more, if one chose to take into consideration the recent circumstances. For Martine's sentient clitoral flesh had earlier rubbed itself against its charming English twin, thereby offering her stimulated palate an even more savory treat. Just the memory of the blushing little mademoiselle's lush silken petal caused the Frenchwoman to whimper with desire, and all at once a surplus of honeyed fluid spurted forth from her unoccupied slit, pooling round the defenseless orange pucker below.

Taking this invitational form of lubrication as his cue, Colin launched himself into the upended and eagerly twinkling bottomhole of the dancer, finding himself reaching depths he had never before believed possible. The exaggerated position of the woman's backside offered him no barriers—he could journey as far as the length of his penis allowed, which would, of course, be considerable. Indeed, the only physical barrier he encountered seemed to be the barrier of his testes, which continued to glow with the orgasm-producing praise of Martine's skillful mouth, its earlier ministrations guaranteeing that his journey would also be a prolonged one. Because of the extremeness of the angle in which she presented her rear thoroughfare to her guest, Colin had to reorient himself toward directing his thrusts sharply downward rather than crossways or upwards as he had grown accustomed to with Celia. It required a fair amount of careful coordination and balance, for he had to position himself in a wide-legged crouch over the entertainer's upended bottom, with only his hands on his knees as support. Since he aimed to take her from the front—a position which allowed for a delicious view of the auburn-haired vixen's hairless female folds and the bright vermilion accouterments of clit and slit—the natural arc of Colin's penis fit at an angle rather at odds with the natural curve of the interior he endeavored to penetrate, thereby necessitating an administration of substantially more vigor than if the encroachment had been attempted from behind. Thus it was no wonder that such forceful interjections of his vengeance-seeking member elicited such fitful moans from the clit-filled mouth of its impassioned recipient. Being of Hardwicke stature, Colin found himself traveling to distant territory, his deeply penetrating thrusts prompting his pleasurer's hungering lips to momentarily lose hold of the swollen pendant of her clitoris. Nevertheless, she quickly recovered, only to resume her previous oral activities with more vehemence than ever before.

Indeed, Colin well remembered the expression of naked shock upon his beloved's flushing face the first time she had witnessed the cancan dancer's special ability to pleasure herself with her own mouth. Had he personally not been so understandably flabbergasted, he might very well have laughed aloud at this bizarre spectacle of self-lust, as had his wicked cousin, who had chuckled lewdly throughout, not to mention interjected a litany of crude comments—all of which had been greatly appreciated by the lady to whom they had been intended. For the sliver of Martine's vagina had flowed like a raging river that day—as Celia's hard-working tongue could most assuredly have attested. Of course none of those gathered in the little salon that day could have known of the spirited performer's secret and longstanding passion for her handsome host. Indeed, even the coarsest of asides had been the sweetest music to her ears—a virtual symphony of Sir Jason's homage to her talents. Although Colin's shrinking ladylove might have given the impression of being extremely appalled by such an act, surely she must have envied the woman to some degree, for who could *not* envy such a remarkable ability? No doubt Celia had wished for the agility of form to do the same. Why, perhaps she was at this very moment folding herself into a facsimile of the dancer, stretching and straining and struggling to grasp her salmon pink clitoris between her desperately seeking lips just as the captivating originator of this erotic production was currently doing for her audience of one—a private audience who found such a lewd display so much more extraordinary now that it had been intended specifically for his eyes. Oh, wherever did his dastardly cousin manage to find such women?

All of a sudden yet another salacious scenario took form in Colin's head—a scenario very nearly the same save for one slight alteration—that of the ignoble presence of his relative. Indeed, could it be that his dainty Celia was performing this bizarre act of self-love upon herself with the encouraging aid of Sir Jason? Yes, the younger Hardwicke could easily imagine his self-serving elder cousin assisting the embarrassed young woman into precisely so vulgar a posture, not stopping until he had bent and twisted the delicate limbs of her tremulous body well beyond their normal physical limits. For the lecherous fellow would surely not have been satisfied until he had forced his ever-humbled captive to nurse upon the needy salmon pink nipple of her own clitoris—an act he would have accepted as a personal victory. Indeed, such unnatural deeds would have been well within the grand scope of Jason's desires...as were many other unnatural deeds. For all too many times had an aggrieved Colin witnessed the anxiously flicking tongue of his flushing ladylove paying bashful homage to the masculine hollow of his cousin's backside. No doubt she had assumed that so shameful an occupation had heretofore remained private —that these too-often errant wanderings of her unfaithful tongue had remained a secret between herself and the man whom she had chosen to degrade herself for. Well, Colin possessed a few secrets of his own—which did not preclude the occasional act of spying upon the lustful pair whenever they believed themselves to be alone and therefore free to indulge in matters which might be considered—even for someone as hopelessly debauched as Sir Jason—as far beyond the dissolute boundaries of everyday Hardwicke propriety. Thus it did not require too taxing a mental under- taking for the young Englishman to envision his clit-suckling betrothed being made to abandon her own flavorful female fruit, only to just as swiftly replace it with a fruit of an exceedingly more masculine and, indeed, forbidden nature.

Be that as it may, on this particular Provençal night, pity for his beloved Celia did not appear to occupy Colin's wildly thudding heart. Clearly he had no time for such wasted emotions. For how could he, with the empyrean delights of the cancan dancer's lush, limber body at his complete disposal? Hence, as the greedily throbbing head of his vengeful penis continued to plumb the innermost recesses of Martine's seemingly fathomless rectum, for the first time since the younger Hardwicke had been made into a fugitive from the law, he actually began to feel himself beholden to his elder cousin. Although naught could compare to Celia's fiery rear conduit, these illicitly gained pleasures from the fiery rear conduit of another proved most congenial—especially considering that the nimble fingers and tongue of his cherished inamorata had only a short while previous performed a most thorough and public probing therein. Colin could have sworn that he had tasted the sweet flavor of Celia's saliva when he had first breached the entertainer's tangy tangerine with his tongue. That had been the moment when he had most hoped for his discovery—most hoped for his delicate ladylove to come in upon them during this highly spirited transaction. Yes, her eyes would have opened wide at seeing the velvety length of his tongue stuck well up the amorous bottomhole of the beautiful dancer, their innocent china blue misting over with bitter tears as she recalled how he had once fought to perform the very same lusty deed upon her. Indeed, if the auburn-haired vixen whose hind passage had been made the avid recipient of his continually charging phallus did not quiet her appreciative moans, Colin might very well have been granted his wish, for Celia's bed was just on the far side of the flower-papered wall—a wall the coral-tipped toes of the Frenchwoman's upended feet tapped a steady and unmistakable rhythm against. *Surely she can hear the succulent sounds of our anal convergence!* mused Colin with vindictive relish. Had he slipped the latch on the door after he had come in?

Martine sucked hard and with great enthusiasm upon the severely reddened knoll of her clitoris, the rich, creamy juices from her slit pouring down onto her well-plugged anus and further lubricating it for this invading Hardwicke shaft. An exhilarated Colin increased the speed of his strokes, finding himself unable to steer his focus away from the hairless puffs of the woman's labia with its bright vermilion flame flickering between them —of which, thanks to a suctioning pair of lips, only the merest hint of elastic root could be glimpsed. Silently damning his fickle betrothed, he concentrated with a scholarly zeal upon the unoccupied sliver of Martine's vagina, for each profound thrust of his penis into her upraised bottom prompted it to pop invitingly open, offering its fascinated observer an unprecedented view of the mysteries of her womanly interior, which would prove to be as intensely shaded as the distending flap of flesh now occupying her mouth. Indeed, Colin had only ever made such an intimate examination of his demure Celia, and her womanly interior had shown itself to be of a slightly pinker nature—rather like the aggrieved flesh of her clitoris after it had benefited from a jolly good rubbing.

Thus it was no wonder that after the younger Hardwicke had finally finished indulging and consequently spending himself with such consummate thoroughness within the cancan dancer's multitalented backside, he should then choose to direct his thirsting tongue toward the central core of her femininity, for it had grown ever more liquescent with her climaxes. Indeed, Martine had suffered one right after the other, the second of which was quickly to be joined by Colin's own as he pumped his manly pleasure deep into the auburn-haired woman's rear chasm until she pleaded for him to stop. For surely she could not swallow any more Hardwicke seed on this eve!

These were heady delights indeed, for, like his older cousin, this Hardwicke's tongue had only ever bathed itself within the nectarous contours of his delicate ladylove. Colin shuddered with undisguised glee as he consumed this forbidden female fare, the subtle differences between the honeyed confection now being offered to his vengeful palate and the honeyed confection he had come to know with such delicious detail a source of much enchantment. For Celia had both felt and tasted like a gentle spring rain against his ardently licking tongue, whereas this première danseuse was a violent storm. Nevertheless, Colin rode out this tempestuous downpour with considerable bravery, only to put forth one of even greater fury that would go splashing hotly against the chafed cheeks of the dancer's still-upraised bottom. Never would he have believed that his well-spent organ could have been capable of providing such a generous bounty of froth in the span of a single evening. Could it be that the younger and less cruel of the Hardwicke cousins had also developed a taste for the distinctive flavor of revenge?

When Colin had finally drunk his fill of his auburn-haired companion—for her juices continued to spill from her with every lustful lap of his tongue and he simply could not bear for the least drop of it to go to waste—it required all the control he could muster to stop himself from crashing through the door of Celia's bedchamber and rousing her from her post-orgasmic slumber which was brought on by her previous indulgences with the exotic creature whom he had just used as a balm for his pain. For Colin so wanted her to smell the fragrant fluids of another female upon him—to taste them on his lips and tongue. Let her know that he had desired the voluptuous flesh of another—and that he had desired that particular other's orifices as well! Yes, he would tell his faithless beloved how enchantingly sleek and satiny were the tangerine crinkles of Martine's insatiable bottomhole against his hungrily licking tongue, and how its well-plundered interior had scorched it. He would describe to her every subtle note of its tangy flavor—and even those not so subtle. He would praise to the heavens the fiery-bottomed vixen's unique ability to nourish herself upon her own clitoris—a robust appendage of substantial beauty and flavor in itself…as was the womanly sliver below whose sweet cream was greedily consumed by the man whose relentlessly thrusting penis had inspired it. Speaking of which, Colin would make absolutely certain to relay to Celia the delicious experience of the cancan dancer's sodomizing in the most vivid of terms—from the excited clutching of her athletic sphincter to the sudden and amusing release of trapped air upon his withdrawal. Indeed, he would spare his fragile ladylove's flushing ears no detail, regardless of its intimacy or the tears it might inspire. Perhaps he would even offer up the moistened length of his manhood to the trembling pout of her mouth so that she might enjoy firsthand the savory fruits of his labors, then dispatch her to the dancer's bedchamber so that she might clean away with her tongue the spumous residue of the pleasure he had left upon the woman's flesh. How sweet his fluids would taste as they trickled out from their guest's well-plundered rear hatchway. Yes, he would treat Celia as his cousin had done. For perhaps *this* was what she desired most of all.

Only Colin did not do any of these things. Instead he returned to his bedchamber, dreading what the light of morning would bring.

an uninvited guest...

Celia failed to hear the clatter of the old coach come to an unsteady halt at the end of the walk…nor did she hear the telltale creak of the front door which immediately followed. She was upstairs overlooking the flowering garden and preparing for the evening's entertainment as orchestrated by her beloved's salacious cousin. Although she possessed no knowledge of the specifics, his unexpected appearance in her bedchamber told her she would be receiving no rest on this fine spring day. For a few minutes earlier the relentless steel of his razor had whisked away all traces of the caramel-shaded nubs darkening the porcelain flesh of her vulva and the satiny fissure between her bottom cheeks. It was a task this discerning gentleman preferred to attend to personally, as it always proved the most supreme of indignities for its embarrassed beneficiary.

As the freshly shaven young woman gazed at the profusion of color below, a tantalizing breeze wafted in through the opened window, cooling the stinging burn left by the blade. She glanced timidly down at her naked mound, only to be cuckolded by the flagrant pink presence of her clitoris. A lavender-scented current of air licked softly and seductively over it, prompting the already-conspicuous bud to blossom with desire. The middle finger of her right hand moved instinctively and unconsciously into place, making slow, leisurely circles as she held the surrounding pods spread with her left. Anyone happening upon the garden could have observed her standing before the undraped window, the distinctive rotations of her finger obvious to even the most naive of passersby. Celia's heart pounded with an inexplicable speed, and all at once she felt overwhelmed with shame at the thought of the anonymous young female who was waiting for her downstairs in the little salon. She did not even need to see her to know that she would be very beautiful—and indeed, very wet for the oral attentions of a member of her own sex. For the wicked Sir Jason would have had it no other way.

Oh, when will these unnatural encounters finally come to an end? Celia cried inwardly, her finger beginning to move with a fierce despair. Her growing enthusiasm for the feel and flavor of her sex frightened her. It seemed so terribly wrong to do to their fragrant, yielding bodies what should only be done by a man—if by anyone at all! She now realized that her failed flight with Colin had wounded Sir Jason deeply, and in his pain, he desired to humiliate her—to make her pay for her fickleness. Yes, she could understand this kind of pain, for had she not experienced the briefest taste of it when her eyes had been held prisoner by the enthusiastic lancings of his penis into the lustful tangerine between Martine's bottom cheeks? Indeed, his seemingly inexhaustible member had doled out an incalculable number of strokes, each like the sharp jab of a knife in her heart. Yet how exquisite was the final pain of taking his throbbing flesh into her mouth immediately afterward and drinking from it the hot frothy ecstasies incited by the welcoming rear hollow of another woman. Sir Jason had come long and hard on that day—longer and harder than she could ever remember him coming. Perhaps there was no going back for any of them....

In the moors a powerful bond had formed between Celia and her enigmatic captor, and in her foolhardiness to believe that she could once again live life like any other normal young woman, she had gone and damaged it. She could only hope that she had not broken it completely. For surely Sir Jason would one day find it in his heart to forgive her once his ruthless dark eyes had finally sated themselves with the sights and sounds of her humbled pink tongue slithering slavishly between the glistening folds of the females he procured for her.

Indeed, she wondered how he ever managed to locate them, let alone lure them back to their unwholesome household in the French countryside. For nary a one had ever expressed surprise at the tremulous Englishwoman's uncertain presence—nor shock at the aberrant transactions which soon took place. Each would shuck her garments easily, not bashful in the least to do so before Celia, let alone before the two handsome gentlemen in attendance. The women demonstrated not the slightest sense of unease when it came to displaying themselves in the highly immodest poses so very essential for executing the dissolute deeds their host expected of them. Perhaps their normal feminine inhibitions had been lessened by the still-intact presence of their pubic locks—a natural phenomenon Sir Jason had stolen from his abashed cageling a long time ago. Although it was apparent upon their disrobing that the majority of these eager callers had introduced a pair of scissors to themselves, no barbering, no matter how precise, could compare to the painstakingly thorough divestiture Celia had undergone—and would continue to undergo for as long as she remained within the elder Hardwicke's realm.

All the women whose most intimate of parts her eyes, fingers, and tongue had thus far been made privy to, she appeared to be the only one, save for Martine, whose distinctive female lips had been sloughed of any covering. Instead, hers were made to parade themselves in all their puffy grandeur, thereby forcing what should stay discreetly hidden into brazen view. Even the demure cleft of Celia's backside underwent similar treatment, the exacting steel of Sir Jason's razor stripping away any last remnants of modesty that might once have been hers to claim. After all these many months of routine paring, she still could not accustom herself to the obscene sight of the fleshy pink tongue projecting so boldly out from the bashful seam of her labia. Nevertheless, this unseemly spectacle appeared to be what this gentleman preferred. Indeed, he always went to great pains to express his lecherous desires for these tantalizingly uncluttered attributes in the most graphic of terms, regardless of who might be present.

And the hours following Celia's latest encounter with the immoderately familiar instrument of her denuding was no different. While she performed her sapphic ritual of shame for the man she had dishonored, she began to sense something different in the little salon—a *something* which caused her to shiver in the comforting warmth of the late Provençal spring. Perhaps it might have been brought on by the provocative newness of the soft womanly folds a slender pairing of fingers held fanned out for their blushing encroacher's ease of consumption. For as Celia had quickly discovered, each lovely lady possessed a uniqueness of taste and texture that provided a highly addictive impetus to prolong and even escalate such oral explorations. Hence, as her industrious tongue continued to execute Sir Jason's dastardly bidding, she felt more naked than ever before, regardless of the fact that she had appeared thusly on numerous similarly staged occasions.

Suddenly the peculiar something that had been troubling her prompted the still-shivering young woman to lift her honey-glossed lips from between the widely flared thighs of the raven-haired female writhing in undisguised pleasure beneath her...only to find that it was not a something, but a *someone*. This afternoon a stranger sat in the high-backed fauteuil normally occupied by the cruel orchestrator of her disgrace. For a moment Celia believed she must surely be imagining things—that her tongue had gotten so carried away with the ambrosial delights being offered up to its velvety surface her eyes had lost their ability to focus. When she finally dared to hazard a second glance at Sir Jason's chair, a cry of such raw shame was ripped from her throat that even the moans of her climaxing partner were silenced.

A masculine image appeared in stark clarity against the darkening window tinted blood red from the setting western sun. Light glinted off the chestnut-colored curls on his head—a light which repeated itself poignantly within the corresponding brown of his attentive eyes. The merest sliver of a cleft marked his chin, an intensity of expression making it appear deeper. He possessed the type of mouth whose well-defined corners looked perpetually turned downward irrespective of mood. Indeed, to call him handsome would undoubtedly be understating the true meaning of the word. Sir Jason stood smiling quietly at his side, his left hand planted companionably upon the man's broad shoulder.

This mysterious stranger's name was Count D'Arcy.

It might have been the unexpected addition of this particular guest that inspired Sir Jason to become all the lewder in his instructions. Or perhaps he simply wished to put forth a dramatic display of his power over the trembling young female on the floor lest his friend get any untoward ideas into his head. Whatever the reason, his orders to Celia elicited a startled intake of breath from the visiting count, which had, of course, been Jason's intent. Even his reticent cousin gasped in wordless protest, for such a proposed demonstration before another of their sex was not only unprecedented, but, indeed, most worrisome. "Show us your clit!" Jason demanded of his bewildered captive, his voice hoarse with the headiness of a man used to controlling and manipulating others for his own personal pleasure.

Certain that further humiliations were in store for her if she did not oblige, the crudely chastened Celia adjusted her hips ever so imperceptibly to comply, feeling the seated gentleman's knowing eyes searing into the still partially hidden snippet of salmon pink the elder Hardwicke had so unceremoniously called attention to. To her horror, she could feel it stretching and pulling away from the root, a sudden gust of air from this new arrival's leg informing her that such an extension had just forced the secret inner pink of her labia outward and hence into exposure. Fortunately her partner blocked it from view by placing her redly rouged mouth over the region, replacing one form of disgrace with another.

It soon became apparent that Sir Jason had decided to perpetrate the most indecent of all humiliations upon his timorous *détenue* in the devastatingly handsome presence of this stranger, for suddenly he began to bark out additional instructions, seemingly unperturbed by their increasing vulgarity. "Wink your arsehole at our guest!" he shouted jubilantly, secure in the knowledge that *this* would impress his thorough possession of the English girl on Count D'Arcy in the event her docile young body might persuade him otherwise. For Jason fully understood the man's dubious character, as it was so very much like his own.

And indeed, there could be no mistaking the totality of Sir Jason Hardwicke's command over Celia as she struggled to imitate the outrageous act she had seen so lewdly executed by another of her sex. However, unlike the auburn-haired dancer whose similarly practiced orifice had achieved fame as well as a myriad of devotees throughout the country, this stand-in's enactment was considerably less gregarious—an actuality which made it necessary for its single-minded petitioner to repeat himself several times and with ever-diminishing patience. By the time Jason had hastened the crimsoning young woman toward the results he sought, the muscular ring of her anus had contracted so many times that she fell forward in exhaustion. Even the seductive presence of her dark-haired companion's far-reaching fingers probing the overexercised dimple failed to rouse her. Had Count D'Arcy not been in attendance that afternoon, Celia might very likely have unfolded herself from the floor and walked out of the blue-shuttered house...*forever.* Yet his elegant presence compelled her to remain and, yes, even to resume her degrading performance under the unremitting orders of her prurient tormentor.

Needless to say, the worldly count was not in the least bit fooled by his longtime friend's grandiose bluster. He knew full well that such coarse asides had been constructed entirely for his benefit...although to give the gentleman his rightful due, they *did* bring the most winsome blush of color to his disconcerted victim's cheeks, not to mention the telltale beacon of lustrous flesh that even now tried in vain to hide! Be that as it may, did Hardwicke honestly believe he could prevent another man from taking possession of this enchanting female if he truly wanted her? For if he did, then Sir Jason was a fool, indeed. No. Count D'Arcy did not need to resort to such obvious ploys to prove his dominance. Nor had he ever found it necessary to order a woman about like a trained animal in a circus. The many charming ladies of his acquaintance did not require any instruction; they were quite capable of deducing for themselves what would best please their distinguished benefactor, very often exceeding his wildest expectations. And after his scrupulous observations of the past few minutes, the count maintained not the slightest doubt that the delectable Celia would prove equally perceptive, if not more so. Why, one needed only to take note of the pinpoint erectness of her tiny pink nipples that so resembled his favorite summer fruit, or the corresponding erectness of an even sweeter fruit lower down—a fruit which, if his eyes did not deceive him, had already been topped with a generous serving of luscious cream. How exquisite it would be to take it into his mouth!

Count D'Arcy was a man who could make things happen by a mere snap of the fingers, as, indeed, the cultured individuals who attended his Paris soirees could wholeheartedly attest to. For not even the most maidenly and devout of females could resist falling under his spell, committing acts of the flesh previously unknown to them and hence unnatural to their natures —and committing them with great relish. An individual did not necessarily require a lengthy acquaintanceship with the count to understand the subtle form of power he wielded. Celia discerned it instantly upon their first meeting—a meeting which had been set into motion by her wanton transaction with the long-fingered and nimble-tongued beauty a vengeful Sir Jason had arranged for her—indeed, ordered for her as if the woman were simply an item on a café menu. Unfortunately, the potency of their mutual attraction made itself known during the one act she wished most *not* to perform before this inscrutable stranger. For just when the last of the afternoon light chose to illuminate the luxurious tangle of feminine nudity upon the floor, the luminous blue of Celia's eyes became inextricably welded to the luminous brown of the count's as the length of her tongue became inextricably welded to the sweltering walls of the proffered backside before her. The villainous Sir Jason could not have devised a more fitting way in which to humble her!

Despite the engaging and, admittedly, highly roguish cleft upon his chin, Count D'Arcy frightened the humiliated young woman more than her beloved's older cousin ever had, and she could feel her fear dribbling like warm cream onto the insides of her quaking thighs. She flushed hotly beneath their visitor's intense scrutiny, her shame all the more poignant and complete at this masculine addition to her audience. For what could be worse than debasing herself before *three* sets of male eyes, the most recent of which having up until this disreputable moment been foreign to her? However, Celia knew better than to cease from her illicit actions; the count's silent presence seemed to have emboldened Sir Jason, priming an already fertile mind and tongue to do their worst. Instead of waiting to be subjected to even further verbal indecencies, she ground her agitated vulva harder against the receptive lips of her partner, suddenly imagining they were the lips of this mysterious stranger. Hence, Celia's orgasm was stealthily gained, its occasion evidenced only by the shyest trickle from her quivering slit, which was hungrily licked away by a tongue expert in such lavings.

Count D'Arcy looked on with a combination of amusement and arousal. Although these sapphic practices were not entirely alien to him, the delicate young thing with the bewildered blue eyes and the gleaming mane of honey-colored silk *was*. Up until now he had only been made privy to the briefest glimpse of her naked form in the upstairs window, and her solitary activities had been mere child's play when compared to these voluptuous goings-on. Indeed, how could she possibly appear so innocent with the greedy tongue of another of her sex lodged so deeply up the streaming tributary of her vagina? This harmless feminine deception—for it could be naught else—showed a great deal of promise.

As if to confirm the count's rather slanted analysis as to the true nature of her character, Celia altered her position. Whether for his benefit or her own, the young woman portraying the aggressor in this delicious drama hauled herself up onto her crooked knees and bent forward over the thrusting dark mound of her partner, the porcelain swells of her bottom rising proudly into the air and splitting into two separate and distinct entities as she concentrated all her efforts on licking the bifurcated tongue of carnelian flesh below. Count D'Arcy's breath snagged in his throat, for whether knowingly or unknowingly, Celia had just provided him with a vista the likes of which would usually have required considerable coercion to behold. At last he could fully appreciate her lush womanly attributes in the manner in which they should be appreciated! Indeed, he was granted a double treat, for the exaggerated V formed by her widely splayed thighs functioned as an open window through which to view the bisected vulva of her impassioned companion and, therefore, every saliva-inducing detail of what was being done to it.

The gentleman occupying Sir Jason's chair leaned dangerously forward, shivering with all the pent-up lust of a man too-long denied from his fleshly objectives as a long carmine tongue fluttered happily within the cream-filled seam Celia's amended position had made available. Raven tendrils of hair snaked and jittered as if charged with electricity, clashing dramatically against the milky thighs held so generously and compliantly open for this highly skilled attendant whose industrious presence the count had been instrumental in providing. A pair of determined hands reached up to further disengage the pliant cheeks above, and they were rapidly followed by several bright flashes of carmine eclipsing the now fully disclosed rosette of Celia's anus.

A turmoil had commenced within Count D'Arcy's pleated trousers, and he breathed slowly and steadily to control himself. It simply would not do for a gentleman such as himself to lose control of his manhood only moments after stepping over the threshold of his host. It was a wonder that his male comrades had not as yet seen fit to plug their straining organs into the nearest available orifice! Had the two Hardwickes not been in attendance, the count would have without doubt already sampled the front and rear entries of both lovely ladies —and *still* have found the time to be entertained by their tongues. For there was nothing he enjoyed better than to have his handsome prick dutifully laved by a pair of reverent tongues after he had just finished indulging himself within the savory inlets of vagina and rectum. And indeed, he knew of no lady whose pleasure at doing so did not equal his own!

This recent witness to Celia's humbling could not believe his good fortune on this warm Provençal afternoon. Instead of listening to the endless cacophony of the Paris streets, his appreciative ears could listen to the succulent symphony of sound being generated from the auspiciously engaged young women on the floor. Although the dark-headed one who now lay in rapturous abandon upon her back was admittedly quite attractive and uninhibited in her actions— attributes which had led him to secure her company for his friend Sir Jason—it was the fledgling English maiden in the inverted crouch above who captured the count's lustful heart. *Ahh. Such an artful tongue,* he mused gleefully, suppressing an impassioned groan as he observed it scooping up a dollop of fresh cream from her partner's discharging slit. *And such a ripe pink clit!* Indeed, it was the most luscious shade of pink this seasoned connoisseur of the appendage had ever seen. How frightfully clever of his host to have arranged for so thorough a divestment of her pubic locks, for this flirtatious feminine accessory spent far too much time concealing itself from inquisitive eyes. Considering its uniqueness of purpose, a predisposition toward shyness was neither beneficial nor warranted, and such behavior should be discouraged at all costs. And judging by the highly tumescent condition of Celia's spirited specimen, it had lost any sense of reserve a long time ago. Suddenly Count D'Arcy knew that he must have her. And it mattered not what he would need to do to get her.

The orally occupied subject of so much attention could not help but notice the naked admiration shining in this stranger's dark eyes, and she vowed to make herself worthy of it. If only he had been there to see her with Martine! For even the often-difficult Sir Jason had been filled with nothing but the highest praise for her performance, as had the orgasmically fatigued dancer.

Indeed, had they both not called her a virtuoso of the tongue? Yes, she would show the count exactly how accomplished she could be!

Jason well recalled his effusive compliment to his humbled captive—a compliment which had been given most sincerely and without any premeditation. How Celia had flushed at hearing it. Only it had been a flush of pleasure as well as of shame. Nevertheless, his anger toward her could not be assuaged by the mere lash of her ingenue's tongue upon the hot flickering slot of another female's bottomhole. No. His ungrateful ward would have to suffer as he had been made to suffer, for her crimes against him were grave, indeed. To think she had chosen his lackluster cousin over himself! Why, Jason's unspoken proposal of marriage had very nearly fallen from his lips as he had watched Celia step aboard the train in York. Rather than divulging the contents of his heart in an icy late-winter English rain, he had decided to wait—to wait until their perspiring bodies were happily intertwined beneath the comforting warmth of the Provençal sun. Strange that his only comfort should now be found in the vendetta of humiliation he waged daily and nightly against the young woman he had once hoped would accept him for her husband. Never again would Sir Jason Hardwicke play the fool!

Oblivious to the masculine turmoil taking place all round her, Celia rolled her raven-headed partner over onto her belly, urging the woman's floor-reddened buttocks upward and thus into a position best suited for what she had in mind. Unlike earlier, she was no longer be concerned with matters of pride. She sensed intuitively that the strikingly handsome count would approve most wholeheartedly of her intentions, as, indeed, would Sir Jason. Yet suddenly she cared not for the good opinion of her vengeful tormentor, nor even of his younger cousin who continued to sit silently by as she carried out the most dissolute of trespasses upon the luxuriant body of another female. For this evening there was only *one* member of the audience whose favor she sought.

A dark anal eye peered stealthily out from between the two supple mounds Celia had upended, and she parted them to further reveal it. Unlike Martine's celebrated orifice, this version had not received the obvious benefits of paring. Dainty ringlets decorated the unlit gateway—ringlets as black and lustrous as the mane atop its ecstatic proprietress's head. With an unshakable sense of purpose that had never before been hers to claim, the English girl smoothed them out of the way with her thumbs—a gesture both aesthetic and practical, for it also served to cast away any last shadows from the discreet little gouge. A brilliant ruby appeared—a ruby which was soon glittering all the more with the uncoerced endorsement of its present admirer's saliva. She pressed the tips of her thumbs against the elastic periphery, inducing the puckered mouth to open wide. Such ease of cooperation indicated that this gaping void had already attained substantial knowledge of a man's penis. For some reason, this excited Celia—indeed, excited her more than she would have cared to admit. Perhaps it made her think of her own equally gaping void and how frequently it, too, had provided recreation for the boisterous male caller. Suddenly she wondered how many men had passed through this hallowed chamber now being offered to her awaiting tongue and whether the handsome count had possibly been one of them.

The mere thought of such an ingress convinced Celia to discard any last restraints she might have had remaining to her on this day. Ensuring that she had total command of Count D'Arcy's attention, she took to her task like one born for it, encircling the enlarged perimeter of the other woman's anus with her tongue. After the initial introduction had been made, she decided to incorporate a few long, deliberate strokes across its twittering surface for variety. Although not quite as sweet as the auburn-haired dancer's ripe tangerine, this rubescent facsimile nevertheless proved a most satisfying repast for the palate—and to those masculine palates partaking of a surreptitious sampling through the organ of sight rather than taste.

The fantasized images of the count's stalwart penis thrusting aggressively into this darkly fringed furrow prompted Celia's tongue to dip deeply and deliriously into her female associate's pulsating fundament in

The Possession of Celia

search of the phantom flavors that might have been left by its visitor, the ragged chaos of her clitoris twitching and surging with desire and all but begging for an obliging fingertip to relieve its suffering. The irrepressible lavishing of such painstaking oral attentions induced the resilient ring to contract uncontrollably, thereby forcing this determined adventuress to tighten the grip of her thumbs so that the yawning mouth would not close up. Indeed, Celia needed this quaking portal to remain unlatched, for her tongue still had a great deal of work left to do.

the count's desires...

Later that same evening as Count D'Arcy lay upon the well-stuffed feather mattress of his bed in preparation for a sleep that seemed elusive in arriving, he reflected further upon the fair young English maiden whose glistening female charms he had become aware of only a few short hours earlier. Despite the warmth of the country air, he shuddered. Rather than pulling the duvet up to cloak his nakedness, he took the throbbing plum crowning his penis into his hand and squeezed the syrupy tears from its single weeping eye. Sufficiently lubricated, he began to rub the unsheathed head against his palm, his fingers creating a snug-fitting vise.

Sadly, the vise of his hand provided a poor replacement for what was at that very moment only a few feet away—indeed, just on the other side of the wall behind him, so tantalizingly near he could almost taste it. Although the count possessed a prick of considerable proportion both breadthwise and longitudinally, and one which had elicited many a startled gasp from a buggered lady, he felt certain that it would fit easily into the rosy furrow which had captured his heart from his first breath-stealing glimpse of it. For now, however, all that appeared to be left for him to do was wait.

Had his curiosity about his highly secretive recluse of a friend, Sir Jason Hardwicke, not gotten the better of him, Count D'Arcy might never even have known of the girl's existence. Why, he would very likely instead have been sitting in the salon of his Paris *maison* sipping a lonely cognac and smoking a lonely cigarette instead of massaging himself to orgasm with the remembered image of that twinkling bottomhole as his inspiration. Oh, most certainly he always had the finest ladies the city had to offer at his constant beck and call, each of whom would do battle just to receive a kind word from his lips. Indeed, no act, regardless of its indecorum, was beneath their dignity. And to the count, the more indecorous, the better! Yet suddenly nary a one could compare to the enchanting little vixen with the glory-seeking tongue he had just observed downstairs. No wonder Sir Jason's behavior had been so mysterious!

Granted, it did strike this unannounced caller as rather odd that a gentleman of Hardwicke's stature should be desiring a simple house in the country—a cottage really when compared to the more stately lines of Moorland House. He should have realized that something untoward was in the works when Sir Jason specifically requested a residence as simple and unobtrusive as could be gotten, and one settled well away from either village or town. Surely the man should have fancied a villa, if not a château! But now that his old friend's felonious motives had been demonstrated to him, it made brilliant sense. As a foreigner in a land frequently inhospitable to and suspicious of foreigners, Sir Jason Hardwicke had made the clever decision to blend in with his surroundings rather than calling attention to himself—and therefore calling attention to the indiscreet and highly illicit nature of his activities. Of course Count D'Arcy had no knowledge as to the fugitive status of the gloomy cousin, whose unsociable presence was far better concealed by such humble rural surroundings. The younger Hardwicke's attendance in the little salon proved equally as baffling to this guest upon his arrival as it would upon his departure.

The sensually down-turned edges of the count's mouth quirked upward into a cryptic smile as he recalled the deliciously widened cleft of the English girl's buttocks—the English girl whom he now knew as *Celia*. He had been momentarily shocked and, indeed, utterly delighted by the complete absence of hair in those regions—a phenomenon undoubtedly instigated by the salaciously minded Sir Jason himself. For only a Hardwicke could have conceived of something so blatantly wicked as to return to a full-grown woman her girlish innocence—and then distort this innocence so that it incited the most lecherous form of prurience possible. Not even a man of Count D'Arcy's experience could have been prepared for the naked vista of blushing pink offered up to both spectator and participant alike—*and* offered with such divinely shamefaced flair! Yes, he would make it his goal to discover how much of this discomfiture had been genuine and how much of it had not.

With the silken curls indigenous to this enchanting feminine landscape of ivory flesh fully shorn, each sleek slope and crevice had been forced to display its most intimate of secrets to the room of approving men—of whom this most recent arrival had become the third and probably the least welcomed. Nevertheless, the sincerity of his host's hospitality mattered not to the count. All that mattered was the exquisite creature before him. Never had he encountered such delicate beauty! The consummately plucked Celia possessed all the tremulous demeanor of a rare bird whose spectacular plumage was seldom glimpsed but greatly sought after by admirers. How ever had Sir Jason managed to cage her?

Count D'Arcy's heart thudded as never before as the nimble pink tongue of his confrere's ingenue ardently swabbed up the honeyed beads of moisture from the unrolled labia of the raven-haired beauty positioned inversely beneath her—a woman whose incessantly moaning presence he had been so instrumental in arranging. He knew well of this enthusiastic recipient's preference for the tongue and folds of her own sex; she had demonstrated them often enough in his Paris salon. Yet perhaps she was not the only one with such preferences. For with each lusty lash of her tongue, the revelatory pendant projecting out from Celia's denuded vulva twitched and surged and grew ever more florid and—if the count's discerning nostrils did not deceive him, *fragrant*. How he envied her female partner as she wrapped her hungering lips round this bold burgeoning bud, the tip of her nose sinking into the aqueous pool below. He, too, would have enjoyed burying his nose within the source of this fragrance—within the burbling little sliver which, upon further perusal, looked as red and glossy as the sweetest candied cherry. Even the pinched dimple of this fair young maiden's bottomhole heralded the same provocative flush—a flush as bashful as it was inviting. No doubt Sir Jason's stately prick had been burned by its flame many times. And indeed, who could blame the gentleman for his recklessness, for the count wished to hurl himself into the conflagration as well.

And, too, who could blame Celia's crafty companion as she stretched out her neck to sample the anxiously twinkling port with her long tongue, only to dive deeply into the unfathomable frontiers beyond. It was a move Count D'Arcy himself always liked to encourage whenever being thusly entertained—and judging from the deep-throated sigh beside him, the sentiment appeared to be shared. It would seem that he and Hardwicke had a great many things in common, the most consequential of which happened to be their single-minded desire to possess the young woman whose frantically bucking backside had just swallowed the entire carmine length of her female accomplice's invading tongue.

To the count's astonishment, the passive player in this two-character drama suddenly took the role of aggressor by hurtling the protagonist with the crest of raven curls atop her mons veneris over onto her belly, only to initiate the same scandalous procedure upon the similarly plumed rear hatchway that had just been employed upon her own. It occurred to this attentive observer that Sir Jason might have somehow engineered his blushing lady friend's aggressive reciprocation via a secret hand signal or through a message mouthed from behind the closed fan of his fingers. For Count D'Arcy harbored a fair amount of skepticism as to Celia's propensity for indulging in such disreputable practices without considerable coercion. Why, he could only imagine the foul

The Possession of Celia

threats wreaked upon her by his wicked associate and, indeed, their painstaking application.

Yet such threats—regardless of how grievous in nature—had made for a most luxuriant and satisfying scenario. How scrupulously the girl had attended to her partner's upended bottomhole! Never had the count seen a tongue plunge so deeply or with so much passion for the deed. All at once he began to fear that it had gotten permanently stuck until she eventually allowed it to slip slowly and teasingly out and—confirming that the bedazzled eyes of her all-male audience were fully upon her—plunge right back in to steal yet another zesty taste of those forbidden delights. This was the moment when he had finally lost himself—when his fluids had gone spewing forth from the spasming pinhole on the unsheathed head of his penis, making a gluey mess in the expensively tailored linen of his trousers. Unlike Sir Jason's taciturn cousin who released his liquescent ecstasies with impunity, this gentleman had no desire to make a public exhibition of himself— not even if that public only consisted of four. He preferred to contend with the sodden repercussions later in the privacy of the tiny accommodation granted him by his host, where he could once again enjoy a renewal of his earlier pleasures courtesy of a keenly accurate memory and a fierce determination to possess the wide-eyed perpetrator whose saliva-moistened specimen nearly drove him to its uninvited ravishment.

The remembered image of Celia's brazen tongue incited the understandably agitated count to increase the speed of his hand, the ancient springs of his bed creaking so loudly they were certain to be heard on the far side of the adjoining wall—and, in turn, heard by the enchanting creature who had sparked such a measure. He came instantly, catching the arcing jet of boiling froth within a silken handkerchief borrowed from Sir Jason. It required a control beyond that of even the most pious of monks to keep from crashing through the door of the young Englishwoman's bedchamber and doing to her what he had earlier witnessed her doing with such solicitous dedication to the raven-haired female downstairs. Count D'Arcy was not at all ashamed to admit his powerful hunger to sample the depilated little ringlet himself. Why, he could already feel it heating up beneath his tongue. How deliciously it would scorch this probing muscle! Yes, he would explore Celia's savory nooks and crannies most thoroughly, putting his carmine competitor to disgrace. Then perhaps afterward the appreciative beneficiary of his oral adoration would return the favor—and return it *in abundance*. For the count simply had to experience the dizzying talents of her lustful pink tongue firsthand.

Indeed, it was a tongue as lustful and pink as the one he had spied thrusting immodestly out from the mouth-watering cleft of her hairless vulva. In this gentleman's learned opinion, the two were irrevocably tied, as were their desires. The gusto with which a woman applied her tongue—regardless of the sex of the recipient—bore a direct and unmistakable relationship to the similarly structured limb of her femininity. A man only had to kiss her to determine what sumptuous riches awaited him lower down. For whatever the age or temperament of the lady in question, these wiggly banners of flesh were not in the least bit bashful to make their needs known. And it had become glaringly apparent to this unexpected caller that Celia's lush little clit possessed a great many needs....

Despite an extremely fruitful acquaintanceship spanning nearly a decade and two countries, Sir Jason Hardwicke actually knew very little about his friend the count. As a matter of fact, he had his suspicions that this *count* business might simply be a false front—that the handsome expatriate Englishman was not really a count at all. Oh, he certainly had the financial means to carry his title, not to mention his decadent modus vivendi. Nonetheless, something about the man just did not ring true; virtually nothing about his background appeared to be known. There was a titled family of D'Arcys living somewhere in Wiltshire, but if they were related, he never made mention of it. Indeed, D'Arcy had materialized as if from out of nowhere. All of a sudden the doors of his Paris *maison* had been thrown open, allowing those of equal means and mystery to enter. Why, Jason could hardly even recall how they had met, only that it was considered a distinct privilege to be granted entrée to one of the count's exotic soirees. For how else could he have managed to procure so much juicy young female flesh for his blushing captive's tongue?

One thing Sir Jason knew with an unshakable certainty—that this gentleman's unexpected appearance on his doorstep would surely bode no good. Despite the rather cramped quarters of the little blue-shuttered house in Provence, Count D'Arcy seemed in no particular haste to depart. Indeed, his grudging host's subtle remarks regarding his presumed eagerness to return home to Paris fell on blocked ears. Summer was quickly approaching and the corresponding increase in temperature made Sir Jason edgy and mistrustful. Suddenly he began to see things that could not possibly be there... like a simmering heat in the attentive brown of D'Arcy's eyes as he looked upon Celia's rose-tinted nakedness—or a telltale licking of his lips when her thighs opened wide and accommodatingly for her most recent partner's serpentine tongue. Instead of putting a halt to these provocative performances, Jason resolved to make his position all the more pronounced. For what if his imaginings were, indeed, not imaginings at all? What if what he thought he saw was really and truly there? As if he did not have enough to worry about what with his lovesick cousin mooning about the house and spraying his thwarted seed in every direction!

The Possession of Celia

Hence, Sir Jason made the difficult decision to do what he had promised himself never again to do—to perform in the presence of another man. Of course he did not place his younger relative in this category; indulging himself before Colin was all part of his plan to punish the ungrateful couple for their transgressions. Unfortunately it had become apparent that the visiting count required a further display of his host's relentless mastery over the demure young woman in his care—a display which would prove once and for all that his possession of her was thorough and complete, and hence could not be shaken by the sudden appearance of some English dandy, regardless of how pleasing to the eye that particular dandy might be.

The following afternoon while Count D'Arcy looked wistfully on at the two female performers—and most specifically at the one whose moist, hairless charms the slight shifting of his chair had placed directly in his line of sight—Sir Jason once again entered into the sexual fray. By the time his manly offerings had been fully discharged from his penis, there would be no question in the count's mind as to his command—nor indeed, in the mind of his lovely captive. It seemed wise to start matters off by spending a few delicious moments humbling Celia—and how better than to indulge himself within the rear passage of her newest partner, whose well-groomed anus glowed like a hot coal from betwixt her hungrily spread buttocks. Jason knew well from his previous encounter with the celebrated cancan dancer how effective such an ingress could be to both observer and recipient alike. And he was not disappointed, for no sooner had he managed to fit the gluttonous head of his prick into the straining ring of muscle before him than a plaintive whimper reached his ears.

To Celia, the raw agony of once again being forced to watch Sir Jason's mammoth member entering the desirous bottomhole of one of her sex proved even more humiliating than it had during that baptismal occasion with Martine—especially with the handsome Count D'Arcy bearing eager witness as she consumed the female folds that dripped so profusely with pleasure. For Sir Jason Hardwicke was nothing if not a true master in the anal arts! With each expert thrust of his penis, the delicate carnelian tissue forming the unoccupied mouth of the woman's vagina and the neighboring knurl of cleaving flesh above distended outward as if to protest the extraordinary dimensions of this masculine intruder. However, no verbal confirmation would be forthcoming—only a series of very encouraging moans that could not be mistaken for anything but the most supreme form of ecstasy. At her tormentor's crude bidding, Celia wedged her tongue inside this severely narrowed opening, the ballooning projectile of her clitoris fluttering wildly in response. With it thusly placed, her nose now hovered directly at the place of convergence, the continually charging cylinder of Sir Jason's penis leaving dozens of wet kisses upon the tip. With the provocative perfume of their union filling her nostrils, Celia believed her shame to be grievous, indeed. Nevertheless, she was soon shown exactly how grievous it could be!

For Colin's dastardly cousin appeared to have many more humiliations in store for her on this fine spring day—and in the fine presence of the distinguished count. "My dear Celia, I believe it might be best if you lick my cock each time it enters your lady friend's charming little arsehole," Jason stated with verbose extravagance, making what had clearly been a demand sound more like the politest of suggestions. One might have thought he had just asked her to pour him a cup of tea, so innocuous was his tone.

With the mortified china blue of her eyes blinded by salty tears, the victim of the elder Hardwicke's explicit cruelty plucked her tongue from the humid confines of the other woman's vagina. As she allowed it shyly to graze the slippery shaft of his in-rushing penis, she could feel the astounded gaze of their male guest upon her face—and, indeed, upon her tentatively flicking tongue. Perhaps she, too, experienced such astonishment, for despite the demeaning nature of her activities, she made no attempt to desist from them. Could she not have thrown herself upon the kind mercy of the count and begged for his aid? Begged for a few francs with which to pay for passage home, even if it might have meant leaving her fugitive beloved behind? Yet rather than putting forth such a plea, Celia put forth the velvety length of her tongue, no longer hesitant to do her duty.

With each far-reaching thrust of his organ, Jason grunted with masculine exaggeration, as if seeking to call attention to the glistening object of his labors and the slavish attention now being paid to it by his submissive *détenue*. Had he not known all along what culinary victuals his shrinking English violet's palate would enjoy? For indeed, she laved the rectally heated surface of his prick most thoroughly. Although sufficiently stimulated, he felt certain he had adequate strokes remaining before he would at last be compelled to forfeit his manly fluids. For what he had planned for his crowning achievement provided all the impetus necessary to challenge his much-availed-upon penis into withholding its final pleasure until he deemed such a release appropriate.

Determining that his attempts to portray both humbler and host had been an undeniable success, Jason withdrew from this recent lady caller's highly agreeable fundament. Indeed, it had provided a most luxuriant accommodation for his discriminating member and one in which he might like to pay a more lengthy return visit when time allowed. At the moment, however, there was still a great deal that needed to be done, and it needed to be done while the auspicious light of day continued to cast away all shadows from the little salon—and from the flooded female folds and furrows present therein. For no lamp, regardless of its brightness, could compare to the natural and brutally honest illumination of the sun. *Nothing*, regardless of how shameful, could be hidden from its unrelenting rays...nor could the total mastery of a certain young woman be in any way misunderstood by an onlooker who desired to believe otherwise.

As the sun poured its radiant judgment onto the floor, Sir Jason placed his dampened pelvis level with his crouching captive's still-dampened nose. "Suck it!" he ordered brusquely, jabbing the pulsating knob of his prick toward her trembling lips. The two startled gasps that immediately followed joined with the liquid sounds of Celia's mouth as she drew upon the throbbing male flesh presented to her with such indecorum. She licked with a surprising and, indeed, *unladylike* hunger up and down the moist, fragrant shaft and even beneath the overburdened sac of her wicked tormentor's testicles, leaving no spot untasted. Jason allowed her to debase herself for as long as he dared before finally removing himself from the heated paradise of her mouth and moving toward the paradise that had been his intended destination from the very beginning. Each lavish lash of Celia's tongue had prompted a bead of viscous fluid to ooze from the tiny pinhole at the crest of his penis. Certain that every lubricating drop would be needed, he distributed them all along the lust-swollen crown, not stopping until he had anointed the thickly ridged corona.

Satisfied he had made his point to all and sundry, Jason urged his humbled quarry's head of honey-colored tresses toward the juicy feast awaiting her between her partner's thighs—a feast he prided himself on being so instrumental in producing—then stationed himself directly behind the divided swells of her outthrust buttocks. To him, Celia never looked more ravishing than when positioned thusly and—if one were to determine by the two desperately craning necks of their audience—it was a sentiment apparently shared. Although keen to commence with the business at hand, he paused momentarily so that his uninvited male guest could fully appreciate the magnitude of what would next transpire. For indeed, Sir Jason Hardwicke had been blessed with a prick of such considerable length and girth that even a gentleman of Count D'Arcy's illustrious reputation would surely have cause to envy. It rose up and away from his muscled abdomen, this well-thickened pillar gleaming evocatively in the late-afternoon sunshine streaming in through the undraped window. Only it was the tumescent growth at the summit that garnered the most attention, for its previous plunderings had induced it to glow greedily with a hunger as yet unslaked. As Jason pointed the unruly bulk of his manhood toward its twinkling target, an incoming bolt of sunlight illuminated the surface, seeming to place the bloated head directly in the uncompromising beam of a spotlight. Droplets of sap dripped from the tiny vermilion sliver on its tip, glittering like diamonds as they pattered to the floor. All at once the indecently posed young woman turned to look hindward, the innocent china blue of her eyes widening with raw fear as she observed this featured player throbbing obscenely behind her. Noting his captive's reaction, Jason squeezed the cumbersome shaft just below the corona, thereby provoking even further turgidity to occur—not to mention further alarm in the eyes of its intended victim. Taking a deep, energizing breath, and without any warning whatsoever, he launched this livid bulb into the distending mouth of Celia's anus.

Despite the startled yelp that ensued, the quivering hatchway this aggressive invader had just broken through was already well primed from the passions spilling over from its neighboring orifice, whose delicate cherry cordial slit Sir Jason's present female invitee had cleverly situated herself beneath and was now in the midst of noisily tonguing. For, above all, he did not wish to appear foolish before his distinguished visitor from Paris by having to poke his way inside the dear girl's fiery bottomhole in small increments. He wanted to be seen as the master he knew himself to be. As if sensing the importance of the occasion, Celia lifted her honey-glossed lips from the similarly glossed lips below, her cries of rapture at this brutal encroachment resonating throughout the sunny salon and echoing for hours to come in the burning ears of its listeners—one of whom vowed that he would very soon inspire cries of even greater rapture by the rigorous dispensation of his own stately member.

Jason could never have guessed that such divine ecstasy at his cageling's anal impalement had been inspired in part by the devastatingly handsome presence of Count D'Arcy. Indeed, Celia could feel his hot eyes upon her...she could feel them riding along the glistening rod of Sir Jason's manhood as it plunged in and out of her upraised backside. Suddenly it seemed as if the count himself moved inside her—as if the weeping knob at the end of his organ left dozens of burning kisses upon the innermost core of her rectum. Frantic with desire, Celia reached back to spread herself wide, her entire body trembling from the strain of absorbing so prodigious a specimen this deeply. Her tongue easily found its way inside the well-stretched aperture of the other woman's anus—a social call made all the juicier and, indeed, all the more shameful by the many viscous tears wept by Sir Jason's traitorous penis. His every punishing thrust served to drive her own eagerly exploring tongue farther and farther into this slippery hearth, thereby amplifying her disgrace. For it would prove impossible for Celia to ignore the sodomistic parallels taking place. Her climax arrived quickly and with much liquescent fanfare, raining profusely into the mouth of her female attendant, whose drowning tongue labored hard to collect every creamy droplet from its burbling fount. Hence she would come yet a second time, imagining that the velvety object consuming her most intimate of secretions belonged instead to the sensually down-turned mouth of a man she had only laid eyes upon the day before.

Later that evening when the much-humbled Englishwoman encountered Sir Jason's mysterious associate in the corridor outside her bedchamber, the sudden explosion of color on her face told him all that he had heretofore suspected. Yes...despite his friend's extravagant performance, it appeared he still had a fighting chance for the possession of Celia!

A temporarily satiated Sir Jason Hardwicke slept most soundly that night, secure in the knowledge that he had finally put his colleague in lust in his place. While casually caressing the deliciously varnished surface of his still-partially erect penis, he began to wonder why he had not taken some appropriate form of action sooner, for this would surely have hastened the inquisitive count's departure. Indeed, Jason fully expected this unwanted guest to be gone by the time he awakened the following morning. But to his astonishment, who should he find seated complacently at the table enjoying a hearty breakfast that an unusually flushed Celia had prepared for him but Count D'Arcy himself. Upon observing his ill-tempered host's handsome, sleep-swollen face, the descending corners of the count's mouth twitched upward into an ingenuous smile, the tiny cleft in his chin growing deeper and more impudent by the moment. Indeed, was there no end to the man's hubris?

Beside this accursed caller who steadfastly refused to leave, Colin slumped morosely in his chair, the smell of spirits palpable amongst the more wholesome odors of fried eggs and herb sausages and freshly brewed coffee. *Whatever had Celia seen in him?* mused Jason in genuine bewilderment. Why, here he was, ready and willing to don his fighting gloves to ward off what he considered to be a rival for her body and heart, whereas his gloomy cousin merely seemed content to douse himself in liquor and witness the woman he professed to love being further humbled and degraded—and indeed, humbled and degraded in the presence of a strange man! Undoubtedly the couple's brief sojourn in Marseilles had been far too much for the hapless lad, for it had become highly apparent that he had given up—that the stuffing had finally been knocked out of him. Could it be that his supposedly quiescent relative had actually come to enjoy his beloved's humiliation? For perhaps such profane tastes ran in the blood.

All at once Jason experienced a brief pang of uncharacteristic pity for his woebegone young cousin...only it was swiftly replaced by disgust at Colin's apparent spinelessness. Why, he had half a mind to invite the handsome count to have his way with the girl just to see what would happen—to see if *this* might spark at least *some* sense of battle within the deflated body of his liquor-soaked relation. Surely Colin would raise himself up off his chair at the sight of another man's prick—indeed, a prick that could not even lay claim to Hardwicke lineage—steaming in and out of Celia's quaking bottomhole or—if the calendar bode favorably—her tender little slit. For perhaps Colin did not consider his dainty ladylove's lusty encounters with others of her sex to be of particular consequence, regardless of the enthusiasm with which she might have participated in these encounters....

Then again, perhaps enlisting the aid of his enigmatic confrere might be going too far to make a point.

If Sir Jason could only have known what thoughts occupied his relative's head, he might not have been so hasty to dismiss him. Indeed, had he been present to witness young Colin's secret night of revenge—a revenge which had resulted in a most unbridled and thorough ravishing of the steamy orifices of the fiery-bottomed Martine's highly limber form, the elder Hardwicke would undoubtedly have reevaluated his somewhat lowly opinion of his seemingly eviscerated cousin. For in his sullen silences, Colin was carefully biding his time, safeguarded by the masculine certitude that he would soon receive his long-awaited opportunity to show up his wicked cousin—*once and for all*. For he had absolutely no intention of allowing the villainous Sir Jason Hardwicke to win in the battle to possess Celia.

Unfortunately this thwarted lover failed to recognize that yet one more male competitor had decided to take up the gauntlet—a competitor as fierce, if not even more so, as the man whose blood coursed through his veins. For the time being, however, the younger Hardwicke sat quietly along the sidelines and observed as the greedy miscreant who was his only living relation grabbed off more and more rope for himself—a rope which would one day hang him, if his present undertakings could be considered any indication. For Jason's unshakable arrogance would eventually do him in. And when it did, Colin vowed to be there to watch him sway!

As for the much-desired young woman in question, her languishing beloved had pretty much resigned himself to the sad fact that she had become lost to him...at least *temporarily*. Perhaps he should have been more attuned to her physical needs during their few blissful moments alone together in the blue-shuttered house in Provence—and hence, a lot less judgmental of their iniquitous nature. For indeed, Celia could not be blamed for the aberrant passions awakened in her by the licentious Sir Jason. Nevertheless, Colin had assumed—and very rightly so—that such unlawful activities were at last over and done with, that his bashful betrothed no longer desired to participate in practices so dreadfully unsuited to a young lady, and that the indulgence in said practices had merely been the result of her unsavory alliance with his blackmailing cousin. Up until recently, he had harbored the comforting belief that Celia had sacrificed herself in order to secure for him his safety. Only Colin's safety was no longer really in question; he had fled from the country in which a queer twist of fate had made of him a hunted man. However, in Provence no one knew him, let alone maintained the slightest bit of interest in his daily affairs. There was no longer any real necessity for his delicate ladylove to once again place herself under Jason's total control. Therefore, why did she continue to do so? Suddenly Colin silenced the derisive voice in his mind, not wanting to hear the answer.

Despite his recent lapse toward sexual puritanism, the younger Hardwicke quickly discovered that he quite fancied his elder cousin's new game in their little Provençal salon. It served to bring back all those deliciously wicked trysts that had transpired in the chilly manor house on the Yorkshire moors—trysts which Colin had fervently observed and, indeed, *participated* in with such private and unwholesome relish. Of course he realized that the salacious scenarios his newly impoverished eyes now witnessed were very, very wrong—that such activities were highly demeaning to his beloved

Celia, not to mention to the other young ladies as well. Yet there seemed to be a certain saturnalian beauty about these unnatural alliances that became highly addictive—that compelled one to keep close vigil irrespective of who might be painted with the brush of degradation. For who could deny the sheer pulchritudinous elegance of a ravishing flash of glistening pink being eclipsed by yet another pink—a pink so divinely skilled in the art of licking? And best of all, such ill-gotten pleasures required virtually no effort whatsoever to enjoy. Indeed, Colin could simply sit back in his chair and relax and hide behind his sullenness instead of being ordered about by his manipulative older relative, his senses aroused by drink and by the libidinous tongues in eager action before him—of which each female participant owned a most charmingly matched set. Perhaps in this sun-baked and lavender-scented Provençal landscape he was growing lazy—complacent even. For in his solitary climaxes, there no longer appeared to be any pressing need to hurry—to expedite his plot to seize Sir Jason's crown.

Oh, yes. Colin had *plenty* of time.

a hasty departure...

The morning sun still had several hours of sleep remaining before it would finally be required to show itself over the deep indigo horizon. Nevertheless, tonight there would be no sleep for Celia—nor would there be any for a certain handsome gentleman who had descended so unexpectedly upon Sir Jason's humble Provençal household. For unbeknownst to his host, Count D'Arcy's private coach had been waiting just down the road from the blue-shuttered house ever since the telling toll of midnight. Indeed, it would not be long before its two passengers were be safely settled upon the plush velvet seat, leaving nothing in their wake save for a hazy cloud of dust and a pair of parallel ruts that a distant breeze from the Mediterranean would eventually obliterate.

Earlier on that tranquil moonlit evening, when the count had stolen into the object of his desire's bedchamber for what would be the very first and the very last time, he had undertaken the precaution of arming himself in advance by bringing along a kerchief with which to stifle the inevitable cries of protest his unexpected presence would undoubtedly elicit. Obviously he had anticipated being met with at least *some* sort of struggle from the alluring female who had so thoroughly captured his fancy. For after all, he would not be asking her to go away with him, but rather *demanding* that she do so. He had planned to take the lovely young Englishwoman by surprise whilst she slept, the tenuous lids curtaining the ethereal blue of her eyes closed against the dangers surrounding her. By the time Celia had realized that her pretty strawberry-hued lips were encased by the length of silk, her quick-witted abductor would have already gotten the leather of his belt cinched snugly round her slender wrists.

Thusly bound, Count D'Arcy would carry his precious spoils over the broad shelf of his shoulder, down the stairs, and outside to the attending coach, with one hand placed strategically up her nightdress in the event any additional impetus to cooperate might be required. For this astute gentleman did not consider himself above using his fingers to execute an occasional torturous tweak in the appropriate locale. Many a stubborn young lady of his acquaintance had been rendered fully and deliciously malleable by such a wily technique and, indeed, even come to crave a dastardly pinch or two upon this fragile flesh, for it never failed to inspire her womanly juices to flow.

Despite the extreme lateness of the hour, Celia was not as yet in bed. However, so preoccupied was she in her wakefulness that she might as well have been fast asleep. Hence, she neglected to hear her caller's stealthy entrance as she stood before the opened window, leaning forward and staring out into the moonlit darkness as if searching for something...or *someone*. Could it be she heard the not-too-distant striking of a match as Count D'Arcy's impatient driver lit his third cigarillo of the night? Or could it be she sensed that something of great magnitude was about to happen—something which could change her life forever?

For all evening the agitated young woman had thought of naught else but the devastatingly handsome count and how he always looked at her each time they met—how his eyes seemed to burn her flesh, melting her body into a helpless puddle and uncovering from its watery depths even her closest-held secrets. Nor had she been able to think of anything else since his arrival. How her heart fluttered whenever he came near—as did the yearning flesh of her clitoris. If only he would touch her! For Celia would have welcomed any form of physical contact from Count D'Arcy, regardless of how fleeting or minor. Even the lightest caress of his refined fingertips would have given some sustenance to her aching heart, not to mention the empty aching shell of her body. Yet she knew this to be a complete and utter impossibility with the ever-vigilant Sir Jason about, for he would never have consented to allowing her to be handled by another man. Why, even her poor cuckolded Colin could no longer lay claim to her female charms; his touch had become but a distant memory from another even-more-distant time. Nevertheless, Celia could not silence her innermost desires—desires which drove her from her bed each night and, indeed, drove her to commit lewd acts of self-love that caused her to burn with shame and guilt. Oh, whatever would become of her?

A warm Provençal breeze rippled the lacy hem of this insomnious young woman's nightdress, scenting the entire room with the comforting springtime smell of lavender. The yellow orb of the moon illuminated her face, turning the guileless china blue of her eyes into two smoldering sapphires and delineating the gentle curves of her petite form beneath the thin white cotton of the garment she had chosen to wear to bed. The count stood behind her in silent reverence, savoring the ingenious way the moonlight shone through her parted thighs, for it served to highlight the delicate cleft formed by the meeting of her pouty labial lips—a cleft which had been made all the more succulently conspicuous by its surrounding and, without doubt, *enforced* hairlessness. Yes, one certainly had to admire Sir Jason's incredible keenness of mind, for a woman such as this was unquestionably at her finest and most appealing with her feminine folds shorn to their polished pale perfection.

As if sensing someone there in the room with her, Celia began to turn slowly away from the window, the limned pear between her thighs metamorphosing into a pair of satiny puffs rent irreparably open by the presence of an audacious tongue of cleaving flesh. She clutched the hem of her wrinkled nightdress in one trembling hand, revealing what had—from the back—been kept mostly shrouded. Upon seeing Count D'Arcy's handsome figure so close behind her, her knees began to give way, and had he not been there to catch her, she would have surely collapsed to the floor.

All at once this stealthy trespasser to the young woman's bedchamber realized that his startled prey had been masturbating, for the formerly salmon pink projectile of her clitoris glowed with a flame which could only have been sparked from a steady and very determined stimulation—a stimulation which, unbeknownst to the gentleman happening upon it, had been inspired entirely by his recent arrival in the blue-shuttered house. For even in such insufficient light as this, its well-rubbed condition would have been impossible for anyone to misunderstand...or mistake.

A closer perusal by its ardent admirer revealed what appeared to be a butterfly in flight. Yet this was no mere creature of flight, but one of a rare and exquisite beauty that would cause even the most jaded gentleman to shiver in its presence. Oh, how heavenly it should be to capture those lustrous wings of fire in his mouth! The count could feel the heat radiating off its disheveled surface, and he breathed slowly and deeply to calm his racing heart, only to discover that the fragrance of lavender wafting in through the opened window had mingled with the fragrance of the startled young woman's need, hence creating a dizzying bouquet for his greedy nostrils.

Had there been sufficient time, Count D'Arcy would have taken her right there—indeed, taken her in every conceivable fashion ever known to one of his sex. Instead he drew Celia's warm, tremulous form into his arms and covered her silently protesting lips with his own. As his searching tongue joined up with its velvety female equivalent, his skillful fingers located the similarly shaped appendage flickering hotly and wetly against his linen-clad thigh, massaging from it the orgasm his unexpected appearance in the lady's bedchamber had impeded. Such silken plushness against the highly sentient pads of his fingers proved almost too much for the enamored count, and he very nearly fell to his knees to absorb the billowy knurl into his mouth. How he longed to tease with the inquisitive tip of his tongue those flavorful pink sinews he knew to be hiding shyly beneath the protective shade of this fair maiden's prepuce! Instead he placated himself by fully retracting the pliant little hood and stroking the exposed glans, only to follow it up with the insertion of his middle finger at the moment of climax, the quivering slit of her sweltering vagina swallowing this invading digit to the third knuckle.

The scantily clad young woman, whose most intimate and disreputable of moments had been interrupted by the catalyst which had provoked them, moaned fitfully, sucking frantically upon this mysterious stranger's provocatively wriggling tongue. Never could she have dreamed of such a kiss! Indeed, Count D'Arcy's mouth tasted of a sweetness Celia had been hungering for all her life, and she drank greedily of his saliva, each precious droplet as fresh and pure as the early morning dew upon the springtime petal of a rose. She wove her trembling fingers through the chestnut curls crowning his head—something she had been longing to do ever since she had first glimpsed the gentleman's elegant figure seated before the sun-reddened salon window as he watched her carry out Sir Jason's iniquitous bidding. The count's hair felt like the finest silk against her acquisitive fingertips, and suddenly Celia began to imagine these dark spirals caressing the pale insides of her thighs as his head moved busily between them. Yes, she would hold herself willingly open for the handsome count...for to do so would bring her no shame!

Indeed, shame had been all too plenteous in this Englishwoman's young and mostly virtuous life. She had entered into an alliance with it—an alliance which had led to endless days and nights of it at the cruel instigation of her beloved's debauched cousin. Shame had seeped into her every pore until she could smell it on herself—until she could see it imprinted upon her flesh. For rather than having the more legitimate mouth of a man upon her, Celia had been forced to unwrap her shaven female folds for the mouth of a woman! And as if committing such a grievous misdeed in the enraptured presences of three male spectators had not been torture enough, she found herself being subjected to even further indignities. The pungent and not altogether *unpleasant* tang of her partner's slit and bottomhole had not even faded from the memory of Celia's tongue before she received instructions to draw back the hairless pods of her labia and touch the engorged petal between them to the equally engorged petal she had just been made to suckle—a performance which an irrepressibly obscene Sir Jason made considerable merriment over.

For the elder Hardwicke had put forth several extremely pointed remarks with regard to his lovely captive's apparent sweet tooth for this fondant of femininity. In fact, he would even go so far as temporarily to intervene in the situation by dribbling a dram of lavender honey onto its twitching sumptuousness with a tiny glass wand, taking care that enough had spilled backward toward the twinkling star to the aft. To make Celia's disgrace all the more deliciously potent and therefore enjoyable to all, Sir Jason inserted the honey-coated wand inside the visiting woman's bottomhole, thereby ensuring that the dear girl's craving for these exotic confections would be fully slaked—as would the thirsting eyes of those who observed its slavish consumption with such masculine ardor. So clever an administration of the sticky nectar provided its salaciously minded disseminator with much to comment upon. It also provided the crimsoning-faced individual imbibing it with what had, through the unique circumstances of its application, become a very fine mead, with much to be humbled by. For this provocative anal honeycomb had yielded a great deal more to this shyly foraging tongue than mere sweetness. Why, just that very morning during breakfast had Celia made casual and quite innocent mention of her lifelong affection for the syrupy substance, only to corroborate her words by spooning a generous portion into her tea and spreading a like portion onto her bread, consequently missing the sly look which passed between the wicked Sir Jason and his equally wicked confrere. Never had two gentlemen been so well suited as friends—or indeed, *rivals*.

All this lustful activity between the two intertwined women had inspired considerable tumescence to take place—a tumescence which quickly extended to those who remained quiescent as well. The drastically distending flames bisecting Celia and her enthusiastic partner's aggressively grinding vulvae fluttered against each other in an erotic dance, the participants' impassioned moans serving as the music. This continuous friction eventually caused the flexible hoods of their clitorises to be pushed up and away from the tubercle tissue they had been intended to protect, creating invisible sparks when the highly sensitive glans beneath them came together in sticky courtship. For apparently the ever-toiling tongue of Sir Jason's subjugated ward had missed the small amount of honey that had gotten wedged up beneath the snug-fitting mantle of the visiting woman's prepuce—an oversight she would pay for dearly with her pride.

Indeed, such sparks soon became far too great for either lovely female participant to bear. However, it was a severely flushed Celia whose cries rang out the loudest and the most anguished of the pair. She came thusly in her humiliation, the swollen pillows of her lips glossed with the golden honey she had been forced to consume from the intimate parts of another, the fingers of both hands peeling away the protective half shells of her labia so the freed flap of salmon pink flesh between them could meet its yearning twin in a shuddering and very public kiss. The bittersweet shame of taking her ecstasy in so degrading a manner brought anguished tears to Celia's eyes, and she turned her head away from those her actions had pleasured. Surely the handsome count did not approve of such illicit matters! Little did the unsuspecting young woman know that the gentleman himself had made the request, whispering it in his associate's earnestly listening ear only a mere heartbeat earlier.

As the clandestinely meeting couple's lips and tongues continued to feed hungrily upon each other in the full light of the moon, a strangled sigh became lodged in this enigmatic visitor's throat. For all at once Count D'Arcy's mind replayed to him the rousing scene of a cherubic tongue ferreting out the mellifluous syrup from the twittering ruby between a dissevered pair of womanly buttocks. As the flustered young female he desired to possess bucked and shuddered against his expertly moving hand, the count decided to supplement his stimulations by thrusting a pairing of fingers as deeply as they could possibly go inside the hot, convulsing slot of Celia's anus, therefore prolonging and intensifying her orgasm. In his experience, such an amiable introduction never once failed to win a lovely lady's heart. The elastic mouth gripped his fingers snugly in what felt to him like a bashful kiss. For Count D'Arcy had fallen passionately in love with the dainty little rosette the first moment he had seen it winking so frantically at him. So talented a muscle had many uses, all of which the count fully intended to explore once they had taken their leave from Sir Jason Hardwicke's little house in Provence.

In a fit of rapturous affection, this gentleman caller to Celia's bedchamber bent to kiss the sweat-dampened indentation of her navel, the tip of his tongue traveling in dizzying circles along the rim. An eloquent shiver coursed throughout his body, for how could he possibly mistake the provocative parallels to another such similarly endowed locale? Indeed, his tongue could hardly wait to make the flavorful and highly rewarding circuit round the scorching perimeter his two fingers now occupied. With a poignant sigh, Count D'Arcy swabbed away the perspiration that had pooled within this shallow firth, tasting of its salty offerings, his thoughts continuing to linger happily upon offerings of a far more nature.

All at once Celia sank to the floor and pressed the trembling pout of her mouth against this stranger's hand in grateful homage, taking his fingers and licking from them the piquant wetness his artful manipulations had elicited. She swallowed each one in its elegant entirety, the strawberry plumpness of her lower lip dragging slowly and enticingly along his opened palm, her breath misting hotly over the pale skin. Such a humble obeisance stirred Count D'Arcy greatly—as it would stir his painfully throbbing penis. *Yes, perhaps a few more moments might be spared,* he mused as he undid the bulging front of his trousers. Thus he released its well-stiffened burden to its supplicant's eagerly awaiting mouth, the voluptuous image of two billowy clits kissing still reflected within the deep dark wells of his eyes.

It was not be long before the kneeling young woman with the disheveled nightdress drank the hot briny fluids of the handsome count. She gulped his manly offerings with an alarming thirst, surprised to find herself craving more. The resourceful tip of her tongue searched out any last droplets from beneath the severely retracted ridge of foreskin, its efforts well rewarded. The flavor of this masculine flesh and its frothy bounties proved similar and yet dissimilar to the only two men whom Celia had ever accepted into her mouth or, indeed, into her body. The wriggly little cowl of flesh surrounding the throbbing crown of his penis was quite foreign to her, for she had only seen and experienced the flawless male cylinders belonging to the Hardwicke cousins. Indeed, perhaps Count D'Arcy's distinguished sex organ might have been in some way special—that this extra piece of skin set him apart from others of his sex much like a distinctive marking upon the body of a god. For in her innocence, Celia knew naught of the procedure of circumcision. However, rather than having this sophisticated aristocrat believe her to be completely ignorant of its value and therefore unworthy of his lustful attentions, the count's perplexed pleasurer continued to pry beneath his foreskin with her tongue, also rolling it back along the shaft with her fingertips so that she could cover as much of his shrinking length as possible. Celia found herself extremely charmed by its uncanny ability to retreat back in a daring disclosure of the amorous purple plum that had been the source of so much juiciness and—in a fit of modesty—come fully forward to form a protective cloak over it. So intent did she become upon her happy endeavors that it required the spent gentleman himself to call attention to the fact that his discharged member had diminished to a size undeserving of such loving devotion.

After the unique tang of so many females upon her tongue, it had proven an unexpected treat to taste a man again—especially the man who had materialized in their little Provençal salon so unexpectedly and mysteriously a mere few days previous. Had Count D'Arcy so wished it from her, Celia would have gladly placed herself before the fine muscular mounds of his backside and honored him in the manner in which her wicked tormentor had so often demanded and, indeed, so often received from her. For she suddenly realized that she would have done anything for the handsome count—she would perform deeds far beyond those of even Sir Jason's twisted imagination. And this realization was the key that freed her from the Hardwicke shackles which had kept her bound.

With the lacy hem of her sleeping garment, the young Englishwoman dabbed daintily from her prick-swollen lips the errant pearls of Count D'Arcy's pleasure, the awakened passage of her rectum still burning with the ghostly impression of his fingers. She wanted desperately for him to continue with such indelicate probings and, indeed, to escalate them to shameless and ever-more unprecedented levels, for she had thought of naught else since that fateful afternoon the startled blue of her eyes had first encountered the gluttonous glitter in his. Nevertheless, Celia sensed an urgency to this nocturnal meeting—an urgency which would prevent her yearning bottom from receiving the total fulfillment of its iniquitous desires. And this urgency was made all the more manifest by the count's husky whisper for her to make haste. Indeed, this whisper caused her to shiver deliciously, for never before had her ears been filled with the mellifluous honey of his voice.

Even after being so thoroughly and skillfully depleted of its fluids, this clandestine caller to Celia's bedchamber could feel his wizened penis beginning to stir once again. And how could it not, for the tantalizing display of the widely flared wings of the tremulous young woman's clitoris served to bring to mind the day's festivities. Yes…this silken butterfly had had much to soar about, as had its somewhat less elegant male counterparts. For the other two gentlemen admirers of this distinctive lobe of salmon pink flesh appeared to have been mightily affected by the lusty events that had led up to its many orgasmic flutters—which only made the count appreciate precisely how important it was for him and this bewitching female whose scent still remained deliciously inscribed upon his fingers to depart quickly and quietly before Sir Jason or his sullen companion came forth to stake their claim. Indeed, Count D'Arcy had fully expected to discover the fair Celia entertaining *both* Hardwicke penises when he had stolen into her bedchamber. Could it be that they were instead enjoying the dusky company of their most recent arrival?

Perhaps if events had not taken the unforeseen turn that they did, such a salacious scenario might have been extremely likely. Only rather than a divine trinity of lust, Sir Jason had envisioned a quartet. And it would be a quartet with one very special addition. For even whilst he slumbered with such seeming peacefulness in his bed, his mind continued to labor feverishly toward just so superbly orgiastic an orchestration—with a freshly shaven Celia at its core. Imagine how delicious it should be to put into use *all* of her dainty openings!

Like her renowned predecessor, the serpentine Gizelle also lived the glamorous life of a performer. She spent her evenings—or at least those that were not being spent in the glittering salons of distinguished ladies and gentleman—dancing in a smoky nightclub on the fringe of the Arab quarter of Paris. However, unlike the more traditional forms of the art one usually encountered in the city, she had devised for herself a far more distinctive style—indeed, a style which brought her nearly as much fame and adulation as a certain auburn-haired cancan dancer whose shapely legs could kick higher than any female who had ever graced a stage. This sultry creature of the *bôite de nuit* would writhe and shimmy behind a series of fans, occasionally lifting one to offer her audience a seductive tease of the tightly wound corkscrews upon her undulating mons veneris or the melonlike swells of her continually swaying bottom. Beneath the unrelenting glare of the spotlights, Gizelle's skin looked as black and shiny as Newcastle coal, stealing the excited breath from the constricting throats of her captivated onlookers. The finest men and women in all of Parisian society would come to see her perform, although only the most fortunate few could actually claim to have knowledge of the exotic mysteries that lay on the other side of the fans. Nevertheless, one more would very soon be added to this very distinguished list.

In the lavender-scented heat of Provence, Gizelle would not be requiring any of her trusty fans. For rather than being the performer, her sinuous body would instead serve as the stage upon which another of somewhat lesser renown would act out a drama—and it would be a drama guaranteed to please both audience and players alike. This invitee's leonine eyes had glimmered goldly in the waning afternoon light as she offered up to a certain blushing young female's trembling tongue a bottomhole the size and shade of a ripe raspberry. A palpable hush had fallen over the small salon as its gentlemen occupants abandoned the stiff-backed formality of their chairs to gather in a tight semicircle round the two women. Even the normally docile Colin took willing leave of both his chair and his glass, resuming his nearly forgotten place at his relative's side. Sensing his presence, Sir Jason smiled with genuine fondness, surprised to discover that he had greatly missed such cousinly camaraderie. Yes, they had enjoyed some fine festivities back in the chilly manor house on the moors! Perhaps the time had finally come for the two Hardwickes to once again enter into the sexual arena.

The close proximity of these three male spectators sparked a sudden renewal of feminine modesty within the blushing subject of the elder Hardwicke's campaign of humiliation, and all at once Celia found herself completely unable to move. Indeed, this now-seasoned performer's pleasure-inducing tongue had frozen in her mouth before it had even commenced its special dance upon the tenebrous stage being offered to it. Despite her cruel tormentor's increasingly impatient orders for her to proceed with the lustful matters at hand, it was the silent and unfathomable presence of Count D'Arcy who affected her the most and therefore thawed the frigid shyness that had happened upon her. Hence, as Celia pressed her reddening face closer to blinking beacon that garnered so much attention, she could feel the fluttering flesh of her clitoris lengthening, its swelling bulk prying apart the barbered lips encasing it until it felt as if two invisible thumbs had reached down to pluck them open. Suddenly the count's dark, searching eyes seemed to be everywhere, both between her thighs, which Sir Jason had demanded she keep spread to their limits, and upon her mouth, which was now only mere centimeters from the visiting woman's widened rear fissure. Oh, the stinging shame of it all!

With nowhere to turn and no one to turn to, ever so slowly Sir Jason's shivering captive unrolled her bashful tongue from its hiding place. At first her innate sense of propriety acted to restrain her, and she permitted only the investigating tip to glance lightly off the crinkly proscenium of Gizelle's anus. However, after hearing Count D'Arcy's ragged intake of breath, she grew further emboldened and began to undertake significantly more extravagant licks which served to encompass the entire aperture. For some inexplicable reason the primitive darkness of the other woman excited Celia, and the actions of her tongue felt even more forbidden than they had during her public introduction to the tangy tangerine nestling between the dance-muscled cheeks of Martine's buttocks. Indeed, perhaps what she experienced might very well have been similar to what the three eager gentlemen huddling before the explicit display of Gizelle's upended bottomhole experienced, for the penumbral furrow had sprouted temptingly open, providing all and sundry with a savory peek into its desirous depths. All at once Sir Jason's humiliated captive could see herself through their eyes. How brightly the pink tip of her tongue glowed against the reddish purple circlet! And how slowly and seductively it skirted the quivering periphery, as if endeavoring to charm an uncertain partner into a waltz. To Celia, being able to envision how she might have looked to her appreciative audience proved every bit as heady a fare as what the sultry fan dancer had just placed at her tongue's disposal.

Unlike previous such occasions, both Sir Jason and the visiting count found themselves totally powerless to contain the fleshy stalks straining and dampening their trouser fronts, and were compelled to join with the less high-minded and -prided Colin in allowing them to spring forth to joyous freedom. Although they made certain to refrain from such blatant improprieties, each gentleman longed with an uncharacteristic desperation to sample the generous coating of rich cream that served as a condiment for the polished pout of Celia's denuded labia—for indeed, it would surely taste all the sweeter from the intriguing actions which had inspired it! Instead they had to content themselves with the provocative perfume wafting upward from this burgeoning flower of femininity, silently praising the heavens for the sensory treat being granted to their unworthy nostrils.

The Possession of Celia

From out of the corner of her eye, Celia was stealthily able to observe Count D'Arcy's elegant hand working the broad shaft of his manhood. Its silken sheath slipped back and forth in a strangely hypnotic rhythm, the rapid movements prompting the inflated plum at the end to burn with a furious fire—a fire much like the one burning with such intense heat between her well-parted thighs. This was the humbled young woman's first-ever glimpse of the count's imposing member. As if to add to her disgrace, she experienced an overwhelming need to have the entirety of its great length and width inside her bottom—indeed, to have it right at that very moment, as her tongue thrust deeply into the well-heated chasm before her. In her frustration, Celia reached behind herself to locate the sadly vacant slot of her own similarly outfitted chasm, inspiring a series of delighted masculine gasps as she urged a pairing of cunt-moistened fingers inside and moved them in and out in a frantic simulation of the manly cylinder she now found herself pining for. As if to placate her oral pleasurer's thwarted desires, Gizelle spread the coal black swells of her buttocks all the wider so that her luscious fruit could be more easily consumed, thereby swallowing what little remained of Celia's frenzied tongue.

That afternoon the fair English maiden of Count D'Arcy's desire had come harder than she could ever remember coming, her anguished sob of release echoing off the palpitating walls of her partner's sympathetically quaking rectum. Her final shudders did not even have time to cease before she felt something hot and wet spraying her submissively posed nakedness in three separate and very distinct jets. She did not even need to turn her head to know what had just transpired, for the triad of men standing behind her and thrusting their wildly spewing organs into the empty air groaned in a symphony of anguished ecstasy, too euphoric in their pleasure to be embarrassed by so wet and communal a climax. A hot, spumy stream of liquid had begun to make its way down Celia's left side—a stream which, because of his proximity, she rightly ascertained belonged to the mysterious count. She halted its progress with her fingertips, bringing them up to her lips when she believed nobody was watching. And indeed, neither Sir Jason nor Colin witnessed the young woman's furtive actions. Nevertheless, there was *one* gentleman who did —and he took a silent vow to be most munificent when the next occasion arose for him to bestow his frothy favors upon so thirsting and appreciative a recipient.

Although this particular gentleman could think of nothing he would have liked better than to rouse from her bed the dusky female whose distinctive bottomhole had created such a stir and demand an immediate replay of the events of only a few short hours earlier, it was growing late and their coach was waiting. Thus, Count D'Arcy hastened the half-clad young Englishwoman along, the remembered image of her lustful pink tongue slithering between the fan dancer's splayed hind-cheeks sparking a raging conflagration inside his head and, indeed, inside his testicles. Yes, the lovely Celia had most assuredly enjoyed her raspberry tart! If the conclusion of this extraordinary night turned out as he hoped, he would see to it that the young lady's sweet tooth would suffer from no shortage of such savory treats.

Perhaps this once-demure captive of Sir Jason Hardwicke should have foreseen this visitation—a visitation as welcome as it was inevitable. And perhaps in a fleeting instant of uncertainty, she should have called out for assistance, for the gentleman had not had cause to silence her lips with his kerchief. Yet as with Sir Jason before him, Celia could not refuse the count. Therefore she went willingly and wordlessly with this enigmatic stranger down the stairs and outside into the flower-scented spring of the predawn blackness of morning—moving willingly and wordlessly to her fate. The grass beneath her bare feet still retained the comforting warmth of the sun, and she stopped for a moment to wriggle her toes in the satiny blades, taking considerable pleasure from so simple and commonplace an act. For thanks to her wicked captor, every part of her had become highly sensitized to even the most subtle forms of stimulation.

Suddenly Celia turned to look back at the darkened windows of the little *maison de campagne* she had spent so many hours of degradation in. The cheerful blue of their shutters had turned to silver in the moonlight, reminding her of many pairs of observant eyes—eyes that perhaps belonged to Sir Jason and Colin. Indeed, she fully expected the elder Hardwicke to come flying out of the front door on a black cloud of fury and wrench her from the evil clutches of this presumptuous brigand. Yet even as she stood there awaiting her rescuer, she realized with a bittersweet finality that it was too late.

"Come, my lady," Count D'Arcy urged softly, reaching out to caress the heat of her cheek with fingertips scented with her most intimate of places.

Celia had brought nothing with her save for the wispy nightdress she now wore. Nevertheless, its lacy hem was soon draped into a loose collar for her slender neck as she found herself straddling the Count's lap in the rear of the careening coach, the thickly heated shaft of his manhood planted well up her welcoming backside. Each sharp jolt of the vehicle along the rutted country road drove him in deeper, marking new territory and, indeed, canceling out those who had traveled that way before. Although the gentleman could have just as easily slipped inside the more traditional thoroughfare of his pirated treasure's womanhood, he desired to lay claim to her in a manner most absolute and, therefore, *irrevocable*. For to a man, such a penetration always proved the ultimate in possession.

And indeed, Celia's possession by the handsome

Count D'Arcy was total and complete, casting away the ghosts of those whose manly members she had received with such unceasing love and humiliation. Strange that at such a significant moment as this her thoughts should suddenly turn to Martine. For something told her that she would be seeing the auburn-haired beauty again, and although her tongue burned in remembered shame, it was a shame which made her very happy.

Thusly impaled, Celia rode bumpily north with Count D'Arcy and his unseen driver—and north to her new life.

MASQUERADE
AN EROTIC JOURNAL

60% OFF THE NEWSSTAND PRICE!

**Get one year (six issues) for only $15
or two years for only $25!**

MASQUERADE: AN EROTIC JOURNAL

a bimonthly review of the best in international erotic art and fiction.

One of the best magazines of this type produced in the USA.
—*The Stockroom*

An intelligent and stimulating must-read....
—*Genesis*

The best photographers and writers in the world are assembled in this little magazine....
—*Selen (Italy)*

A very well put-together publication that you will read from cover to cover—at least once!
—*Redemption*

For artistic and literary quality, this is about as good as porn gets.
—*Alternative Press Review*

MASQUERADE/DIRECT • 801 SECOND AVENUE • NY, NY 10017
Fax: 212.906.7355/E-Mail: MasqBks@aol.com/WWW.MASQUERADEBOOKS.COM
MC/VISA orders can be placed by calling our toll-free number: 800.375.2356

YES! I'd like to subscribe to MASQUERADE: AN EROTIC JOURNAL

☐ 2 issues for $5   ☐ one year for $15   ☐ two years for $25

NAME _____

ADDRESS _____

CITY _____ STATE _____ ZIP _____

E-MAIL _____

PAYMENT: ☐ CHECK   ☐ MONEY ORDER   ☐ VISA   ☐ MC

CARD # _____ EXP. DATE _____

No C.O.D. orders. Please make all checks payable to Masquerade/Direct. Payable in U.S. currency only.

1-800-375-2356

Masquerade

RICHARD MANTON

THE DAYS AT FLORAVILLE
$6.95/691-X
Lesley, an emancipated young beauty, tires of middle-class respectability. Accompanied by her young friend, Judith, Lesley embarks on a journey to the French resort of Floraville. There, in the confines of a secluded villa, Lesley learns the many thrilling techniques she will need to please the demanding men who have taken her in hand. Other young women accompany Lesley on this journey into utter submission—including Maggie, a vulgar shopgirl, and Claire, a voracious redhead. Together they embark on an erotic odyssey that has captivated readers worldwide.

THE GARDENS OF THE NIGHT
$6.95/678-2
A sequel to the cult classic *The Days at Floraville*. Lesley, an independent young beauty, has surrendered herself completely to Anton and Mano, who challenge her to unflinchingly obey their most extreme commands. Lesley is renowned for selflessly pleasuring others—and it is precisely this reputation that hangs in the balance. Faced with numerous depravities, Lesley performs with abandon. Traveling to increasingly remote locations, the willing young woman finds herself the plaything of many, until finally she encounters a vengeful face from the past.

WILMA KAUFFEN

SPANKED FOR BEING GOOD
$6.95/692-8
Poor Noodles! This voluptuous, green-eyed blonde can't seem to avoid being spanked. Her boyfriend Tony, initially thrilled that Noodles shares his interest in erotic spanking, soon disciplines her for her attentions to his rival. Later, as a dental assistant, Noodles is punished for being "too kind" to a patient—despite having made the doctor's practice an enormous success. Moving on to porn stardom, Noodles is again paddled for a minor transgression—even while helping her director become incredibly famous. It seems that no matter how nice Noodles tries to be, she's destined to be over some guy's knee at the end of the day....

OUR SCENE
$6.95/682-0
The chronicle of one man's exploits as a spanking aficionado. From early experiments as college graduate possessed of more enthusiasm than experience, to his no-holds-barred relationship with Lucy—a licentious beauty who responds best to the stinging kiss of an old-fashioned hairbrush—*Our Scene* is filled with encounters certain to please the most demanding reader.

CHET ROTHWELL

KISS ME, KATHERINE
$6.95/657-X
Husband—or slave? Beautiful Katherine can hardly believe her luck. Not only is she married to the charming and oh-so-agreeable Nelson, she's free to live out all her erotic fantasies with other men as well. Katherine has discovered Nelson to be far more devoted than the average spouse—and the duo soon begin exploring a relationship that could prove more demanding than marriage! Nelson becomes increasingly enthralled by Katherine's dominance—finally being reduced to mere voyeurism as his lusty wife pleasures herself with numerous others. An incredible chronicle of one woman's transformation into the unquestioned Mistress of her domain.

ANN BLAKELY & JULIA MOORE

THE OTHER RULES: Never Wear Panties on a First Date and Other Tips
$6.95/658-8
By now you've read (or at least heard about) *The Rules*, the old-fashioned "marriage manual" that's been getting so much attention. But what is a *modern* woman to do when it comes to dealing with the Opposite Sex? Ann Blakely and Julia Moore divulge the dating techniques that Mama never taught you...*The Other Rules*.

CLAIRE BAEDER, ED.

LA DOMME: A Dominatrix Anthology
$6.95/649-9
Erotic literature has long been filled with heart-stopping portraits of domineering women, and now Claire Baeder has assembled the most memorable in one beautifully brutal volume. No fan of real woman-power can afford to miss this ultimate compendium of dominatrix fiction.

MASQUERADE BOOKS

WWW.MASQUERADEBOOKS.COM

P. N. DEDEAUX

THE NOTHING THINGS
$6.95/653-7
Beta Beta Rho has taken on a new group of pledges. Five women elect to put themselves through the most grueling of ordeals, during which all their defenses will be stripped away—much to the delight of their stern pledgemistresses! The pleasure mounts as these young women leave behind the lowly status of nothing things....

THE TERRITORY WITHIN
$6.95/640-5
Dedeaux sets his tale within the boundaries of "The Territory," the ultimate fantasy patriarchy. While residing there, all women are strongly encouraged to live by its unusual system. As they discover, it's hard to tell what's more enjoyable: strict obedience or thrilling chastisement!

J. P. KANSAS

THE HOUSE GUEST and Other Stories
$6.95/638-3
A collection of stories from the author of the best-selling *Andrea at the Center*. From the tale of one woman's stay with an unusually welcoming—and horny—young couple to an encounter with a pair of identical women possessed by decidedly carnal desires, the tales of J. P. Kansas will set your senses aflame!

STEVE RICHARDSON, ED.

THE SWEET SPOT
$6.95/628-6
A collection of red-hot spanking stories. Twelve titillating tales designed to appeal to devotees of this popular fetish, the stories in *The Sweet Spot* will please all readers of erotica.

CLAIRE THOMPSON

SARAH'S SURRENDER
$6.95/620-0
Lovely Sarah denies her true desires for many years, hoping to find happiness with the pallid men who court her. Finally, Sarah explores the SM scene—and tastes fulfillment for the first time. Gradually, her desires lead her to Lawrence, a discriminating man whose course of erotic training bring Sarah to a fuller realization of her submissive nature—and a deeper love—than she had ever imagined possible....

ANAÏS NIN AND FRIENDS

WHITE STAINS
$6.95/609-X
Written by Anaïs Nin, Virginia Admiral, Caresse Crosby, and others for a dollar per page, this breathtaking volume was printed privately and soon became an underground legend. After more than fifty years, this collection of explicit but sophisticated musings is back in print.

DENISE HALL

THE COMPANION
$6.95/676-6
Carla spends her days answering phones in a sterile workplace she'd be happy to leave. One day, an anonymous admirer calls with an intriguing proposition. How would she like working for him—as his personal phone sex operator? In no time, Carla becomes the ultimate exhibitionist!

JUDGMENT
$6.95/590-2
A blistering tale of the ultimate disciplinary establishment. Judgment—a forbidding edifice where unfortunate young women find themselves subject to the wiles of their masters. Abandoned to the whims of Judgment's thrilling masters, Callie descends into the depths of this prison, discovering a new capacity for sensuality....

ALISON TYLER & DANTE DAVIDSON

BONDAGE ON A BUDGET
$6.95/570-0
The ultimate guide to low cost lust! Filled with delicious scenarios requiring no more than simple household items and a little imagination, this guide to DIY S&M will explode the myth that adventurous sex requires a dungeonful of expensive paraphernalia. A must for anyone determined to get the most bang for their buck.

JEAN SADDLER

THE FASCINATING TYRANT
$6.95/569-7
A reprint of a classic tale from the 1930s. *The Fascinating Tyrant* is a riveting glimpse of sexual extravagance in which a curious young man discovers his penchant for flagellation and sadomasochism.

BUY ANY 4 BOOKS & CHOOSE 1 ADDITIONAL BOOK, OF EQUAL OR LESSER VALUE, AS YOUR FREE GIFT

1-800-375-2356

ROBERT SEWALL

THE DEVIL'S ADVOCATE
$6.95/553-0
One of the America's earliest erotic novels. Clara Reeves appeals to Conrad Garnett, a New York district attorney, for help in tracking down her missing sister, Rita. Clara soon finds herself being "persuaded" to accompany Conrad on his descent into a shocking demimonde where unspeakable pleasures await....

ERICA BRONTE

LUST, INC.
$6.50/467-4
Explore the extremes of passion that lurk beneath even the most businesslike exteriors. Join in the sexy escapades of a group of professionals whose idea of office decorum is like nothing you've ever encountered!

OLIVIA M. RAVENSWORTH

DOMESTIC SERVICE
$6.95/615-4
Though married for twenty-five years, Alan and Janet still manage to find sensual excitement in each other's arms. Sexy magazines fan the flames of their desire—so much so that Janet yearns to bring her own most private fantasy to life. Janet persuades Alan to hire live-in domestic help—and their home soon becomes a most infamous household!

GERALD GREY

NEW YORK SECRETS
$6.95/675-8
A young woman arrives in Old New York, intent on realizing her dream of being a writer. She meets with Mr. Keating, an established and influential magazine editor and publisher. To her shock, Keating suggests that she turn her talents to sex fiction. She agrees—not knowing that Keating actually has the most severe erotic training in mind for his new authoress.

THE QUALITY OF MERCY
$6.95/650-2
James Adams arrives in Vienna intent upon receiving a thorough university education. All seems in order until he encounters Gizelle, a randy servant. With James, Gizelle is anything but subservient—little by little, she gains control of the young man's raging libido, until he is powerless in her hands!

LONDON GIRLS
$6.50/531-X
In 1875, Samuel Brown arrives in London, determined to take the glorious city by storm. Randy Samuel quickly distinguishes himself as one of the city's most notorious rakehells. Young Mr. Brown knows well the many ways of making a lady weak at the knees—and uses them not only to his delight, but to his enormous profit. The incredibly explicit account of a rake's progress!

ATAULLAH MARDAAN

KAMA HOURI/DEVA DASI
$7.95/512-3
A scintillating look at the sexual habits of another time and place. *Kama Houri* details the life of a sheltered Western woman who finds herself living within the confines of a harem. *Deva Dasi* is a tale dedicated to the sacred women of India who devoted their lives to the fulfillment of the senses.

J. A. GUERRA, ED.

COME QUICKLY: For Couples on the Go
$6.50/461-5
The increasing pace of daily life is no reason to forego a little carnal pleasure whenever the mood strikes. Here are over sixty of the hottest fantasies around, in one extraordinary all designed especially for modern couples on a hectic schedule.

VISCOUNT LADYWOOD

GYNECOCRACY
$9.95/511-5
A new edition of this timeless erotic classic! Julian is sent to a private school, and discovers that his program of study has been devised by stern Mademoiselle de Chambonnard. In no time, Julian is learning the many ways of pleasure and pain—under the firm hand of this beautifully demanding headmistress.

N. T. MORLEY

THE SECRETARY
$6.95/690-1
Suzette is a voluptuous young secretary at a leading fetish publication. While working in this highly arousing environment, Suzette can barely control herself—finally going so far as to submit to the caresses of her co-worker, Sasha. Incredible scenarios abound in this exploration of corporate lust!

MASQUERADE BOOKS

WWW.MASQUERADEBOOKS.COM

THE LIBRARY
$6.95/683-9
Monique, a virginal young librarian, entertains herself with fantasies of complete submission. One night, Monique meets a mysterious man who might be able to help her live out her fantasies—if she follows his instructions to the letter. As the young beauty prepares to commit herself to this ultimate figure of domination, numerous others entertain themselves by participating in her development.

THE APPOINTMENT
$6.95/667-7
Vanya Garrison is married to a wealthy man, but she's beautiful enough to have plenty of fun on her own. It takes a firm hand to control this pampered nymphomaniac; luckily, Dr. Rachel Quarry—Vanya's favorite shrink—provides a type of restraint and guidance unmatched in contemporary psychology. Despite the raging nymphomania that stands in the way of Vanya's progress, Dr. Quarry makes certain that all of her patient's deep-seated issues are thoroughly exposed and explored!

THE CIRCLE
$6.95/627-8
The story of one woman's ever-broadening horizons. Gina, a high-class "working girl," encounters a mysterious woman who pays her to indulge her kinky whims. Gina finds herself increasingly aroused by her encounters with Miranda, expanding her limits further than she could ever have imagined. Gradually, additional partners join in the fun, creating a circle of friends who just couldn't be closer!

THE OFFICE
$6.95/616-2
Lovely Suzette interviews for a desirable new position on the staff of a bondage magazine. Once hired, she discovers that her new employer's interest in dominance and submission extends beyond the printed page. Soon, Suzette is putting in plenty of overtime—as the bound sextoy of her demanding superior.

THE CONTRACT
$6.95/575-1
Beautiful Sarah is experiencing some difficulty in training her current submissive. Carlton proposes an unusual wager: if Carlton is unsuccessful in bringing Tina to a full appreciation of Sarah's domination, Carlton himself will become Sarah's devoted slave....

THE LIMOUSINE
$6.95/555-7
Brenda was enthralled with her roommate Kristi's desire to be dominated. Brenda decides to embark on a trip into submission, beginning in the long, white limousine where Kristi first met the Master.

VANESSA DURIÈS

THE TIES THAT BIND
$6.95/688-X
This best-selling account of real-life dominance and submission will keep you gasping with its vivid depictions of sensual abandon. At the hand of Masters Georges, Patrick, Pierre and others, this submissive seductress experiences pleasures she never knew existed....

M. S. VALENTINE

THE POSSESSION OF CELIA
$6.95/666-9
The story of Celia and the lusty cousins Hardwicke continues. Jason releases Celia from her obligation and arranges for the couple's passage to safety in France. But Celia cannot easily forget the man who has awakened so many desires within her—even as she struggles to restore normalcy to her relationship with Colin. Can Colin compete with the memory of Jason's virility—or must Celia finally choose between them?

THE CAPTIVITY OF CELIA
$6.95/654-4
A scorching tale of erotic blackmail. Beautiful Celia wants nothing more than to be with her lover, Colin. But Colin is mistakenly considered the prime suspect in a murder, forcing him to seek refuge with his cousin, Sir Jason Hardwicke. In exchange for Colin's safety, Jason demands Celia's unquestioning submission—knowing she will do anything to protect the man she loves.

CHARISSE VAN DER LYN

SEX ON THE NET
$5.95/399-6
Electrifying sex tales from one of the Internet's hottest authors. Encounters of all kinds—straight, lesbian, dominant/submissive and all sorts of extreme passions—are explored in thrilling detail.

BUY ANY 4 BOOKS & CHOOSE 1 ADDITIONAL BOOK, OF EQUAL OR LESSER VALUE, AS YOUR FREE GIFT

1-800-375-2356

SACHI MIZUNO

SHINJUKU NIGHTS
$6.50/493-3
Using Tokyo's infamous red light district as his backdrop, Sachi Mizuno weaves an intricate web of sensual desire, wherein many characters are ensnared by the demands of their carnal natures.

PASSION IN TOKYO
$6.50/454-2
Tokyo—one of Asia's most historic and seductive cities. Come behind the closed doors of its citizens, and witness the many pleasures that await intrepid explorers. Men and women from every stratum of society free themselves of all inhibitions in this thrilling tour through the libidinous East.

MARTINE GLOWINSKI

POINT OF VIEW
$6.50/433-X
After her divorce, a lonely woman decides to expand her sexual horizons. With the assistance of a new, unexpectedly kinky lover, she discovers and explores her exhibitionist tendencies—until there is virtually nothing she won't do before the horny audiences her man arranges. Soon she is infamous for her unabashed sexual performances.

AMANDA WARE

BOUND TO THE PAST
$6.50/452-6
Doing research in an old Tudor mansion, beautiful Anne finds herself aroused by James, a descendant of the property's owners. Together they uncover the perverse desires of the mansion's long-dead master—desires that bind Anne inexorably to the past—not to mention the bedpost!

RICHARD McGOWAN

A HARLOT OF VENUS
$6.50/425-9
A highly fanciful, epic tale of lust on Mars! Cavortia—the most famous and sought-after courtesan in the cosmopolitan city of Venus—finds love and much more during her adventures with some cosmic characters. A sexy, sci-fi fairytale, McGowan's interstellar epic is an unforgettable exploration of the outer limits of the sexual imagination.

M. ORLANDO

THE SLEEPING PALACE
$6.95/582-4
Maison Bizarre is the scene of unspeakable erotic cruelty; the *Lust Akademie* holds captive only the most luscious students of the sensual arts; *Baden-Eros* is the luxurious retreat of one's nastiest dreams.

CAROLE REMY

FANTASY IMPROMPTU
$6.50/513-1
Kidnapped to a remote island retreat, Chantal finds herself catering to every sexual whim of the mysterious Bran. Bran is determined to bring Chantal to a full embracing of her sensual nature, even while revealing himself to be something far more than human....

CHARLES G. WOOD

HELLFIRE
$5.95/358-9
A vicious murderer is running amok in New York's sexual underground—and Nick O'Shay, a virile detective with the NYPD, plunges into the case. He soon becomes embroiled in the Big Apple's notorious nightworld of dungeons and sex clubs, hunting a madman seeking to purge America with fire and blood sacrifices.

MARCO VASSI

THE STONED APOCALYPSE
$5.95/401-1/Mass market
"Marco Vassi is our champion sexual energist." —*VLS*

During his lifetime, Marco Vassi's reputation as a champion of sexual experimentation was worldwide. Funded by his groundbreaking erotic writing, *The Stoned Apocalypse* is Vassi's autobiography; chronicling a cross-country trip on America's erotic byways.

THE SALINE SOLUTION
$6.95/568-9/Mass market
"I've always read Marco's work with interest and I have the highest opinion not only of his talent but his intellectual boldness." —Norman Mailer

Through this story of one couple's brief affair and the events that lead them to desperately reassess their lives, Vassi examines the dangers of intimacy in an age of extraordinary freedom.

MASQUERADE BOOKS

WWW.MASQUERADEBOOKS.COM

TINY ALICE

THE GEEK
$5.95/341-4
An offbeat classic of modern erotica, *The Geek* is told from the point of view of, well, a chicken who reports on the various perversities he witnesses as part of a traveling carnival. When a gang of renegade lesbians kidnaps Chicken and his geek, all hell breaks loose. A strange but highly arousing tale, filled with outrageous erotic oddities.

ROBIN WILDE

TABITHA'S TEASE
$6.95/597-2
A best-selling sorority romp, featuring a cast of hyper-sexed coeds with mischief on their minds! When poor Robin arrives at The Valentine Academy, he finds himself subject to the torturous teasing of Tabitha—the Academy's most notoriously domineering co-ed. Adding to Robin's delicious suffering is the fact that Tabitha is pledge-mistress of a secret sorority dedicated to enslaving young men. Men suffer deliciously at the hands of Tabitha and her wicked beauties.

ANONYMOUS

DIARY OF AN ANGEL
$6.95/641-3
Lovely young Victoria comes to adulthood with little in the way of worldly experience and she never guesses how her life will change when she begins to investigate the delights of woman-hood. With the encouragement of her cousins, Angela and Kenneth, Victoria begins a descent into utter depravity.

LADY F
$6.95/642-1
Master Kidrodstock—full as he is of wicked and uncontrollable impulses and urges—soon discovers just how high the price is when he encounters Lady F. Stunningly cruel and sensuous, this haughty lady leaves all men gasping—for more!

THE YELLOW ROOM
$6.95/631-6
The "yellow room" holds the secrets of lust, lechery, and the lash. There, demure Alice Darvell soon experiences a variety of extraordinary experiences. Another story follows the perversions of a sadistic heiress and her two lusty ladies.

DANIELLE: Diary of a Slave Girl
$6.95/591-3
At the age of 19, Danielle Appleton vanishes. The frantic efforts of her family notwithstanding, she is never seen by them again. After her disappearance, Danielle finds herself doomed to a life of sexual slavery, obliged to become the ultimate instrument of pleasure to the man—or men—who own her.

ROMANCE OF LUST
$9.95/604-9
"Truly remarkable...all the pleasure of fine historical fiction combined with the most intimate descriptions of explicit love-making."
—*The Times*

One of the most famous erotic novels of the century! This collaborative work of sexual awakening in Victorian England was repeatedly been banned for its "immorality"—and much sought after for its vivid portrayals of sodomy, sexual initiation, and flagellation.

PROTESTS, PLEASURES AND RAPTURES
$4.95/204-3
Invited for an allegedly quiet weekend at a country Vicarage, a young woman is stunned to find herself surrounded by shocking acts of sexual sadism. Soon her curiosity is piqued, and she begins to explore her own capacities for cruelty.

SUBURBAN SOULS
$9.95/563-8
Focusing on the May–December sexual relationship of nubile Lillian and the more experienced Jack, all three volumes of *Suburban Souls* now appear in one special edition—guaranteed to enrapture readers with its detail.

THE MISFORTUNES OF COLETTE
$7.95/564-6
Beautiful Colette is the victim of a plot guaranteed to keep her in erotic servitude. Passed from one lustful tormentor to another, Colette wonders whether she is destined to find her greatest pleasures in punishment!

TITIAN BERESFORD

CINDERELLA
$6.95/606-5
Castle dungeons and tightly corseted ladies-in-waiting, naughty viscounts and cruel masturbatrixes—nearly every conceivable method of kinky arousal is explored and described in lush, vivid detail. A fetishist's dream and a masochist's delight!

BUY ANY 4 BOOKS & CHOOSE 1 ADDITIONAL BOOK, OF EQUAL OR LESSER VALUE, AS YOUR FREE GIFT

1-800-375-2356

CHIDEWELL HOUSE and Other Stories
$6.95/554-9
What keeps Cecil a virtual, if willing, prisoner of Chidewell House? One man has been sent to investigate the sexy situation—and reports back with tales of such depravity that no expense is spared in attempting Cecil's rescue. But what man would possibly desire release from the breathtakingly corrupt Elizabeth?

JUDITH BOSTON
$6.50/525-5
Edward would have been lucky to get the stodgy companion he thought his parents had hired for him. But an exquisite woman arrives at his door, and Edward finds that his lewd behavior never goes unpunished by the unflinchingly severe Judith Boston!

MARY LOVE

ANGELA
$6.95/545-X
Angela's game is "look but don't touch," and she drives everyone mad with desire, dancing for their pleasure but never allowing a single caress. Soon her sensual spell is cast, and she's the only one who can break it!

MASTERING MARY SUE
$6.95/660-X
Mary Sue is a rich nymphomaniac whose husband is determined to have her declared mentally incompetent and gain control of her fortune. He brings her to a castle where, to Mary Sue's delight, she is unleashed for a veritable sex-fest!

LIZBETH DUSSEAU

SPANISH HOLIDAY
$6.95/673-1
Lauren finds herself on an unexpected journey when her boyfriend Sam secretly books the couple on a luxury cruise. Little did he know that Lauren would take the opportunity to plan some below-decks activities of her own—in the company of another man. Soon, the couple's vacation heats up beyond all expectations, as Lauren falls under the spell of dark and mysterious Dominick, and Sam begins to wonder if he shouldn't seek excitement with the willing and available Chris.

CAROLINE'S CONTRACT
$6.95/672-3
After a long life of repression, luscious Caroline goes out on a limb. On the advice of a friend, Caroline meets with the dark and alluring Max Burton—a man willing to indulge her deepest fantasies of domination and discipline. Max demands that Caroline live up to his extraordinarily high expectations, with delightful correction her sole enticement. Caroline soon learns to love the ministrations of Max—with red cheeks her delicious reward!

THE APPLICANT
$6.95/670-7
Hilary answers a personal ad, hoping to find someone who can meet her very special erotic needs. She makes an appointment to meet the couple behind the advertisement, and is thrilled to find them abundantly skilled in sensual domination. Liza is a flawless mistress and, together with her husband, Oliver, she trains Hilary to be the perfect servant.

TRINKETS
$6.95/668-5
A woman toys with the idea of erotic submission, never thinking her dream might come true. But it does, and Tessa finds herself subordinate to an eccentric artist's every whim. In no time, the domineering Miles fashions her into the ultimate erotic bauble—to be shown off in public, but fully enjoyed in private.

THE BEST OF LIZBETH DUSSEAU
$6.95/630-8
Dusseau's explorations of male-dominant lust have made her a favorite with fans of contemporary erotica. This volume is full of heroines who are unafraid to put everything on the line in order to experience pleasure at the hands of a virile man...

LYN DAVENPORT

THE GUARDIAN II
$6.50/505-0
The tale of submissive Felicia Brookes continues. No sooner has Felicia come to love Rodney than she discovers that she has been sold—and must now accustom herself to the guardianship of the debauched Duke of Smithton. Surely Rodney will rescue her from the domination of this depraved stranger. Won't he?

MASQUERADE BOOKS

WWW.MASQUERADEBOOKS.COM

AMARANTHA KNIGHT

The Darker Passions:
THE PIT AND THE PENDULUM
$6.95/639-1
Edgar Allen Poe's deadly pit is trans- formed into the site of a thousand unbearable pleasures, a carnal playground frequented by the perverse members of a secret society devoted to sensual experimentation. One young woman is about to discover what has made the Pit of Delights a legend....

The Darker Passions:
FRANKENSTEIN
$6.95/617-0
What if you could create a living, breathing human? What shocking acts could it be taught to perform, to desire, to love? Find out what pleasures await those who play God....

The Darker Passions: CARMILLA
$6.95/578-6
Captivated by the portrait of a beautiful woman, a young man finds himself becoming obsessed with her remarkable story. Little by little, he uncovers the many blasphemies and debaucheries with which the beauteous Laura filled her hours—even as an otherworldly presence began feasting upon her....

THE PAUL LITTLE LIBRARY

LUST OF THE COSSACKS
$6.95/664-2
A countess enjoys watching lovely peasant girls submit to her perverse lesbian manias. She tutors her only male lover in the joys of erotic torture and in return he lures an innocent ballerina to the estate, intent on presenting her to the countess as a plaything.

THE ESSENTIAL PAUL LITTLE
$6.95/629-4
A collection of Little's hottest moments. From the simplest of pleasures to the most extravagant fetishism, Little's heroines indulge each desire—to not only their own delight, but that of their randy suitors!

SLAVE ISLAND
$6.95/655-3
A perennially best-selling title from this master of eroticism. A leisure cruise is waylaid by Lord Henry Philbrock, a sadistic genius. The ship's passengers are kidnapped and spirited to his island prison, where the women are trained to accommodate the most bizarre sexual cravings of the rich and perverted.

DOUBLE NOVEL
$7.95/647-2
Two incredible novels in one volume. *The Metamorphosis of Lisette Joyaux* tells the story of an innocent young woman seduced by a group of beautiful and experienced lesbians. *The Story of Monique* explores an underground society's clandestine rituals.

CHINESE JUSTICE
$6.95/596-4
Chinese Justice is already a classic—the story of the excruciating pleasures and delicious punishments inflicted on foreigners under the tyrannical leaders of the Boxer Rebellion.

FIT FOR A KING/BEGINNER'S LUST
$8.95/571-9/Trade paperback
Two complete novels. Voluptuous and exquisite, she is a woman *Fit for a King*—but could she withstand the fantastic force of his carnality? *Beginner's Lust* pays off handsomely for a novice in the many ways of sensuality.

SENTENCED TO SERVITUDE
$8.95/565-4/Trade paperback
Trained to accept her submissive state, an icy young woman soon melts under the heat of her owners, discovering a talent for love she never knew existed....

ROOMMATE'S SECRET
$8.95/557-3/Trade paperback
A woman is forced to make ends meet by the most ancient of methods. A beautiful young woman learns to rely on her considerable sensual talents.

TUTORED IN LUST
$6.95/547-6
This tale of the initiation and instruction of a carnal college co-ed and her fellow students unlocks the sex secrets of the classroom.

LOVE SLAVE/
PECULIAR PASSIONS OF MEG
$8.95/529-8/Trade paperback
What does it take to acquire a willing *Love Slave* of one's own? What are the appetites that lurk within *Meg*? Paul Little spares no lascivious detail in these two relentless tales!

ALL THE WAY
$6.95/509-3
Going All the Way features an unhappy man who tries to purge himself of the memory of his lover with a series of quirky and uninhibited vixens. *Pushover* tells the story of a serial spanker and his celebrated exploits.

BUY ANY 4 BOOKS & CHOOSE 1 ADDITIONAL BOOK, OF EQUAL OR LESSER VALUE, AS YOUR FREE GIFT

1-800-375-2356

THE END OF INNOCENCE
$6.95/546-8
The days of Women's Emancipation are the setting for this story. These women were willing to go to any lengths to fight for their sexual freedom, and willing to endure any punishment in their desire for liberation.

THE BEST OF PAUL LITTLE
$6.50/469-0
Known for his portrayals of punishment and pleasure, Little never fails to push readers over the edge of sensual excitement.

CAPTIVE MAIDENS
$5.95/440-2
The story of three beautiful young women who find themselves powerless against the landowners of their time. They find themselves banished to a sex colony, where they are subjected to unspeakable perversions.

ALIZARIN LAKE

THE INSTRUMENTS OF THE PASSION
$6.95/659-6
All that remains is the diary of a young initiate, detailing the rituals of a mysterious cult institution known only as "Rossiter." Behind sinister walls, a beautiful woman performs an unending drama of desire and submission.

MISS HIGH HEELS
$6.95/632-4
It was a delightful punishment few men dared to dream of. Forced by his wicked sisters to dress and behave like a proper lady, Dennis Beryl finds he enjoys life as Denise much more! Petticoats and punishments!

CLARA
$6.95/548-4
The mysterious death of a beautiful woman leads her old boyfriend on a harrowing journey of discovery. His search uncovers an unimaginably sensuous woman embarked on a quest for deeper and more unusual sensations!

LUSCIDIA WALLACE

THE ICE MAIDEN
$6.95/613-8
Edward Canton has everything he wants in life, with one exception: Rebecca Esterbrook. He whisks her away to his remote island compound, where she learns to shed her inhibitions. Fully aroused for the first time in her life, she becomes a slave to desire!

SARA H. FRENCH

MASTER OF TIMBERLAND
$6.95/595-6
A tale of sexual slavery at the ultimate paradise resort—where sizzling submissives serve their masters without question. Each lucky visitor lives out her fantasy of complete submission to a dominant man. No one leaves Timberland without exploring the furthest reaches of desire. One of our best-selling titles, this trek to Timberland has ignited passions the world over.

JOHN NORMAN

TRIBESMEN OF GOR
$6.95/677-4
"Surrender Gor"—so read the message received by the Priest-Kings. The gauntlet had been thrown: either Gor submits to the Others, or resigns itself to destruction. Tarl Cabot rouses himself to action on behalf of the Priest-Kings and the world they rule. Cabot heads to the great wasteland of the Tahari, fighting his way amongst feuding clans, treacherous slavers, a voluptuous woman warlord, and the ferocious powers from the worlds of steel.

MARAUDERS OF GOR
$6.95/662-6
Tarl Cabot has struggled to free himself from the control of Gor's powerful Priest-Kings, but to no avail. Now he finds that mission challenged by a threat emanating from the planet's forbidding northern lands. There, a menacing alien force waits for Tarl, who faces an awesome choice: protect his own position as a rich merchant-slaver, or risk everything to defend the freedom of his world....

HUNTERS OF GOR
$6.95/592-1
Tarl Cabot ventures into the wilderness of Gor, pitting his skill against brutal outlaws and sly warriors. His life on Gor been complicated by three beautiful, very different women: Talena, Tarl's one-time queen; Elizabeth, his fearless comrade; and Verna, chief of the feral panther women. In this installment of Norman's million-selling sci-fi phenomenon, the fates of these uncommon women are finally revealed....

MASQUERADE BOOKS

WWW.MASQUERADEBOOKS.COM

CAPTIVE OF GOR
$6.95/581-6
On Earth, Elinor Brinton was accustomed to having it all—wealth, beauty, and a host of men wrapped around her little finger. But Elinor is now a pleasure slave of Gor, a world whose society insists on her subservience, and Elinor finds herself succumbing—with pleasure—to her powerful Master....

RAIDERS OF GOR
$6.95/558-7
Tarl Cabot descends into the depths of Port Kar—the most degenerate port city of the Counter-Earth. There Cabot learns the ways of Kar, whose residents are renowned for the grip in which they hold their voluptuous slaves....

ASSASSIN OF GOR
$6.95/538-7
The chronicles of Counter-Earth continue with this examination of Gorean society. Here is the brutal caste system of Gor: from the Assassin Kuurus, on a mission of vengeance, to Pleasure Slaves, trained in the ways of personal ecstasy.

NOMADS OF GOR
$6.95/527-1
Cabot finds his way across Gor, pledged to serve the Priest-Kings. Unfortunately for Cabot, his mission leads him to the savage Wagon People—nomads who may very well kill before surrendering any secrets....

PRIEST-KINGS OF GOR
$6.95/488-7
Tarl Cabot searches for his lovely wife Talena. Does she live, or was she destroyed by the all-powerful Priest-Kings? Cabot is determined to find out—though no one who has approached the mountain stronghold of the Priest-Kings has ever returned alive....

OUTLAW OF GOR
$6.95/487-9
Tarl Cabot returns to Gor. Upon arriving, he discovers that his name, his city and the names of those he loves have become unspeakable. Once a respected Tarnsman, Cabot has become an outlaw, and must discover his new purpose on this strange planet, where even simple answers have their price....

TARNSMAN OF GOR
$6.95/486-0
This controversial series returns! Tarl Cabot is transported to Gor. He must quickly accustom himself to the ways of this world, including the caste system which exalts some as Warriors, and debases others as slaves.

DON WINSLOW

THE MANY PLEASURES OF IRONWOOD
$6.95/661-8
Welcome to the Ironwood Sportsmen's Club, specifically designed for the erotic entertainment of gentlemen. Charli, Robin, Kitteridge, Nikki, Annie, Diane and Meredith—seven lovely young women who, employed by the small and exclusive club, consider it their vocation to provide the members of Ironwood with the time of their lives.

THE BEST OF DON WINSLOW
$6.95/607-3
Internationally best-selling fetish author Don Winslow personally selected his hottest passages for this special collection. Sizzling excerpts are woven together to make this an extraordinary overview of Winslow's work.

SLAVE GIRLS OF ROME
$6.95/577-8
Never were women so relentlessly used as were ancient Rome's voluptuous slaves! With no choice but to serve their lustful masters, these captive beauties learn to perform their duties with the passion of Venus herself.

SECRETS OF CHEATEM MANOR
$6.50/434-8
Young Edward returns to his late father's estate, to find it being run by the majestic Lady Amanda Longleigh. Edward can hardly believe his luck—Lady Amanda is assisted by her two beautiful, lonely wards, Catherine and Prudence. All three beauties share a love of perverse erotic discipline.

THE INSATIABLE MISTRESS OF ROSEDALE
$6.50/494-1
Edward and Lady Penelope reside in Rosedale manor. While Edward is a connoisseur of sexual perversion, it is Lady Penelope whose mastery of complete sensual pleasure makes their home infamous.

BUY ANY 4 BOOKS & CHOOSE 1 ADDITIONAL BOOK, OF EQUAL OR LESSER VALUE, AS YOUR FREE GIFT

1-800-375-2356

N. WHALLEN

THE EDUCATION OF SITA MANSOOR
$6.95/567-0

On the eve of her wedding, Sita Mansoor is left without a bridegroom. Sita travels to America, where she hopes to become educated in the ways of a permissive society. She could never have imagined the wide variety of tutors—both male and female—who would be waiting to take on so beautiful a pupil.

THE CLASSIC COLLECTION

MAN WITH A MAID
$4.95/307-4

The adventures of Jack and Alice have delighted readers for eight decades! *Man with a Maid* tells a tale of desire and submission. Join Jack in the Snuggery, where many lovely women learn the ways of pleasure.

THE ENGLISH GOVERNESS
$6.95/622-7

When Lord Lovell's son was expelled from his prep school for masturbation, he hired a very proper governess to tutor the boy—giving her strict instructions not to spare the rod to break him of his bad habits. Upon her arrival in Lord Lovell's home, governess Harriet Marwood reveals herself a force to be reckoned with—particularly by her randy charge. In no time, Master Lovell's onanism is under control—as are all other aspects of his life.

MASQUERADE READERS

THE 50 BEST PLAYGIRL FANTASIES
$7.95/648-0

A steamy selection of women's fantasies straight from the pages of *PLAYGIRL*—the leading magazine of sexy entertainment for women. Contemporary heroines pursue liaisons with horny men from every walk of life in these tales of modern lust.

Rhinoceros

CHRISTA FAUST

CONTROL FREAK
$7.95/633-2

"Christa Faust is a Veronica in a world of Betties."
—Quentin Tarantino

"Takes the reader on an odyssey of the spirit leading to places that most of us have neither the imagination nor the courage to envision." —John Pelan

Caitlin McCullough, an author of cheap detective novels who has a nose for the sensational, is fascinated by the grisly particulars of a brutal murder. As Caitlin's investigation into Eva's wild life and brutal death draws her deeper into the labyrinth of New York's infamous sexual playground, she finds herself perversely attracted to the killing's prime suspect—a notorious SM club owner.

LEOPOLD VON SACHER-MASOCH

VENUS IN FURS
$7.95/589-1

The alliance of Severin and Wanda epitomizes Sacher-Masoch's obsession with a cruel goddess and the urges that drive the man held in her thrall. Exclusive to this edition are letters exchanged between Sacher-Masoch and Emilie Mataja—an aspiring writer he sought as the avatar of his desires.

M. CHRISTIAN, ED.

A MIDSUMMER NIGHT'S DREAM: Many Tales From One Story
$7.95/679-0

"This is a book about—and yet not about—William Shakespeare's play, *A Midsummer Night's Dream*. It is...a book of expositions on the intertwining love lives of a dozen or so beings, some of this earth, others not—all creations of the Bard, all living in one of his most imaginative works. An anthology of erotic interpretations on the play, on Theseus and Hippolyta, Hermia and Lysander, Demetrius and Helena, Oberon and Titania, Bottom and, not least of which, Puck—this is a place where remarkable writers have taken these wonderful characters and pushed them out, beyond their familiarity in *A Midsummer Night's Dream*." —from the Introduction

MASQUERADE BOOKS

MASQUERADE BOOKS

EROS EX MACHINA:
Eroticizing the Mechanical
$7.95/593-X

As the millennium approaches, technology is not only an inevitable, but a desirable addition to daily life. *Eros Ex Machina* explores the thrill and danger of machines—our literal and literary love of technology. Join over 25 of today's hottest writers as they explore erotic relationships with all kinds of gadgets, and devices.

THOMAS S. ROCHE

NOIROTICA: An Anthology of Erotic Crime Stories (Ed.)
$6.95/390-2

A collection of darkly sexy tales, taking place at the crossroads of the crime and erotic genres. Here are some of today's finest writers, all of whom explore the extraordinary and arousing terrain where desire runs irrevocably afoul of the law. A groundbreaking collection of contemporary erotica.

NOIROTICA 2: Pulp Friction (Ed.)
$7.95/584-0

Another volume of criminally seductive stories set in the murky terrain of the erotic and noir genres. Thomas Roche has gathered the darkest jewels from today's edgiest writers to create this provocative collection.

DARK MATTER
$6.95/484-4

"*Dark Matter* is sure to please gender outlaws, bodymod junkies, goth vampires, boys who wish they were dykes, and anybody who's not to sure where the fine line should be drawn between pleasure and pain. It's a handful." —Pat Califia

"Here is the erotica of the cumming millennium.... You will be deliciously disturbed, but never disappointed."
—Poppy Z. Brite

DAVID MELTZER

UNDER
$6.95/290-6

A new novel from the acclaimed author of the legendary Agency Trilogy. *Under* is the story of a 21st century sex professional living at the bottom of the social heap. After surgeries designed to increase his physical allure, corrupt government forces drive the cybergigolo underground, where even more bizarre cultures await.... A challenging look at the price of sexual excess in a world devoid of values.

ORF
$6.95/110-1

He is the ultimate musician-hero—the idol of thousands, the fevered dream of many more. And like many musicians before him, he is misunderstood, misused—and totally out of control. From agony to lust, every last drop of feeling is squeezed from a modern-day troubadour and his lady love in their relentless descent into hell. Long out of print, Meltzer's frank, poetic look at the dark side of the sixties returns.

KATHLEEN K.

SWEET TALKERS
$6.95/516-6

"If you enjoy eavesdropping on explicit conversations about sex... this book is for you." —*Spectator*

A explicit look at the burgeoning phenomenon of phone sex. Kathleen K. ran a phone-sex company in the late 80s, and she opens up her diary for a peek at the life of a phone-sex operator. Transcripts of actual conversations are included.
Trade /$12.95/192-6

GARY BOWEN

DIARY OF A VAMPIRE
$6.95/331-7

"Gifted with a darkly sensual vision and a fresh voice, [Bowen] is a writer to watch out for." —Cecilia Tan

Rafael, a red-blooded male with an insatiable hunger for the same, is the perfect antidote to the effete malcontents haunting bookstores today. A thrillingly erotic tale of a gay vampire.

LAURA ANTONIOU, ED.

SOME WOMEN
$7.95/573-5
Introduction by Pat Califia

"Makes the reader think about the wide range of SM experiences, beyond the glamour of fiction and fantasy, or the clever-clever prose of the perverati." —*SKIN TWO*

Over forty essays written by women actively involved in consensual dominance and submission. Women from every conceivable walk of life lay bare their true feelings about issues as explosive as feminism, abuse, pleasure and public image. An important and uncompromising look at contemporary sexuality, from a little-seen perspective.

BUY ANY 4 BOOKS & CHOOSE 1 ADDITIONAL BOOK, OF EQUAL OR LESSER VALUE, AS YOUR FREE GIFT

1-800-375-2356

NO OTHER TRIBUTE: Erotic Tales of Women in Submission
$7.95/603-0

Tales of women kept in bondage to their lovers by their deepest passions. Love pushes these women beyond acceptable limits, rendering them helpless to deny anything to the men and women they adore.

ROMY ROSEN

SPUNK
$6.95/492-5

Casey, a lovely model poised upon the verge of super-celebrity, falls for an insatiable young rock singer—not suspecting that his sexual appetite has led him to experiment with a dangerous new aphrodisiac. Soon, Casey becomes addicted to the drug, and her craving plunges her into a strange underworld....

MOLLY WEATHERFIELD

SAFE WORD: CARRIE'S STORY II
$7.95/665-0

The sequel to Molly Weatherfield's best-selling look at contemporary dominance and submission, *Carrie's Story*. Carrie leaves behind her life with Jonathan, intent on proving herself with the demanding gentleman who has chosen her as his own. Whisked away to Greece, Carrie learns new, more rigorous methods of sexual satisfaction. When her year of training is complete, Carrie faces a decision—life on her own, or in the embrace of her beloved but estranged Jonathan.... A compelling, thought-provoking follow-up to Weatherfield's groundbreaking debut.

CARRIE'S STORY
$7.95/652-9

"I was stunned by how well it was written and how intensely foreign I found its sexual world.... And, since this is a world I don't frequent... I thoroughly enjoyed the National Geo tour."
—*bOING bOING*

Weatherfield's bestselling examination of contemporary dominance and submission. "I had been Jonathan's slave for about a year when he told me he wanted to sell me at an auction...." A rare piece of erotica, both thoughtful and hot!

AMELIA G, ED.

BACKSTAGE PASSES: Rock 'n' Roll Erotica from the Pages of *Blue Blood* Magazine
$6.95/438-0

Amelia G, editor of the goth-sex journal *Blue Blood*, has brought together some of today's most irreverent writers, each of whom has outdone themselves with an edgy, antic tale of modern lust.

CYBERSEX CONSORTIUM

CYBERSEX: The Perv's Guide to Finding Sex on the Internet
$6.95/471-2

You've heard the objections: cyberspace is soaked with sex, mired in immorality. Okay—so where is it!? Tracking down the good stuff—the real good stuff—can waste an awful lot of expensive time, and frequently leave you high and dry. An easy-to-use guide for those intrepid adults who know what they want.

GERI NETTICK WITH BETH ELLIOT

MIRRORS: Portrait of a Lesbian Transsexual
$6.95/435-6

Born a male, Geri Nettick knew something just didn't fit. Even after coming to terms with her own gender dysphoria, and taking steps to correct it, she still fought to be accepted by the lesbian feminist community to which she felt she belonged. An inspiring true story of self-discovery and acceptance.

LAURA ANTONIOU ("Sara Adamson")

"Ms. Adamson creates a wonderfully diverse world of lesbian, gay, straight, bi and transgendered characters, all mixing delightfully in the melting pot of sadomasochism and planting the genre more firmly in the culture at large. I for one am cheering her on!"
—Kate Bornstein

THE MARKETPLACE
$7.95/602-2

The first title in Antoniou's thrilling Marketplace Trilogy, following the lives an lusts of those who have been deemed worthy to participate in the Marketplace—the ultimate BD/SM arena.

MASQUERADE BOOKS

WWW.MASQUERADEBOOKS.COM

THE SLAVE
$7.95/601-4
The Slave covers the experience of one submissive who longs to join the ranks of those who have proven themselves worthy of entry into the Marketplace. But the price of admission, while delicious, is staggeringly high....

THE TRAINER
$7.95/686-3
The Marketplace Trilogy concludes with the story of the trainers, and the desires and paths that led them to become the ultimate figures of authority.

THE CATALYST
$6.95/621-9
Different from a lot of SM smut in that it depicts actual consensual SM scenes between just plain folks rather than wild impossible fantasies, *The Catalyst* is both sweet-natured and nastily perverse. —*Blowfish*

After viewing an explicitly kinky film full of images of bondage and submission, several audience members find themselves deeply moved by the erotic suggestions they've seen on the screen. A modern BD/SM classic, and this popular author's debut.

JOHN NORMAN

IMAGINATIVE SEX
$7.95/561-1
The author of the Gor novels outlines his philosophy on relations between the sexes, and presents fifty-three scenarios designed to reintroduce fantasy to the bedroom.

JOHN WARREN

THE TORQUEMADA KILLER
$6.95/367-8
Detective Eva Hernandez gets her first "big case": a string of murders taking place within New York's SM community. Eva assembles the evidence, revealing a picture of a world misunderstood and under attack—and gradually comes to face her own hidden longings.

THE LOVING DOMINANT
$7.95/600-6
Everything you need to know about an infamous sexual variation, and an unspoken type of love. Warren, a scene veteran, guides readers through this rarely seen world, and offers clear-eyed advice guaranteed to enlighten the novice and seasoned erotic explorer alike. A best-selling erotic manual.

TAMMY JO ECKHART

AMAZONS: Erotic Explorations of Ancient Myths
$7.95/534-4
The Amazon—the fierce woman warrior—appears in the traditions of many cultures, but never before has the erotic potential of this archetype been explored with such energy and imagination. Powerful pleasures await anyone lucky enough to encounter Eckhart's legendary spitfires.

PUNISHMENT FOR THE CRIME
$6.95/427-5
Stories that explore dominance and submission. From an encounter between two of society's most despised individuals, to the explorations of longtime friends, these tales take you where few others have ever dared....

GRANT ANTREWS

LEGACIES
$7.95/605-7
Kathi Lawton discovers that she has inherited the troubling secret of her late mother's scandalous sexuality. In an effort to understand what motivated her mother's desires, Kathi embarks on an exploration of SM that leads her into the arms of Horace Moore, a mysterious man who seems to see into her very soul. As she begins falling for her new master, Kathi finds herself wondering just how far she'll go to prove her love.

SUBMISSIONS
$7.95/618-9
The moving story of a lonely man, a lottery ticket, and a demanding but sensitive dominatrix. Suddenly finding himself a millionaire, Kevin Donovan thinks his worries are over—until his restless soul tires of the high life. He turns to the icy Maitresse Genevieve, hoping that her ministrations will guide him to some deeper peace....

ROGUES GALLERY
$6.95/522-0
A stirring evocation of dominant/submissive love. Two doctors meet and slowly fall in love. Once lovely Beth reveals her hidden, kinky desires to Jim, the two explore the forbidden acts that will come to define their affair.

BUY ANY 4 BOOKS & CHOOSE 1 ADDITIONAL BOOK, OF EQUAL OR LESSER VALUE, AS YOUR FREE GIFT

1-800-375-2356

MY DARLING DOMINATRIX
$7.95/566-2

When a man and a woman fall in love, it's supposed to be simple, uncomplicated, easy —unless that woman happens to be a dominatrix. One couple exlores the outer limits and inner depths of desire in this unpretentious love story that captures the richness of this special kind of love without leering or smirking.

T. TAORMINO & D. A. CLARK, EDS.

RITUAL SEX
$6.95/391-0

These writers understand that body and soul share more common ground than society feels comfortable acknowledging. From memoirs of ecstatic revelation, to quests to reconcile sex and spirit, *Ritual Sex* provides an unprecedented look at private ritual.

AMARANTHA KNIGHT, ED.

DEMON SEX
$7.95/594-8

Examining the dark forces of humankind's oldest stories, the contributors to *Demon Sex* reveal the strange symbiosis of dread and desire. Stories include a streetwalker's deal with the devil; a visit with the stripper from Hell; the secrets behind an aging rocker's timeless appeal; and many more.

SEDUCTIVE SPECTRES
$6.95/464-X

Tours through the erotic supernatural via the imaginations of today's best writers. Never have ghostly encounters been so alluring, thanks to otherworldly characters well-acquainted with the pleasures of the flesh.

SEX MACABRE
$6.95/392-9

Horror tales designed for dark and sexy nights —sure to make your skin crawl, and heart beat faster. A cast of stellar talents makes this a compelling volume, and an important title in the emerging genre of erotic horror.

FLESH FANTASTIC
$6.95/352-X

Humans have long toyed with the idea of "playing God": creating life from nothingness, bringing life to the inanimate. Now Amarantha Knight collects stories exploring not only the act of Creation, but the lust that follows.

JEAN STINE

THRILL CITY
$6.95/411-9

Thrill City is the seat of the world's increasing depravity, and this classic novel transports you there with a vivid style you'd be hard pressed to ignore. Raging passions bring together lonely, desperate souls in this vision of contemporary Babylon.

PHILIP JOSÉ FARMER

A FEAST UNKNOWN
$6.95/276-0

Lord Grandrith—armed with the belief that he is the son of Jack the Ripper—tells the story of his remarkable life. His story progresses to encompass the furthest extremes of human behavior.

FLESH
$6.95/303-1

Commander Stagg explored the galaxies for 800 years. Upon his return, the hero Stagg is made the centerpiece of an incredible public ritual—one that will take him to the heights of ecstasy, and the depths of hell.

ALICE JOANOU

THE BEST OF ALICE JOANOU
$7.95/623-5

"Outstanding erotic fiction." —*Susie Bright*

The best from this major name in the renaissance of American erotica.

BLACK TONGUE
$6.95/258-2

"Joanou has created a series of sumptuous, brooding, dark visions of sexual obsession, and is undoubtedly a name to look out for in the future." —*Redeemer*

Exploring lust at its most florid and unsparing, *Black Tongue* is redolent of forbidden passions.

SOPHIE GALLEYMORE BIRD

MANEATER
$6.95/103-9

Through a bizarre act of creation, a man attains the "perfect" lover—by all appearances a beautiful, sensuous woman, but in reality something far darker. Once brought to life she will accept no mate, seeking instead the prey that will sate her hunger.

MASQUERADE BOOKS

WWW.MASQUERADEBOOKS.COM

LIESEL KULIG

LOVE IN WARTIME
$6.95/3044-X

Madeleine knew that the handsome SS officer was dangerous, but she was just a cabaret singer in Nazi-occupied Paris, trying to survive in a perilous time. When Josef fell in love with her, he discovered that a beautiful woman can be as dangerous as any warrior.

SAMUEL R. DELANY

THE MAD MAN
$8.99/408-9/Mass market

"Delany develops an insightful dichotomy between [his protagonist]'s two worlds: the one of cerebral philosophy and dry academia, the other of heedless, 'impersonal' obsessive sexual extremism. When these worlds finally collide...the novel achieves a surprisingly satisfying resolution...."
—*Publishers Weekly*

Graduate student John Marr researches the life of Timothy Hasler: a philosopher whose career was cut tragically short over a decade earlier. Marr begins to find himself increasingly drawn toward shocking sexual encounters with the homeless men, until it begins to seem that Hasler's death might hold some key to his own life as a gay man in the age of AIDS. Surely this legendary writer's most mind-blowing and explicit novel.

MICHAEL PERKINS

THE SECRET RECORD:
Modern Erotic Literature
$6.95/3039-3

An authoritative and insightful overview. Updated and revised to include the latest trends, tastes, and developments in this misunderstood genre.

AN ANTHOLOGY OF CLASSIC ANONYMOUS EROTIC WRITING
$6.95/140-3

The best passages from the world's erotic writing. "Anonymous" is one of the most infamous bylines in publishing history—and these excerpts show why!

Badboy

MICHAEL BRONSKI, ED.

FLASHPOINT: Gay Male Sexual Writing
$7.95/687-1

Well-written, and in most cases, even excellently so.... Savor this worthy assortment of gay male sexual writing. And believe you me, you will desire repeated visits to Michael Bronski's excellent collection. —*Lambda Book Report*

Today's hottest volume collection of contemporary gay erotica. Cultural critic Michael Bronski presents work from more than twenty of the genre's best writers, exploring areas such as enlightenment, violence, true life adventures, trans- formations and more.

DAVID MAY

MADRUGADA
$6.95/574-3

"...Real literary talent....May clearly has a deep and complex view of his characters..." —*Lambda Book Report*

Set in San Francisco's gay leather community, *Madrugada* follows the lives of a group of friends—and their many acquaintances—as they tangle with the thorny issues of love and lust. Uncompromising, mysterious, and arousing, David May weaves a complex web of relationships in this unique story cycle.

PETER HEISTER

ISLANDS OF DESIRE
$6.95/480-1

Red-blooded lust on the wine-dark seas of classical Greece. Anacraeon yearns to leave his small, isolated island and find adventure in one of the overseas kingdoms. Accompanied by some randy friends, Anacraeon makes his dream come true—and discovers pleasures he never dreamed of!

KITTY TSUI ("Eric Norton")

SPARKS FLY
$6.95/551-4

A chronicle of the highest highs—and most wretched depths—of life as Eric Norton, a beautiful wanton living San Francisco's high life. *Sparks Fly* traces Norton's rise, fall, and resurrection, vividly marking the way with the personal affairs that give life meaning.

BUY ANY 4 BOOKS & CHOOSE 1 ADDITIONAL BOOK, OF EQUAL OR LESSER VALUE, AS YOUR FREE GIFT

1-800-375-2356

SCOTT O'HARA

DO-IT-YOURSELF PISTON POLISHING
$6.50/489-5
Sex-pro Scott O'Hara drew upon his powers of seduction to lure you into a world of hard, horny men long overdue for a tune-up.

JOHN PRESTON

MR. BENSON
With a new introduction by Michael Bronski
$6.95/637-5
"Something in the character of Jamie and Aristotle Benson struck a nerve in adventuresome gay America that has simply never been duplicated.... This seminal work of American SM literature is now back in print in its unexpurgated entirety to be savored as both a piece of history and a damn good read."
—*Inches*

A classic erotic novel from a time when there was no limit to what a man could dream of doing.

HUSTLING: A Gentleman's Guide to the Fine Art of Homosexual Prostitution
$6.50/517-4
"Fun and highly literary. What more could you expect form such an accomplished activist, author and editor?" —*Drummer*

John Preston solicited the advice and opinions of "working boys" from across the country in his effort to produce the ultimate guide to the hustler's world.
Trade $12.95/137-3

THE ARENA
$4.95/3083-0
Preston's take on the ultimate sex club. One young man is introduced to the pleasures that await members of the Arena—and soon establishes himself as one of the club's most dedicated members. Only the author of *Mr. Benson* could have imagined so perfect an institution for the satisfaction of male desire.

TALES FROM THE DARK LORD
$5.95/323-6
Twelve stunning works from the man *Lambda Book Report* called "the Dark Lord of gay erotica." The ritual of lust and surrender is explored in all its manifestations in this heart-stopping triumph of authority and vision.

TALES FROM THE DARK LORD II
$4.95/176-4

THE HEIR•THE KING
$4.95/3048-2
The Heir, written in the lyric voice of the ancient myths, tells the story of a world where slaves and masters create a new sexual society. *The King* tells the story of a soldier who discovers his monarch's most secret desires.

The Mission of Alex Kane

DEADLY LIES
$4.95/3076-8
Politics is a dirty business and the dirt becomes deadly when a smear campaign targets gay men. Who better to clean things up than Alex Kane!

STOLEN MOMENTS
$4.95/3098-9
A malicious newspaper editor who is more than willing to boost circulation by printing homophobic slander. He never counted on Alex Kane!

SECRET DANGER
$4.95/111-X
Alex Kane and the faithful Danny are called to a small European country, where a group of gay tourists is being held hostage by brutal terrorists.

LETHAL SILENCE
$4.95/125-X
Chicago becomes the scene of the right-wing's most homophobic plan. Alex and Danny face off with the mercenaries who would squash gay men underfoot.

WILLIAM J. MANN, ED.

GRAVE PASSIONS: Gay Tales of the Supernatural
$6.50/405-4
A collection of the most chilling tales of passion currently being penned by today's most provocative gay writers. Unnatural transformations, otherworldly encounters, and deathless desires make for a collection sure to keep readers up late at night.

JAY SHAFFER

ANIMAL HANDLERS
$4.95/264-7
A terrific collection of stories from this acclaimed writer. In Shaffer's world, every man finally succumbs to the animal urges deep inside.

MASQUERADE BOOKS

WWW.MASQUERADEBOOKS.COM

FULL SERVICE
$4.95/150-0
One of today's best chroniclers of masculine passion. No-nonsense guys bear down hard on each other as they work their way toward release in this fine assortment of fantasies.

BARRY ALEXANDER

ALL THE RIGHT PLACES
$6.95/482-8
Stunningly sexy stories filled with hot studs in lust and love. From modern masters and slaves to medieval royals and their subjects, Alexander explores the mating rituals men have engaged in for centuries.

J. A. GUERRA, ED.

THE BADBOY BOOK OF WAR STORIES
$6.95/693-6
A special volume of gay erotic tales set during the Gulf War. Despite the U.S. Government's policy of "don't ask, don't tell," plenty of hot guys are getting what they need at the hands of their fellow warriors. Included are stories about lusty seamen (everything you've heard is true!); the hot antics behind the scenes of the USO; the outrageous adventures of an irrepressible chopper pilot.

COME QUICKLY: For Boys on the Go
$6.50/413-5
Here are over sixty of the hottest fantasies around. J. A. Guerra has put together this volume especially for you—a busy man on a modern schedule, who still appreciates a little old-fashioned action.

D. V. SADERO

IN THE ALLEY
$4.95/144-6
A breathtaking collection of stories from this popular writer. Hardworking men bring their special skills and impressive tools to the most satisfying job of all: capturing and breaking the male animal.

SUTTER POWELL

EXECUTIVE PRIVILEGES
$6.50/383-X
No matter how serious or sexy a predicament his characters find themselves in, Powell conveys the sheer exuberance of their encounters with a warm humor rarely seen in contemporary gay erotica.

GARY BOWEN

WESTERN TRAILS
$6.50/477-1
Gay lit's brightest stars tell the sexy truth about the many ways a stud found to satisfy himself—and his buddy—in the Wild West.

MAN HUNGRY
$5.95/374-0
A riveting collection of stories from one of gay erotica's new stars. Dipping into a variety of genres, Bowen crafts tales of lust unlike anything being published today.

ROBERT BAHR

SEX SHOW
$4.95/225-6
A thrilling collection of erotic tales, highlighting luscious dancing boys. Brazen, explicit acts. Take a seat, and get very comfortable, because the curtain's going up on a very special show no discriminating appetite can afford to miss.

KYLE STONE

THE HIDDEN SLAVE
$6.95/580-8
"This perceptive and finely-crafted work is a joy to discover. Kyle Stone's fiction belongs on the shelf of every serious fan of gay literature." —Pat Califia

A young man searches for the perfect master. An electrifying tale of erotic discovery.

HOT BAUDS 2
$6.50/479-8
Stone conducted another heated search through the world's randiest gay bulletin boards, resulting in one of the most scalding follow-ups ever published.

HOT BAUDS
$5.95/285-X
Stone combed cyberspace for the hottest fantasies of the world's horniest hackers. A collection of sexy, shameless, and eminently user-friendly tales.

FIRE & ICE
$5.95/297-3
A collection of stories from the author of the adventures of PB 500. Stone's characters always promise one thing: enough hot action to burn away your desire for anyone else....

BUY ANY 4 BOOKS & CHOOSE 1 ADDITIONAL BOOK, OF EQUAL OR LESSER VALUE, AS YOUR FREE GIFT

1-800-375-2356

FANTASY BOARD
$4.95/212-4
Explore the future—through the intertwined lives of a collection of randy computer hackers. On the Lambda Gate BBS, every horny male is in search of virtual satisfaction—and no one goes away unsatisfied!

THE CITADEL
$4.95/198-5
The sequel to the legendary gay scifi epic *PB 500*. Micah faces new challenges after entering the Citadel. Only his master knows what awaits....

THE INITIATION OF PB 500
$4.95/141-1
An interstellar traveller crash lands on a strange planet—where he is held and trained as the sexual slave of a powerful warrior. Soon, he takes pride in the extent of his servitude.

RITUALS
$4.95/168-3
Via a computer bulletin board, a young man finds himself drawn into sexual rites that transform him into the willing slave of a mysterious stranger. His former life is thrown off, and he learns to live for his Master's touch....

JASON FURY

THE ROPE ABOVE, THE BED BELOW
$4.95/269-8
A vicious murderer is preying upon New York's go-go boys. In order to solve this mystery and save lives, each studly suspect must lay bare his soul—and more!

LARS EIGHNER

WANK: THE TAPES
$6.95/588-3
A look at every guy's favorite pastime. Studs bare it all and work up a healthy sweat during these provocative discussions about masturbation. All secrets are revealed by this cast of hunks, as each relates his thrilling experiences in an oversexed college dorm.

WHISPERED IN THE DARK
$5.95/286-8
A volume demonstrating Eighner's unique combination of strengths: poetic descriptive power, an unfailing ear for dialogue, and a finely tuned feeling for the nuances of male passion.

AMERICAN PRELUDE
$4.95/170-5
Eighner is one of gay erotica's true masters, producing wonderfully written tales of all-American lust, peopled with red-blooded, oversexed studs. This volume is one of his best, exploring the many manifestastions of gay lust.

1 900 745-HUNG

THE connection for hot handfuls of eager guys! No credit card needed—so call now for access to the hottest party line available. Spill it all to bad boys from across the country! (Must be over 18.) Pick one up now.... $3.98 per min.

TOM BACCHUS

RAHM
$5.95/315-5
Tom Bacchus brings to life an extraordinary assortment of characters, from the Father of Us All to the cowpoke next door, the early gay literati to rude, queercore mosh rats.

BONE
$4.95/177-2
Queer musings from the pen of one of today's hottest young talents. Tom Bacchus maps out the tricking ground of a new generation.

BOB VICKERY

SKIN DEEP
$4.95/265-5
So many varied beauties no one will go away unsatisfied. No tantalizing morsel of manflesh is overlooked—or left unexplored!

DAVID LAURENTS, ED.

SOUTHERN COMFORT
$6.50/466-6
A collection of tales focusing on the American South— sexy stories reflecting the many sexy contributions the region has made to the iconography of the American Male.

WANDERLUST:
Homoerotic Tales of Travel
$5.95/395-3
A volume dedicated to the special pleasures of faraway places. Celebrate the freedom of the open road, and the allure of men who stray from the beaten path....

MASQUERADE BOOKS

WWW.MASQUERADEBOOKS.COM

THE BADBOY BOOK OF EROTIC POETRY
$5.95/382-1
Erotic poetry has long been the problem child of the literary world—highly creative and provocative, but somehow too frank to be considered "art." *The Badboy Book of Erotic Poetry* restores eros to its place of honor in gay writing. A groundbreaking volume.

AARON TRAVIS

SLAVES OF THE EMPIRE
$6.95/646-4
"Aaron Travis' epic of gladiator sex, slavery and sadism is not good porn—it's great. Not only is the story told well, but it is populated by real people who are at once pornographic archetypes and complex models of psychology. Caught between the real and the fantastic, Travis has given us the best of both worlds."
—Michael Bronski

"Aaron Travis' masterpiece." —*Drummer*

BIG SHOTS
$5.95/448-8
Two fierce tales in one electrifying volume. In *Beirut*, Travis tells the story of ultimate military power and erotic subjugation; *Kip*, Travis' hypersexed and sinister take on film noir, appears in unexpurgated form for the first time.

EXPOSED
$4.95/126-8
Cops, college jocks, ancient Romans—even Sherlock Holmes and his loyal Watson—cruise these pages, fresh from the pen of one of our hottest authors.

IN THE BLOOD
$5.95/283-3
Early tales from this master of the genre. Includes "In the Blood"—a heart-pounding descent into sexual vampirism.

THE FLESH FABLES
$4.95/243-4
One of Travis's best collections. Includes "Blue Light," as well as other stories that established him as one of gay erotica's masters.

KEY LINCOLN

SUBMISSION HOLDS
$4.95/266-3
From tough to tender, the men between these covers stop at nothing to get what they want. A collection of originality and scalding sensuality.

JR

FRENCH QUARTER NIGHTS
$5.95/337-6
Sensual snapshots of the many places where men get down and dirty—from the steamy French Quarter to the steam room at the old Everard baths.

CLAY CALDWELL

SOME LIKE IT ROUGH
$6.95/544-1
Here are the best of Caldwell's darkest tales—filled with enough virile masters and slaves to satisfy the most demanding reader.

JOCK STUDS
$6.95/472-0
Swimmers, football players—whatever your sport might be, there's a man here waiting to peel off his uniform, and claim his reward for a game well-played....

ASK OL' BUDDY
$5.95/346-5
Set in the underground SM world—where men initiate one another into the secrets of the rawest sexual realm of all. And when each stud's initiation is complete, he takes part in the training of another hungry soul....

STUD SHORTS
$5.95/320-1
"If anything, Caldwell's charm is more powerful, his nostalgia more poignant, the hominess he captures more sweetly, achingly acute than ever."
—Aaron Travis

A new collection of this legend's latest sex-fiction. Caldwell tells all about cops, cadets, truckers, farmboys (and many more) in these dirty jewels.

TAILPIPE TRUCKER
$5.95/296-5
Trucker porn! Caldwell tells the truth about Trag and Curly—two men hot for the feeling of sweaty manflesh. Together, they pick up—and turn out—a couple of thrill-seeking punks.

SERVICE, STUD
$5.95/336-8
Another look at the gay future. The setting is the Los Angeles of a distant future. Here the all-male populace is divided between the served and the servants—guaranteeing the erotic satisfaction of all involved.

BUY ANY 4 BOOKS & CHOOSE 1 ADDITIONAL BOOK, OF EQUAL OR LESSER VALUE, AS YOUR FREE GIFT

1-800-375-2356

QUEERS LIKE US
$4.95/262-0
For years the name Clay Caldwell has been synonymous with the hottest, most finely crafted gay tales available. *Queers Like Us* is one of his best: the story of a randy mailman's trek through a landscape of available studs.

CALDWELL/EIGHNER

QSFX2
$5.95/278-7
Other-worldly yarns from two master storytellers—Clay Caldwell and Lars Eighner. Both eroticists take a trip to the furthest reaches of the sexual imagination, sending back ten scalding sci-fi stories of male desire.

CALDWELL & AARON TRAVIS

TAG TEAM STUDS
$6.50/465-8
Two legendary talents team up for a volume of high impact erotica. Wrestling will never seem the same, once you've made your way through this assortment of sweaty studs. But you'd better be wary—should one catch you off guard, you might spend the night pinned to the mat....

LARRY TOWNSEND

MIND MASTER
$4.95/209-4
One psychically gifted man exploits his ability to control others. Soon, studs of every strip are catering to his perverse whims.

LEATHER AD: M
$5.95/380-5
An eager young man seeks experience at the hands of numerous leatherclad studs.

LEATHER AD: S
$5.95/407-0
The story of one man's discovery of leathersex continues, as he takes on the Top man's role.

BEWARE THE GOD WHO SMILES
$5.95/321-X
A mindblowing trip through the gay past, via this author's notoriously twisted imagination. Two lusty young Americans are transported to ancient Egypt—where they are embroiled in warfare and taken as slaves by barbarians. The two finally discover that the key to escape lies within their own rampant libidos.

THE CONSTRUCTION WORKER
$5.95/298-1
A young, hung construction worker is sent to a building project in Central America, where he is shocked to find some ancient and unusual traditions in practice. Of special interest are the sexual ways of the men he encounters—all of whom believe man-to-man sex to be the only acceptable norm!

THE LONG LEATHER CORD
$4.95/201-9
Chuck's stepfather never lacks money or male visitors with whom he enacts intense sexual rituals. As Chuck comes to terms with his own desires, he begins to unravel the mystery behind his stepfather's secret life.

THE SCORPIUS EQUATION
$4.95/119-5
The story of a man caught between the demands of two galactic empires. Our randy hero must match wits—and more—with the incredible forces that rule his world.

MAN SWORD
$4.95/188-8
The *trés gai* tale of France's King Henri III, who encounters enough sexual schemers and politicos to alter one's picture of history forever! Witness the unbridled licentiousness of one of Europe's most notorious courts.

THE FAUSTUS CONTRACT
$4.95/167-5
Another thrilling tale of leather lust. Two cocky young hustlers get more than they bargained for in this story of lust and its discontents.

CHAINS
$4.95/158-6
Picking up street punks has always been risky, but here it sets off a string of events that must be read to be believed. The legendary Townsend at his grittiest.

RUN NO MORE
$4.95/152-7
The sequel to *Run, Little Leather Boy*. This volume follows the further adventures of Townsend's leatherclad narrator as he travels every sexual byway available to the S/M male. Soon, Wayne's experiencing more than even he had dreamed possible....

MASQUERADE BOOKS

WWW.MASQUERADEBOOKS.COM

THE GAY ADV. OF CAPTAIN GOOSE
$4.95/169-1
A rollicking tale of gay lust on the high seas. Handsome Jerome Gander is sentenced to serve aboard a ship manned by the most hardened criminals. In no time, Gander becomes one of the most notorious rakehells Olde England had ever seen. On land or sea, Gander hunts down the Empire's hottest studs.

DONALD VINING

CABIN FEVER AND OTHER STORIES
$5.95/338-4
"Demonstrates the wisdom experience combined with insight and optimism can create." —*Bay Area Reporter*

Eighteen blistering stories in celebration of the most intimate of male bonding, reaffirming the importance of both love and lust in modern gay life.

DEREK ADAMS

FORBIDDEN LOVE
$6.95/645-6
Forbidden Love contains a baker's dozen of this writer's best, most passion-packed tales. A horny cop becomes far too involved with a mysterious hunk; a struggling artist supports himself by immersing himself in the all-male culture of pro wrestling; an unemployed construction worker finds a position posing for a voyeuristic photographer; and many other delicious scenarios make this one of Adams' wildest volumes.

THE MARK OF THE WOLF
$5.95/361-9
The past comes back to haunt one well-off stud, whose desires lead him into the arms of many men—and the midst of a mystery.

MY DOUBLE LIFE
$5.95/314-7
Every man leads a double life, dividing his hours between the mundanities of the day and the pursuits of the night. Derek Adams shines a little light on the wicked things men do when no one's looking.

HEAT WAVE
$4.95/159-4
Derek Adams sexy short stories are guaranteed to jump start any libido—and *Heatwave* contains his very best.

MILES DIAMOND & THE CASE OF THE CRETAN APOLLO
$6.95/381-3
Hired to track a cheating lover, Miles finds himself involved in a highly unprofessional capacity! When the jealous Callahan threatens not only Diamond but his studly assistant, Miles counters with a little horny undercover work.

MILES DIAMOND & THE DEMON OF DEATH
$4.95/251-5
The return of the intrepid Miles Diamond. Miles always find himself in the stickiest situations—with any stud he meets! This adventure promises another carnal carnival, as Diamond investigates a host of horny guys.

KELVIN BELIELE

IF THE SHOE FITS
$4.95/223-X
An essential volume of tales exploring a world where randy boys can't help but do what comes naturally—as often as possible! Sweaty male bodies grapple in pleasure.

BERT McKENZIE

FRINGE BENEFITS
$5.95/354-6
From the pen of a widely published short story writer comes a volume of highly immodest tales. Not afraid of getting down and dirty, McKenzie produces some of today's most visceral sextales.

JAMES MEDLEY

THE REVOLUTIONARY and Other Stories
$6.50/417-8
Billy, the son of the station chief of the American Embassy in Guatemala, is kidnapped and held for ransom. Billy gradually develops a close relationship with Juan, the revolutionary assigned to guard him—and soon, lust complicates an already explosive situation.

HUCK AND BILLY
$4.95/245-0
Young lust knows no bounds—and is often the hottest of one's life! Huck and Billy explore the desires that course through their bodies, determined to plumb the depths of passion. A thrilling look at desire between men.

BUY ANY 4 BOOKS & CHOOSE 1 ADDITIONAL BOOK, OF EQUAL OR LESSER VALUE, AS YOUR FREE GIFT

1-800-375-2356

FLEDERMAUS

FLEDERFICTION:
Stories of Men and Torture
$5.95/355-4
Fifteen blistering paeans to men and their suffering. Unafraid of exploring the furthest reaches of pain and pleasure, Fledermaus unleashes his most thrilling tales in this volume.

"BIG" BILL JACKSON

EIGHTH WONDER
$4.95/200-0
"Big" Bill Jackson's always the randiest guy in town. From the bright lights and back rooms of New York to the open fields and sweaty bods of a small Southern town, "Big" Bill always manages to cause a scene!

VICTOR TERRY

TYING KNOTS
$6.95/636-7
From an encounter with a lusty German who begs a position of service on the farm of a horny American couple, to a gay leather couple who test the limits of their love and lust in an effort to secure a hefty inheritance, these stories are among the very best and hottest of this veteran eroticist's career.

MASTERS
$6.50/418-6
Terry's butchest tales. A powerhouse volume of boot-wearing, whip-wielding, bone-crunching bruisers who've got what it takes to make a grown man grovel.

SM/SD
$6.50/406-2
Set around a South Dakota town called Prairie, these tales offer evidence that the real rough stuff can still be found where men take what they want despite all rules.

WHIPS
$4.95/254-X
Cruising for a hot man? You'd better be, because these WHiPs—officers of the Wyoming Highway Patrol—are gonna pull you over for a little impromptu interrogation....

MAX EXANDER

DEEDS OF THE NIGHT:
Tales of Eros and Passion
$5.95/348-1
MAXimum porn! Exander's a writer who's seen it all—and is more than happy to describe every inch of it in pulsating detail. A whirlwind tour of the hypermasculine libido.

LEATHERSEX
$4.95/210-8
Leather clad lust draws together only the most willing and talented of tops and bottoms—for an all-out orgy of limitless surrender and control....

MANSEX
$4.95/160-8
Unrelenting tales of men who like to take control—and those who so willingly abandon themselves to desire.

TORSTEN BARRING

CONFESSIONS OF A
NAKED PIANO PLAYER
$6.95/626-X
Frederic Danton is a musical prodigy—and currently the highest paid and most sought-after concert pianist in the world. At the height of his fame, Frederic withdraws from the limelight, setting off for the isle of Corrigia—home of the most perverse gay sex resort known to man!

GUY TRAYNOR
$6.50/414-3
Some call Guy Traynor a theatrical genius; others say he was a madman. All anyone knows for certain is that his productions were the result of blood, sweat and outrageous erotic torture! Never have so many handsome young men suffered so for their art.

SHADOWMAN
$4.95/178-0
From spoiled aristocrats to randy youths sowing wild oats at the local picture show, Barring's imagination works overtime in these steamy vignettes of homolust.

MASQUERADE BOOKS

WWW.MASQUERADEBOOKS.COM

PETER THORNWELL
$4.95/149-7
Follow the exploits of Peter Thornwell and his outrageously horny cohorts as he goes from misspent youth to scandalous stardom, all thanks to an insatiable libido and love for the lash.

CHRISTOPHER MORGAN

STEAM GAUGE
$6.50/473-9
This volume abounds in manly men doing what they do best—to, with, or for any hot stud who crosses their paths.

THE SPORTSMEN
$5.95/385-6
A collection of super-hot stories dedicated to the timeless archetype of the all-American athlete. These writers know just the type of guys that make up every red-blooded male's starting line-up....

TOM CAFFREY

HITTING HOME & OTHER STORIES
$4.95/222-1
Titillating and compelling, the stories in *Hitting Home* make a strong case for there being only one thing on a man's mind. Hot studs via the imagination of this new talent.

ROGER HARMAN

FIRST PERSON
$4.95/179-9
Each story takes the form of a confessional—told by men who've got plenty to confess! From the "first time ever" to firsts of different kinds....

SEAN MARTIN

SCRAPBOOK
$4.95/224-8
From the creator of *Doc and Raider* comes this hot collection of life's horniest moments—all involving studs sure to set your pulse racing!

MICHAEL LOWENTHAL, ED.

THE BADBOY EROTIC LIBRARY Vol. 2
$4.95/211-8
A second volume of scalding outtakes, taken from *Mike and Me, Muscle Bound, Men at Work, Badboy Fantasies,* and *Slowburn.*

ERIC BOYD

MIKE AND ME
$5.95/419-4
Mike joined the gym squad to bulk up on muscle. Little did he know he'd be turning on every sexy muscle jock in Minnesota! Hard bodies collide in a series of horny workouts.

MIKE AND THE MARINES
$6.50/497-6
Mike takes on America's most elite corps of studs! Join in on the never-ending sexual escapades of this singularly lustful platoon!

ANONYMOUS

A SECRET LIFE
$4.95/3017-2
Meet Master Charles: eighteen and quite innocent, until his arrival at the Sir Percival's Academy, where the lessons are supplemented with a crash course in pure sexual heat!

SINS OF THE CITIES OF THE PLAIN
$5.95/322-8
indulge yourself in the scorching memoirs of young man-about-town Jack Saul. Jack's sinful escapades grow wilder with every chapter!

THE SCARLET PANSY
$4.95/189-6
Randall Etrange travels the world in search of true love. Along the way, his journey becomes a sexual odyssey of truly epic proportions.

HARD CANDY

SIMON LEVAY

ALBRICK'S GOLD
$7.95/644-8
"Well-plotted and imaginative... Original and engaging."
—*Publishers Weekly*

Violence is on the rise at ultraconservative Leviticun University—and Dr. Roger Cavendish becomes a reluctant gumshoe, busily involved in discovering what lies beneath this sudden rise in brutal crime. The truth seems to lie somewhere in the laboratory of Dr. Guy Albrick—a mysterious scientist who claims to "cure" homosexuals. Soon, Cavendish is in a race with time, struggling to unlock the secrets of Albrick's work as the wave of violence threatens to overtake him and all others in its path.

BUY ANY 4 BOOKS & CHOOSE 1 ADDITIONAL BOOK, OF EQUAL OR LESSER VALUE, AS YOUR FREE GIFT

1-800-375-2356

STAN LEVENTHAL

BARBIE IN BONDAGE
$6.95/415-1
Widely regarded as one of the most clear-eyed interpreters of big city gay male life, Leventhal here provides a series of explorations of love and desire between men.

SKYDIVING ON CHRISTOPHER STREET
$6.95/287-6
"Positively addictive." —Dennis Cooper

Aside from a hateful job, a hateful apartment, a hateful world and an increasingly hateful lover, life seems, well, all right for the protagonist of Stan Leventhal's latest novel. An insightful tale of contemporary urban gay life.

CHEA VILLANUEVA

BULLETPROOF BUTCHES
$7.95/560-3
"...Gutsy, hungry, and outrageous, but with a tender core... Villanueva is a writer to watch out for: she will teach us something." —Joan Nestle

One of lesbian literature's most uncompromising voices. Never afraid to address the harsh realities of working-class lesbian life, Chea Villanueva charts territory frequently overlooked in the age of "lesbian chic."

ROBERT PATRICK

TEMPLE SLAVE
$7.95/635-9
"Genuinely original—a story of triumph."
—Harvard Gay & Lesbian Review

Temple Slave tells the story of the Espresso Buono and the wildly talented misfits who called it home in the 60s. The Buono became the birthplace of underground theater—and the personal and social consciousness that would lead to Stonewall and the modern gay and lesbian movement.

KEVIN KILLIAN

ARCTIC SUMMER
$6.95/514-X
An examination of the emptiness lying beneath the rich exterior of America in the 50s. With the story of Liam Reilly—a young gay man of considerable means and numerous secrets—Killian exposes the complexities and contradictions of the American Dream.

PATRICK MOORE

IOWA
$7.95/702-9
"A lot of clatter has accompanied the publication of Patrick Moore's second book, Iowa. It is deserved.... It is as fine a small town coming out story as I have ever read."
—Lambda Book Report

Moving from his small town to New York City, Wayne knows he's actually going farther away than his family could ever imagine. And it is only the inevitable return to Iowa that brings about a coming of age more complete, more essential than any experience in his life. Because if coming out, finding, and losing love are the most important events in life, going home may still be the hardest.

PAUL T. ROGERS

SAUL'S BOOK
$7.95/462-3
Winner of the Editors' Book Award

"A first novel of considerable power... Speaks to us all."
—New York Times Book Review

The story of a Times Square hustler, Sinbad the Sailor, and Saul, a brilliant, self-destructive, dominating character who may be the only love Sinbad will ever know. A classic tale of desire, obsession and the wages of love.

ELISE D'HAENE

LICKING OUR WOUNDS
$7.95/605-7
Winner of a 1998 Firecracker Alternative Book Award
"A fresh, engagingly sarcastic and determinedly bawdy voice. D'Haene is blessed with a savvy, iconoclastic view of the world that is mordant but never mean." —Publisher's Weekly

This acclaimed debut novel is the story of Maria, a young woman coming to terms with the complexities of life in the age of AIDS. Abandoned by her lover and faced with the deaths of her friends, Maria struggles along with the help of Peter, HIV-positive and deeply conflicted about the changes in his own life, and Christie, a lover who is full of her own ideas about truth and the meaning of life.

MASQUERADE BOOKS

WWW.MASQUERADEBOOKS.COM

LARS EIGHNER

GAY COSMOS
$6.95/236-1
A collection of this author's provocative essays looking at the state of contemporary gay culture. Praised by the press, *Gay Cosmos* is an important contribution to the area of Gay and Lesbian Studies.

MICHAEL ROWE

WRITING BELOW THE BELT: Conversations with Erotic Authors
$7.95/540-9
"An in-depth and enlightening tour of society's love/hate relationship with sex, morality, and censorship."
—*James White Review*

Michael Rowe interviewed the best and brightest erotic writers and presents the collected wisdom in *Writing Below the Belt*. Includes interviews with such cult sensations as John Preston, Larry Townsend, Pat Califia, as well as new voices such as Will Leber, Michael Lowenthal and others. An acclaimed look at the lives and work of today's most important erotic artists.

WALTER R. HOLLAND

THE MARCH
$6.95/429-1
Beginning on a hot summer night in 1980, *The March* revolves around a circle of young gay men, and the many others their lives touch. Over time, each character changes in unexpected ways; lives and loves come together and fall apart, as society itself is horribly altered by the onslaught of AIDS.

BRAD GOOCH

THE GOLDEN AGE OF PROMISCUITY
$7.95/550-6
"The next best thing to taking a time-machine trip to grovel in the glorious '70s gutter." —*San Francisco Chronicle*

"A solid, unblinking, unsentimental look at a vanished era. Gooch tells us everything we ever wanted to know about the dark and decadent gay subculture in Manhattan before AIDS altered the landscape." —*Kirkus Reviews*

A controversial look at life during the decadent 70s, *The Golden Age of Promiscuity* follows a young gay artist from rags to riches.

JAMES COLTON

TODD
$6.95/312-0
A remarkably frank novel from an earlier age. With Todd, Colton took on the complexities of American race relations, becoming one of the first gay writers to explore interracial love between men.

THE OUTWARD SIDE
$6.95/304-X
Marc Lingard, a handsome, respected young minister, finds himself at a crossroads. Unnerved by the homophobic persecution of a local resident, Marc finds himself caving in to the desires he has so long denied.

RED JORDAN AROBATEAU

WHERE THE WORD IS NO
$7.95/674-5
"Like the characters in her stories, Red Jordan Arobateau's writing is raucous and raw and rough-hewn.... Beautiful, crackling with a kind of sparse energy." —*Nisa Donnelly*

The story of Jesse, a young African-American man struggling with his dream of becoming a "player." Jesse wrestles with his sexual identity, choosing to hide his nascent bisexuality behind a bluff macho exterior. All that changes when Miss La-Di-Da, a fierce, unafraid drag goddess of the streets pierces the young man's armor—leaving Jesse no choice but to confront his own truths....

LUCY AND MICKEY
$6.95/311-2
"A necessary reminder to all who blissfully—some may say ignorantly—ride the wave of lesbian chic into the mainstream." —*Heather Findlay*

The volume that made Red Jordan a sensation. Here are the exploits of Mickey—an uncompromising butch—and her long affair with Lucy, the femme she loves.

FELICE PICANO

AMBIDEXTROUS
$6.95/275-2
"Makes us remember what it feels like to be a child..." —*The Advocate*

Picano tells all about his formative years: home life, school face-offs, the ingenuous sophistications of his first sexual steps.

BUY ANY 4 BOOKS & CHOOSE 1 ADDITIONAL BOOK, OF EQUAL OR LESSER VALUE, AS YOUR FREE GIFT

1-800-375-2356

MEN WHO LOVED ME
$6.95/274-4
"Zesty...spiked with adventure and romance...a distinguished and humorous portrait of a vanished age." —*Publishers Weekly*

In 1966, Picano abandoned New York, determined to find true love in Europe. He becomes embroiled in a romance with Djanko, and lives *la dolce vita* to the fullest. Upon returning to the US, he plunges into the city's thriving gay community of the 1970s.

THE LURE
$6.95/398-8
A Book-of-the-Month-Club Selection
"The subject matter plus the authenticity of Picano's research are, combined, explosive. Felice Picano is one hell of a writer."
—Stephen King

After witnessing a brutal murder, Noel is recruited by the police, to assist as a lure for the homophobic killer. Provided with a false identity, he moves deep into the freneticism of gay highlife in 1970s Manhattan—where he discovers his own hidden desires.

DONALD VINING

A GAY DIARY
$8.95/451-8
"*A Gay Diary* is, unquestionably, the richest historical document of gay male life in the United States that I have ever encountered...." —*Body Politic*

Vining's *Diary* portrays a vanished age and the lifestyle of a generation frequently forgotten. An unprecedented look at the lifestyle of a pre-Stonewall gay man.

Rosebud

ARTEMIS OAKGROVE

WARCLOUDS
$6.95/643-X
Silky, an outsider who's found grudging acceptance in her small community, suddenly finds her staid life changed by the arrival of Cloud—a thrilling but troubled butch still stinging from a recent defeat. In the meantime, Nighthawk, the woman who single-handedly removed Cloud from her turf, rules her hard-won kingdom—and the women in it —with an iron fist, not knowing her greatest battles are yet to come....

NIGHTHAWK
$6.95/634-0
Artemis OakGrove follows the Nighthawk through various adventures. Butcher than butch, 'Hawk leaves her lovers indelibly marked and begging for more—even while she herself moves on in search of tomorrow's conquest. Tough, street-smart and unsentimental, Nighthawk is a figure of unforgettable power and sensuality.

DANIELLE ENGLE

LAVENDER EXCURSIONS
$6.95/689-8
"Whether buried within the recesses of her mind or appearing in her wildest daydreams, it was Lavender Excursions' philosophy that fantasies were treasures, personal riches waiting to be discovered and exploited...." Carol Washington contacts Lavender Excursions, interested in hiring them to fulfill the desires of her best friend, Sheryl. As a former client, Carol knows that the women behind Lavender Excursions are well-versed in addressing a woman's deepest needs, and feels sure that Sheryl will benefit from their hard work....

UNCENSORED FANTASIES
$6.95/572-7
In a world where so many stifle their emotions, who doesn't find themselves yearning for honesty—even if it means bearing one's own secret desires? Danielle Engle's heroines do just that—and a great deal more—in their quest for total sexual pleasure.

RACHEL PEREZ

ODD WOMEN
$6.50/526-3
These women are sexy, smart, tough—some say odd. But who cares! An assortment of Sapphic sirens proves once and for all that comely ladies come best in pairs.

AARONA GRIFFIN

LEDA/THE HOUSE OF SPIRITS
$6.95/585-9
Two novellas in one volume. Though in a relationship with Chrys, *Leda* decides to take a one-night vacation—at a local lesbian sex club. In the second story, lovely Lydia thinks she has her grand new home all to herself—but this *House of Spirits* harbors other souls, determined to do some serious partying.

MASQUERADE BOOKS

WWW.MASQUERADEBOOKS.COM

PASSAGE & OTHER STORIES
$6.95/599-9
A story of one woman's awakening to true desire. Nina finds herself infatuated with a woman she spots at a local café. One night, Nina follows her, only to find herself enmeshed in an maze leading to a mysterious world where women test the edges of sexuality and power.

RED JORDAN AROBATEAU

COME WITH ME, LUCY
$6.95/684-7
"The graffiti artist of lesbian literature."
—*Lambda Book Report*

"Like the characters in her stories, Red Jordan Arobateau's writing is raucous and raw and rough-hewn...[and] beautiful, crackling with a kind of sparse energy." —Nisa Donnelly

"Red Jordan Arobateau is more than a writer of raw, steamy, no-holds-barred sex stories—she's also a deep-thinking dyke philosopher with a style all her own, a Kerouackian eye for detail, and plenty to say about race and class, life and death, sex and love." —Carol Queen

Red Jordan Arobateau returns to the tale of Mickey, the street-smart butch Everydyke of her groundbreaking novel *Lucy & Mickey*. Now in her forties, Mickey has settled into a relationship with Marsha, a young woman with whom she shares the responsibility for two children. But Mickey's notorious roaming eye soon leads her into the arms of others. Determined to keep their family together, Mickey and Marsha take off cross-country—and encounter an old flame of Mickey's who will turn their world upside down.

THE BLACK BIKER
$6.95/624-3
Once again, the Oils Club witnesses the outrageous antics of the Outlaws—a gang of brave and uncompromising rebels, banded together against a hostile world. One day, a mysterious biker walks into Oils, looking for love, driven by lust, and hoping to leave a sorry past behind.

STREET FIGHTER
$6.95/583-2
Another blast of truth from one of today's most notorious plain-speakers. An unsentimental look at the life of a street butch—Woody, the consummate outsider, living on the fringes of San Francisco.

ROUGH TRADE
$6.50/470-4
Arobateau outdoes herself with these tales of butch/femme affairs and unrelenting passions.

BOYS NIGHT OUT
$6.50/463-1
Incendiary short fiction from this lesbian sensation. As always, Arobateau takes a hard look at the lives of everyday women, noting well the struggles and triumphs each experiences.

ALISON TYLER

THE SILVER KEY: Madame Victoria's Finishing School
$6.95/614-6
In a Victorian finishing school, a circle of randy young ladies share a diary. Molly records an explicit description of her initiation into the ways of physical love; Eden tells of how it feels to wield a switch; and Katherine transcribes the journey of her love affair with the wickedly wanton Eden.

COME QUICKLY: For Girls on the Go
$6.95/428-3
Here are over sixty of the hottest lesbian fantasies around. A volume of "quickies" designed for a modern girl on a modern schedule—who still appreciates a little old-fashioned action.

VENUS ONLINE
$6.50/521-2
Lovely Alexa spends her days in a boring bank job, saving her energies for the night—when she goes online, searching chat rooms for a partner willing to satisfy her kinky sexual desires. Soon Alexa—a.k.a. Venus—finds her real and online lives colliding sexily.

DARK ROOM: An Online Adventure
$6.50/455-0
Dani can't bring herself to face the death of her lover, Kate. Determined to keep the memory of her lover alive, Dani goes online under Kate's screen alias—where she discovers Kate's secret life, and the ways in which it led to her untimely death....

BLUE SKY SIDEWAYS & OTHER STORIES
$6.50/394-5
A variety of women, and their many breathtaking experiences with lovers, friends—and even the occasional sexy stranger. Short, sexy fiction from this acclaimed writer.

BUY ANY 4 BOOKS & CHOOSE 1 ADDITIONAL BOOK, OF EQUAL OR LESSER VALUE, AS YOUR FREE GIFT

1-800-375-2356

DIAL "L" FOR LOVELESS
$5.95/386-4
Katrina Loveless—a sexy private eye talented enough to give Sam Spade a run for his money. In her first case, Katrina investigates a murder implicating a host of lovely, lusty ladies.

ANNABELLE BARKER

MOROCCO
$6.50/541-7
A young woman stands to inherit a fortune—if she can only withstand the ministrations of her guardian until her twentieth birthday. Ultimately, she breaks free, finally able to attempt to enjoy all that life has to offer. But liberty has its own delicious price....

RANDY TUROFF

LUST NEVER SLEEPS
$6.50/475-5
Highly erotic, powerfully real fiction. Turoff depicts a circle of modern women connected through the enduring bonds of love, friendship, ambition, and lust with accuracy and compassion. An acclaimed look at modern lesbian life and lust.

VALENTINA CILESCU

DARK VENUS:
Mistress with a Maid, Volume 2
$6.50/481-X
Claudia Dungarrow's quest for ultimate erotic dominance continues in this scalding second volume! How many maidens will fall prey to her insatiable appetite?

BODY AND SOUL:
Mistress with a Maid, Volume 3
$6.50/515-8
Dr. Claudia Dungarrow returns for yet another tour of depravity, subjugating every maiden in sight to her sexual whims. Though many young women have fallen victim to her unquenchable lusts, she has yet to hold Elizabeth in submission. Will she ever?

MISTRESS MINE
$6.50/502-6
Sophia sits in prison, accused of authoring the "obscene" *Mistress Mine*—the chronicle of her life under the hand of Mistress Malin.

LOVECHILD

GAG
$5.95/369-4
Fearless verse addressing sex and freedom at the Millennium. These poems take on hypocrisy with uncommon energy, and announce Lovechild as a writer of unforgettable rage.

LINDSAY WELSH

BAD HABITS
$6.95/625-1
When some dominant and discerning women begin to detect tell-tale signs of poor training in their servants, they know there's only one remedy. In no time, a certain group of young ladies is back in school, joyfully learning the real, burning truth of submission to Woman.

PROVINCETOWN SUMMER
508-8/$6.96
This original collection is devoted exclusively to white-hot desire between women. From the casual encounters of women on the prowl to the enduring erotic bonds between old lovers, the women of *Provincetown Summer* will set your senses on fire!

SECOND SIGHT
$6.50/507-7
The debut of lesbian superhero Dana Steel! During an attack by a gang of homophobic youths, Dana is thrown onto subway tracks. Miraculously, she survives—and finds herself possessing powers that make her the world's first lesbian superhero.

NASTY PERSUASIONS
$6.50/436-4
A hot peek into the behind-the-scenes operations of Rough Trade—one of the world's most famous lesbian clubs. Join Slash, Ramone, Cherry and many others as they bring one another to the height of ecstasy.

MILITARY SECRETS
$5.95/397-X
Colonel Candice Sproule heads a specialized boot camp. Assisted by three dominatrix sergeants, Colonel Sproule takes on the submissives sent to her by military contacts. Then along comes Jesse—a butch recruit whose pleasure in being served matches the Colonel's own.

MASQUERADE BOOKS

WWW.MASQUERADEBOOKS.COM

THE BEST OF LINDSAY WELSH
$5.95/368-6
Welsh was one of Rosebud's early bestsellers, and remains one of our most popular writers. This sampler is set to introduce some of today's hottest lesbian erotica to a wider audience.

NECESSARY EVIL
$5.95/277-9
One lovely submissive decides to create a Mistress who'll fulfill her heart's desire. Little did she know how difficult it would be—and, in the end, rewarding....

A VICTORIAN ROMANCE
$5.95/365-1
A young woman realizes her dream—a trip abroad! Soon, Elaine comes to discover her own sexual talents, as a hot-blooded Parisian named Madelaine takes her Sapphic education in hand.

A CIRCLE OF FRIENDS
$6.50/524-7
A close-knit group of women pair off to explore all the possibilities of lesbian passion, until finally it seems that there is nothing—and no one—they have not dabbled in.

SEXUAL FANTASIES (ED.)
$6.95/586-7
Bestselling author Lindsay Welsh selects a dozen sexy stories, ranging from sweet to spicy, from her favorite up-and-coming writers. *Sexual Fantasies* offers a look at the many desires of modern women.

LAURA ANTONIOU, ED.

**LEATHERWOMEN III:
The Clash of the Cultures**
$6.95/619-7
Antoniou gathers the very best of today's cutting-edge women's erotica—concentrating on multicultural stories involving characters not frequently seen in this genre.

LEATHERWOMEN
$6.95/598-0
"...a great new collection of fiction by and about SM dykes."
—SKIN TWO

A groundbreaking anthology. These fantasies, from the pens of new or emerging authors, break every rule imposed on women's fantasies. An unforgettable exploration of the female libido.

A Richard Kasak Book

PAT CALIFIA

DIESEL FUEL: Passionate Poetry
$12.95/535-2
"Dead-on direct, these poems burn, pierce, penetrate, soak, and sting.... Califia leaves no sexual stone unturned, clearing new ground for us all."
—Gerry Gomez Pearlberg

Califia's first collection of verse. A must-read exploration of underground culture.

MICHAEL BRONSKI, ED.

TAKING LIBERTIES: Gay Men's Essays on Politics, Culture and Sex
$12.95/456-9
Lambda Literary Award Winner
"Offers undeniable proof of a heady, sophisticated, diverse new culture of gay intellectual debate. I cannot recommend it too highly."
—Christopher Bram

America's gay community is, in many ways, stronger than ever before—due largely to the diversity of opinions on the history and future of the tribe. Some of the gay community's foremost essayists—from radical left to neo-conservative—weigh in on such slippery topics as outing, pornography, pedophilia, and much more. One of the most acclaimed anthologies in the field.

FLASHPOINT: Gay Male Sexual Writing
$12.95/424-0
A thrilling and enlightening look at contemporary gay porn. Accompanied by Bronski's insightful analysis, each story illustrates the many approaches to sexuality used by today's gay writers.

SHAR REDNOUR, ED.

VIRGIN TERRITORY 2
$12.95/506-9
Focusing on the many "firsts" of a woman's erotic life, *VT2* provides one of the sole outlets for serious discussion of the myriad possibilities available to and chosen by many lesbians.

VIRGIN TERRITORY
$12.95/457-7
An anthology of writing by women about their first-time erotic experiences with other women. A groundbreaking and influential examination of contemporary lesbian desire.

BUY ANY 4 BOOKS & CHOOSE 1 ADDITIONAL BOOK, OF EQUAL OR LESSER VALUE, AS YOUR FREE GIFT

1-800-375-2356

HEATHER FINDLAY, ED.

A MOVEMENT OF EROS: 25 Years of Lesbian Erotica
$12.95/421-6

Tracing the course of the genre from its pre-Stonewall roots to its current renaissance, Findlay examines each piece, placing it within the context of lesbian community and politics.

LARRY TOWNSEND

THE LEATHERMAN'S HANDBOOK
$12.95/559-X

With introductions by John Preston, Jack Fritscher and Victor Terry. A special twenty-fifth anniversary edition of this guide to the gay leather world, with contemporary updates.

ASK LARRY
$12.95/289-2

For many years, Townsend wrote the "Leather Notebook" column for *Drummer* magazine. Now read Townsend's collected wisdom, as well as the author's careful consideration of the way life has changed in the AIDS era.

AMARANTHA KNIGHT, ED.

LOVE BITES
$12.95/234-5

A volume of tales dedicated to legend's sexiest demon—the Vampire. A virtual who's who of promising new talent.

GUILLERMO BOSCH

RAIN
$12.95/232-9

In a quest to sate his hunger for some knowledge of the world, one man is taken through a series of extraordinary encounters that change the course of civilization around him.

MICHAEL FORD, ED.

ONCE UPON A TIME: Erotic Fairy Tales for Women
$12.95/449-6

Many young women are introduced to cultural values through the timeless tradition of the fairy tale. But how relevant to contemporary lesbians are traditional fairy tales? Some of the biggest names in lesbian literature retell their favorites, adding their own sexy twists.

HAPPILY EVER AFTER: Erotic Fairy Tales for Men
$12.95/450-X

Adapting some of childhood's beloved stories for the adult gay reader, the contributors to *Happily Ever After* dig up the erotic subtext of these hitherto "innocent" diversions. A playfully arousing volume.

CHARLES H. FORD & PARKER TYLER

THE YOUNG AND EVIL
$12.95/431-3

"*The Young and Evil* creates [its] generation as *This Side of Paradise* by Fitzgerald created his generation."—Gertrude Stein

Originally published in 1933, *The Young and Evil* was a sensation due to its portrayal of young gay artists living in Greenwich Village. From drag balls to bohemian flats, these characters followed love wherever it led them.

JOHN PRESTON

MY LIFE AS A PORNOGRAPHER AND OTHER INDECENT ACTS
$12.95/135-7

"...essential and enlightening... *My Life as a Pornographer* is a bridge from the sexually liberated 1970s to the more cautious 1990s, and Preston has walked much of that way as a standard-bearer to the cause for equal rights...." —*Library Journal*

A collection of author and social critic John Preston's essays, focusing on his work as an erotic writer, and proponent of gay rights.

BARRY HOFFMAN, ED.

THE BEST OF GAUNTLET
$12.95/202-7

Gauntlet has always published the widest possible range of opinions. The most provocative articles have been gathered by editor-in-chief Barry Hoffman, to make *The Best of Gauntlet* a riveting exploration of society's limits.

MICHAEL LASSELL

THE HARD WAY
$12.95/231-0

"Lassell is a master of the necessary word. In an age of tepid and whining verse, his bawdy and bittersweet songs are like a plunge in cold champagne." —Paul Monette

The first collection of renowned gay writer Michael Lassell's poetry, fiction and essays.

MASQUERADE BOOKS

WWW.MASQUERADEBOOKS.COM

WILLIAM CARNEY

THE REAL THING
$10.95/280-9
A chilling epistolary novel set in the gay leather clubs of California, circa 1968. *The Real Thing* returns to thrill and enlighten a new audience with its tale of the attitudes and practices of an earlier generation of gay leather-men.

EURYDICE

F/32
$10.95/350-3
"It's wonderful to see a woman...celebrating her body and her sexuality by creating a fabulous and funny tale."
—Kathy Acker

A funny, disturbing quest for unity, *f/32* tells the story of Ela and her vagina—the latter of whom embarks on one of the most hilarious road trips in recent fiction.

SAMUEL R. DELANY

THE MOTION OF LIGHT IN WATER
$12.95/133-0
"A very moving, intensely fascinating literary biography from an extraordinary writer....The artist as a young man and a memorable picture of an age." —William Gibson

Delany's autobiography covers the early years of one of scifi's most important voices.

RANDY TUROFF, ED.

LESBIAN WORDS: State of the Art
$10.95/340-6
"This is a terrific book that should be on every thinking lesbian's bookshelf." —Nisa Donnelly

The best of lesbian nonfiction looking at not only the current fashionability the media has brought to the lesbian "image," but considerations of the lesbian past via historical inquiry and personal recollections.

ASSOTTO SAINT

SPELLS OF A VOODOO DOLL
$12.95/393-7
Lambda Literary Award Nominee.
"Angelic and brazen." —Jewelle Gomez

A spellbinding collection of the poetry, lyrics, essays and performance texts by one of the most important voices in the renaissance of black gay writing.

FELICE PICANO

DRYLAND'S END
$12.95/279-5
Dryland's End takes place in a fabulous techno-empire ruled by intelligent, powerful women. While the Matriarchy has ruled for over two thousand years and altered human society, it is now unraveling. Military rivalries, religious fanaticism and economic competition threaten to destroy the mighty empire.

DAVID MELTZER

THE AGENCY TRILOGY
$12.95/216-7
"...'The Agency' is clearly Meltzer's paradigm of society; a mindless machine of which we are all 'agents,' including those whom the machine supposedly serves..." —Norman Spinrad

A vision of an America consumed and dehumanized by a lust for power.

CECILIA TAN, ED.

SM VISIONS: The Best of Circlet Press
$10.95/339-2
Circlet Press, publisher of erotic science fiction and fantasy genre, is now represented by the best of its very best—a most thrilling and eye-opening rides through the erotic imagination.

CARO SOLES, ED.

MELTDOWN! An Anth. of Erotic SF and Dark Fantasy for Gay Men
$12.95/203-5
The very best examples of the increasingly popular sub-genre of erotic sci-fi/dark fantasy: stories meant to send a shiver down the spine and start a fire down below.

LARS EIGHNER

ELEMENTS OF AROUSAL
$12.95/230-2
A guideline for success with one of publishing's best kept secrets: the novice-friendly field of gay erotic writing.

MICHAEL PERKINS

THE GOOD PARTS: An Uncensored Guide to Literary Sexuality
$12.95/186-1
A survey of sex as seen/written about in the pages of over 100 major fiction and nonfiction volumes from the past twenty years.

BUY ANY 4 BOOKS & CHOOSE 1 ADDITIONAL BOOK, OF EQUAL OR LESSER VALUE, AS YOUR FREE GIFT

1-800-375-2356

COMING UP: The World's Best Erotic Writing
$12.95/370-8
An anthology of today's most provocative erotic writing, including work by some of the genre's biggest names. Sure to challenge the limits of the most seasoned reader.

MICHAEL LOWENTHAL, ED.

THE BEST OF THE BADBOYS
$12.95/233-7
A virtual primer of gay erotic writing, including work by John Preston, Clay Caldwell, Aaron Travis, and others.

MARCO VASSI

THE EROTIC COMEDIES
$12.95/136-5
Scathing and humorous, these stories reflect Vassi's belief in the power and primacy of Eros in American life.

A DRiVING PASSION
$12.95/134-9
Famous for the lectures he gave regarding sexuality, A Driving Passion collects these lectures, and distills the philosophy that made him a sensation.

THE SALINE SOLUTION
$12.95/180-2
The story of one couple's affair and the events that lead them to reassess their lives.

CHEA VILLANUEVA

JESSIE'S SONG
$9.95/235-3
"It conjures up the strobe-light confusion and excitement of urban dyke life.... Read about these dykes and you'll love them."
—Rebecca Ripley

Touching, arousing portraits of working class butch/femme relations. An underground hit.

ORDERING IS EASY

MC/VISA orders can be placed by calling our toll-free number: 800-375-2356
HOURS M-F 9am–12am EDT Sat & Sun 12pm–8pm EDT
E-Mail: MASQBKS@AOL.COM /Fax: 212-986-7355
or mail this coupon to:
MASQUERADE DIRECT
DEPT. BMMQ98 801 2ND AVE., NY, NY 10017
Visit our Website: WWW.MASQUERADEBOOKS.COM

BUY ANY FOUR BOOKS AND CHOOSE ONE ADDITIONAL BOOK, OF EQUAL OR LESSER VALUE, AS YOUR FREE GIFT

QTY.	TITLE	NO.	PRICE
			FREE

DEPT. BMMQ98 (please have this code available when placing your order)

We never sell, give or trade any customer's name.

SUBTOTAL
POSTAGE AND HANDLING
TOTAL

In the U.S., please add $1.50 for the first book and 75¢ for each additional book; in Canada, add $2.00 for the first book and $1.25 for each additional book. Foreign countries: add $4.00 for the first book and $2.00 for each additional book. No C.O.D. orders. Please make all checks payable to Masquerade/Direct. Payable in U.S. currency only. NY state residents add 8.25% sales tax. Please allow 4–6 weeks for delivery. Payable in U.S. currency only.

NAME _____
ADDRESS _____
CITY _____ STATE _____ ZIP _____
TEL( ) _____
E-MAIL _____
PAYMENT: ☐ CHECK   ☐ MONEY ORDER   ☐ VISA   ☐ MC
CARD NO. _____ EXP. DATE _____